ACCIDENTALLY JOINING HIS CULT

CHICAGO AWAKENINGS BOOK ONE

LEXI AMBER

DEDICATION

For any author who's ever written "that one time you almost joined a cult" to show how oblivious a character is, and for any reader who wished they could read more about it.

CONTENT WARNING

This book contains mentions of multi-level-marketing, and cult practices and behaviors that may be disturbing to some readers. A reference to the Jonestown Massacre is made. For a more in-depth list of warnings please visit my website at lexiamber.com

This is a romance with explicit content that is inappropriate for anyone who is under the age of 18, or is related to me.

CONTENTS

CHAPTER ONE

Beckett

Murder was not previously on my list of things to do today. But if the person in line behind me doesn't stop making so much fucking noise before I can even order my coffee, it's getting added right to the top.

In the few minutes since I arrived at Joe's Coffee Shop, they've alternated between zipping and unzipping something incessantly, tapping on the display table like it's a drum set, and humming what I can only describe as pure nonsense.

Whoever this person is clearly doesn't need any more caffeine and should leave before I snap—and I'm usually not a violent person.

Not that anyone would describe me as nice, either. I know how people see me: tattoo sleeves, dark hair, and a resting bitch face that says don't even try me. Judgy assholes take one look and make their assumptions.

My last name comes with its own baggage—a whole other list of assumptions I never signed up for.

Most people don't connect the dots just by looking at me, though.

And okay, maybe I'm being a little judgy right now, plotting this stranger's demise just because they're annoying. But at least I'm judging actions, not appearances. That counts for something, right?

I'm much nicer after I've had my coffee. I promise.

I finally turn my glare in their direction, ready to obliterate them with a look, and—

Poof.

All my irritation evaporates.

In fact, all thoughts of anything other than how hot this guy is are impossible right now.

He's easily the most attractive human that I've ever seen in person. At least three or four inches taller than my six-foot frame. His long golden hair and tan skin make him look like he spends his life on a beach, and I swear, his muscles must have muscles. They're testing the seams of his perfectly fitted suit jacket, and I really want to see what he looks like without it on. His suit looks expensive, but he still seems approachable, not giving off any of the stuck-up vibes most of the men I work with do.

The stylish laptop bag slung over his shoulder must have the loud zipper that's been inspiring my dark fantasies. Now, all I can think about is how his biceps bulge as he continues to move.

By the time our eyes meet, I have no idea what expression I'm wearing. Judging by the amused smile he flashes me, I've been very obvious about checking him out. That smile definitely belongs in a toothpaste ad.

Or in my bedroom.

And don't even get me started on his eyes, they're the most fascinating mix of browns, golds, and greens. They make me feel like I'm lost in a forest during golden hour, and I can't look away.

He chuckles and, yup, he *definitely* caught me checking him out. He doesn't seem annoyed, though. If anything, his smile might be flirty.

Should I give him my number? Do people even do that in person anymore? Nearly all of my hookups start with apps and end with a blurry memory and a hasty goodbye.

This man seems like he could hold my attention for way longer than that, though, *so maybe I should?* But before I can get my thoughts together to say anything, he beats me to it.

"Do you know what you'd like?" he asks in a friendly tone.

"You," I blurt out before I can stop it. *Did I really just say that?* I usually have no trouble flirting, and I'm a fairly confident person, but that was blunt even for me.

Somehow, his smile grows wider, like he didn't hear the word vomit that just escaped my mouth. "Yeah, I'm ready," he replies smoothly, like I'd asked him the question instead. "Did you need a minute? Want me to go in front of you?"

Even his deep voice manages to be upbeat and full of energy.

Seriously, why does this man need caffeine?

He points behind me, and the world around us comes back into focus. Right. I'm still in line at the coffee shop. At some point, I must have completely turned to face him, and I still can't pry my eyes away from his gorgeous smile.

"Go ahead." I open my arm out toward the register, stepping to the side and gesturing for him to go in front of me to order from the very annoyed-looking employee. I guess I've been holding up the line, staring for longer than I'd realized.

It takes me a few moments to pull myself together. I have never had this strong of a reaction to a man. What is it about him that has me acting like this? When the next register opens on the opposite end, I quickly order and practically jog to the pickup counter, scanning the crowd of commuters.

But he's gone.

Any chance I had of being nice today officially disappears with him.

AFTER WALKING the two blocks to Caldwell Tower, I head past security and use my badge to scan into the private elevator on the right, which only goes directly to the top three floors.

My younger brother, Oakley, is the only one waiting with me, which means I can avoid awkward small talk with employees. They're usually either trying to impress a Caldwell—or worse, shrinking into themselves like I'm the Big Bad Brother to avoid.

"Good morning," he says around a sip of his coffee once we're inside. He looks a lot like me, but slightly shorter and with fewer tattoos. Oakley's one of my favorite people, but I'm still too distracted by my coffee shop experience to be polite.

"Is it though?" I ask with more attitude than I'd intended.

"Your shining disposition is always so refreshing first thing in the morning."

"Fuck off."

"Do everyone a favor and finish that coffee before you talk to someone you're not related to," he says with a smile, used to my shit. "See ya." He waves as we exit, heading toward his own office.

Our whole family works here. My father is the current owner and CEO of Caldwell Corporation, which my great-grandfather founded after making some lucky real estate investments back in his day. My grandfather still likes to show up occasionally to "see how things are going" when he's in town and not away on some extravagant golf trip or cruise my grandmother has planned.

The Caldwell Corporation is a successful holding company with ownership or controlling interest in dozens of other companies. My siblings and I each act as president of one of these companies. And if they're not done with their degrees, they still spend all of their free time at "their" future company learning the inner workings.

Most of them are headquartered in this building, with offices taking up as many floors as fit their needs. Each sibling has an office in their respective company's dedicated space and a second office on the top level, where official Caldwell business is conducted.

I always start my day up here in the Caldwell offices to check in with my assistant, Adrian, and to see if any of my family members are around. Then I make my way down to my much cooler office inside the Werewolves headquarters.

I usually bring Adrian his favorite coffee in the mornings. Technically, he's my employee, but he's also my best friend and one of the only people I've ever met who's never cared about my last name.

He grew up in a small town in Arkansas, so it's possible that he didn't know the Caldwell name when we met during freshman year of college, but as time went on, his attitude toward me never changed. When his homophobic roommate started harassing him, my childhood best friend, Jordan, and I insisted he move in with us, and he's been a constant in my life ever since.

Then we graduated, I went to grad school, and Adrian worked for my dad for a few years. When it was time for me to take over with the Werewolves, Adrian had made himself so valuable as one of my father's assistants that I had to win a bet against my dad *and* agree to find his replacement before Adrian could officially come to work for me.

Despite my protests, he always arrives over an hour before me and seems to do way more actual work than I do. So, I like to show him how much I appreciate everything he does by bringing him his favorite fancy drinks as a small thank you.

"Shit, I had a weird morning and forgot your coffee," I say as soon as I see him at his desk in the reception area outside of my office. "I'd offer you mine, but I know you'd never drink plain black."

"Eww." Rolling his eyes, Adrian gives me a disgusted look despite the fact that we've had this exact conversation a few hundred times. "I'll never understand why you choose to torture yourself with that garbage when you can literally add chocolate. Who turns down chocolate?"

I roll my eyes right back. "Do you want me to go get you your fancy mocha and pretend I was running late?"

He dramatically sinks into his chair, the disappointment on his face evident.

"First, you need to stop doing nice things for me, or people are going to realize that you're not a scary asshole," he starts, and I shoot him a small smirk. "Second, you don't have time. You'll be at the executive empowerment program thing all day."

I drop into the seat across from him, groaning loudly. "Pleeeease tell me that this isn't another bullshit HR seminar that we're all required to go to so that they can post pictures on the company's socials about how we're 'Such a fun place to work!' and how we 'Encourage personal success for all of our employees'." I use air quotes and a fake peppy voice to really get my point across.

Adrian doesn't even pretend to feel sorry for me as he replies with an enthusiastic, "That's exactly what it is! Have fuuuun."

"How is it that you always seem to get out of these things when my siblings' assistants will no doubt be there?"

He grins conspiratorially. "I tell them you've excused me to handle 'very important Werewolves business' with Hudson Roy. Nobody questions me when I name-drop the star players."

Being the eldest child meant I had my pick of which company I wanted to work for back in high school. The goal was to start early and learn everything that I possibly could so that I was prepared to take over after graduating with my master's.

Naturally, my fifteen-year-old self chose the NHL team, and I have spent every day since being grateful for that decision. Now, I'm acting CEO of the Chicago Werewolves Hockey Team, which is still the coolest job in the world.

The team manager, president of business operations, and

coaches handle most of the actual hockey stuff. My dad is also still the official owner of the team. My job is everything behind the scenes—financial strategies, operational success, and long-term goals.

"I swear you know the players better than I do." *Not grumpy about that at all. Not even a little bit.*

"I do," he happily agrees. "Because I'm not their boss, and I'm way less scowly than you are. They're all afraid of you. I'm harmless."

His innocent, doe-eyed expression might work on other people, but I know him too well for that. "Sure you are."

He drops the act and returns to professional mode the next second. "You should already be on your way to the seminar if you don't want to be late."

"God forbid."

I'M DEFINITELY RUNNING LATE, but still take my time getting to the conference center where the seminar is being held. *Maybe I should skip this bullshit too and get some actual work done.* But the last time I tried that, Oakley made it his personal mission to drag me there himself, and I don't feel like dealing with that again.

When I enter the room, my first instinct is to grab a chair in the last row and ignore this entire pointless presentation, but familiar golden curls draw my attention to the stage.

Holy shit. It's the coffee shop guy.

On second thought, this is obviously too far from the stage to properly enjoy the seminar.

CHAPTER TWO

Cody

'm having the *best* day, and it's not even nine a.m.

When I checked into my hotel room yesterday, the friendly clerk, Rachel, asked me why I was in town. I told her I was running a seminar for the Caldwell Corporation, and she upgraded me to a suite! Apparently, the Caldwells own the hotel, and she wanted me to experience everything it has to offer.

She even volunteered to show me around the city or come up to my room to help me practice my presentation. *So nice.*

I give these presentations all the time, so I thanked her and explained I didn't need to practice, but that I really appreciated her kindness. She looked pretty disappointed until I invited her to the Individual Empowerment Program I'm running this weekend.

She seemed excited when I told her how the company I work for, Kyla, has developed these specialized classes to help people achieve personal success in whatever they aspire to do in life. We've helped everyone from celebrities, politicians, billionaire

CEOs, and so many regular people find the tools to unlock their full potential.

I know it sounds cheesy, but over the years, I've witnessed so many people improve their lives with these classes, and I know they really work. I seriously have the best job. I get to meet incredible people from all over the world and share in their joy as they work toward their goals.

This morning, I kicked things off with a workout at the hotel's amazing gym. I met some fantastic guys who were really interested in my fitness routine, asking questions and complimenting my dedication. We started talking about why we were all in town, and when I told them about my seminar, they signed up right on the spot!

Harold and Roger could apply it perfectly to elevate their new business. And William sounded so deserving of that promotion at work. I'm confident these classes will give them all the tools they need to succeed.

Back in my suite, I got to use the most incredible shower I've ever seen. There were shower heads facing every direction and a rainfall overhead, deep benches built into three sides, and even a Bluetooth speaker. It's probably big enough for like six people in there, *not sure why six people would ever need to shower at the same time in a hotel room*, but I certainly enjoyed the experience, so I'm not complaining.

Then on the way to my presentation, I decided to grab a coffee, and the man in front of me generously let me go ahead of him in the line. I only drink black coffee because it's healthier, so I was in and out in no time.

With the extra few minutes, I decided to take a longer route to the venue. The walk was spectacular, I was able to enjoy the gorgeous Chicago River and the city's incredible architecture.

I love that my job allows me to travel and see so many beautiful places. I can never decide if I like big cities or smaller remote places more. I also really like it when I get to see the ocean and beaches. Mountains might actually be my favorite, though. It's so hard to choose the best when there are only good options.

Caldwell Tower is a tall, gleaming, all-glass building on the river. Checking in with security was a breeze; everyone was so kind and welcoming. Now I'm all set up in a swanky ballroom, ready to share the Kyla Corporate Empowerment Program with all of the people who work here.

I've got a microphone clipped to my suit jacket, and there are screens on either side of the stage with a camera set up in front of me to project my image for the entire space to see more clearly.

Our company has a lot of different programs tailored to the specific needs of the people taking the classes. Big companies' HR departments will hire us to come in with corporate-focused programs, as a way to show support for their employees and inspire individually driven success. When one person is succeeding within a corporate setting, it benefits everyone around them, as well as the company as a whole.

The ballroom is filling up, but I want to give everyone a chance to get settled so that they don't miss any of the presentation.

Corporate attendees, while sometimes more skeptical, still receive my full effort. Even if not everyone takes advantage of the information, I know I've done my part. Every corporate seminar I've led has inspired at least a few people to join the individual programs, and knowing I've helped improve someone's life is both humbling and incredibly rewarding.

There are hundreds of people in this room, the crowd for this presentation is one of the biggest ones that I've had in a while. The Caldwells own a lot of other companies that all operate out of this building, and most of their employees were encouraged to attend this program.

To me, it doesn't matter if I'm talking to one person or five hundred. I know what I'm saying is important, and I absolutely love what I do.

As I launch into my speech about our plan for the day, movement in the crowd catches my attention. It isn't unusual for people to trickle in late, especially in these larger groups, but most people who do, don't confidently approach the stage.

For a moment, I think the man strutting up the aisle is going to join me up here, which would be a first. At the front row, he stops, resting his hand on the person's shoulder to his left, and looks down at them. They glance up and look like they've seen a ghost. I've never seen someone jump up so quickly. They offer their chair without him saying a word, and scurry to the back where there's open seating.

That was a little strange.

Maybe this man needed to sit up front for some reason, and there weren't any other seats open. You never know what someone else is dealing with in their own life, so I always try my best not to judge anyone without all of the information. That was really nice of the other person to switch with them.

I could give this presentation in my sleep, so the distraction does nothing to slow me down as I give a brief intro. "Okay, now for the fun part! Everyone please get up, and, if you're physically able, stand on your chair."

We always warn the facility ahead of time that this is the plan and are assured of the quality of their furniture before making this request. Companies also sign over liability in case anyone were to get hurt, so we won't be blamed.

As usual, everyone hesitates. There are hushed questions and looks of confusion all around the massive space. A lot of people have stood up, but most people don't seem very excited to jump up on their chairs.

Except for the man in the front row. He steps onto his

without hesitation, his boldness creating a ripple effect. People around him follow suit, and soon the entire room is standing on chairs, eyeing him. He must be someone important at the company.

As I give him my full attention, I realize that I recognize this mystery man. He let me cut him in line at the coffee shop this morning. *Small world.*

I beam at him. "Do you always do what you're told, or are you so bored of me already that you want to speed along the workshop?"

His answering grin is a little wicked, "I like to look down on everyone else, and this seemed like an advantageous position to do so."

I can't tell if he's serious. The slightly less intimidating but similar-looking man next to him barks a laugh, and those around him echo with their own laughter. They must be used to his darker brand of humor.

Are they the Caldwells? It would explain why everyone around them is so captivated. They certainly seem to hold a lot of influence in this massive crowd, I don't think I've ever had everyone up so quickly.

My boss always gets excited when influential celebrity types take an interest in the programs. Viktor thinks they can inspire larger numbers of members to join us because people tend to trust the recommendations of those that they look up to. I don't think that means we should necessarily give anyone special treatment to get them to join, they're not more important than anyone else, which is why I never bother to look up pictures of those people before meeting them. But if we can inspire more people to improve their lives, who am I to question the man who designed the programs?

I still can't believe I get to work with him at all.

Apparently, I have high recruitment and retention percentages, so he likes to have me run the workshops that have these potential influencers in them. I'm not sure what's so special about me. Every coach who runs these seminars does a fantastic job helping people. I'm just honored that Viktor wants me to help spread his ideas and knowledge.

I draw my attention away from my coffee shop friend, addressing the room. "The idea of this opening exercise is to force you out of your comfort zone." I pace across the stage to my own chair, circling it. "To encourage you to question the motivation behind your actions." I spin the chair around so that the back is now closer to the audience. "Do you do things because they're considered 'normal'?" I use air quotes, pausing as I speak. Then step up onto the chair. "Or, do you do things because you want to? Because they bring you joy?"

Then I do a backflip off the chair, landing calmly on my feet as some people gasp, and others start to clap. I've also done this enough times to know what suits work for flips, and I love how surprised people always look.

I wait for everyone to settle down before continuing. "I apologize if that was a bit obnoxious. I'm not trying to show off or impress anyone," I say. Smirking, I straddle the chair, leaning forward on its back toward the audience in a relaxed stance. "I know it's early, I'm simply trying to get everyone's attention so that we can have some fun today." I flash them all a cheeky grin. "Plus, I think flips are fun."

My opening works like I hoped it would, people seem more relaxed and engaged, and I talk for about twenty more minutes before I have them break off into smaller groups to work on exercises while I walk around to some of the groups that seem like they could use the extra encouragement.

Once they're done with that portion and back in their original seats, I play videos that Viktor and some of the highest-level coaches have put together. No matter how many times I watch them, I never get bored with their insights and teachings. But, I skip the ones I'm featured in—I prefer engaging with the audience live rather than relying on pre-recorded material.

We work through lunch. Kyla always requires businesses to supply food for their employees during our corporate seminars to keep people engaged and reward them for their active participation during these day-long events. Time flies like it always does when I'm working, and before I know it, I'm giving my closing remarks.

"Thank you to every single one of you for showing up today! I hope that our time together has allowed you to reflect on your personal aspirations and to begin a new chapter of growth in your life," I say, meaning every word. I'm always so bummed when the day is over. "If today inspired you, I would be absolutely thrilled to see you again for our Individual Empowerment Program that I'm hosting on Saturday. Please feel free to come up and chat with me if you have any questions, and links to the sign up should already be in your company email. I sincerely hope to see you again, and that today has made a positive impact on your life."

We offer a lot of smaller classes to individuals, like the one I'll be hosting this weekend. Anyone can sign up for them. We work with each person to determine what their goals are and help them overcome whatever hurdles may be a barrier on their path to success.

For some people, it's career-related: starting a business, working toward a promotion, or earning a degree. Others hope to improve their personal lives, relationships with partners or family members, or to change personal habits with fitness, food, or drugs. We've also helped countless people improve their anxiety and depression.

Really, whatever is holding a person back from reaching their full potential, we can empower them with the knowledge and tools to overcome and succeed.

The smaller classes are my favorite because they foster

deeper, more personal connections with participants who actively choose to engage. Limited to a hundred people, these sessions prioritize meaningful interaction, where engagement is key to success.

Waving, I walk down to stand in front of the stage where there's already a small group gathering to ask about the classes. Smiling, I answer a few questions, confirming details and expressing my gratitude that so many people are showing interest. After about fifteen minutes of chatting with everyone, they disperse with promises to see me this weekend.

As I unclip my microphone and turn to pack up my laptop, a deep voice surprises me.

"How much money for a one-on-one lesson?"

Startled, I glance up to see my coffee buddy. He's a few inches shorter than my six four, and I can tell he's into fitness with his broad shoulders and trim waist. He's got dark hair with an expensive-looking style, longer on top and faded on the sides. Shockingly blue eyes. Blue eyes always fascinate me. No one in my family has them and I find myself staring at people a little too long to study the endless shades of blue that are out there. I think that he was clean-shaven this morning, but a hint of a five o'clock shadow is already evident on his sharp jawline.

"The programs are designed for group participation," I finally answer. "But, I'm always happy to talk more about it with people individually, free of charge."

I know that other coaches would probably insist they only talk about it in the structured class environment, but I'm passionate about my job and am happy to talk about it whenever someone will listen.

"I'm Beckett," he says as he holds out his hand for me to shake. "Is it too forward if I ask you out to dinner and drinks tonight?" His gaze drops to my mouth, and I feel my cheeks heat. *Do I have something in my teeth?* That would be embarrassing.

"Cody," I say, laughing a little because he probably gathered that during the presentation. "Sadly, I have plans tonight." I really would love to spend more time talking with him about the Kyla programs. But I already promised the guys from the gym this morning that I'd grab dinner with them at our hotel. "Maybe we could go out Saturday, hook up after my class?" I offer, perking up at the idea. "Were you planning to attend?"

He grins back at me. "Absolutely."

CHAPTER THREE

Beckett

The horn blares, and Adrian and Jordan are out of their seats on either side of me, clapping and cheering along with the rest of the Caldwell Center. My friends glance down at me with mirrored looks of concern as they realize that I'm still sitting, and I belatedly lift my gaze to the giant scoreboard above center ice to watch the replay of the goal I just missed.

Our captain, Hudson Roy, streaks down the ice, faking a shot before passing the puck around a defenseman to our star rookie on the far side of the net. He sends it clean past their goalie, who's still focused on Hudson. It's a perfect setup and an even better finish. Beautiful play. *Damn, I can't believe I missed it.*

That ties the score 2–2 in the third period, with just over six minutes left in regulation time. The energy in the arena is electric, but I can't seem to focus.

When everyone settles down, Jordan is the first to question my behavior. "Seriously, what's wrong with you? Are you sick or something?" He's been my best friend since middle school when we were paired up for a class project and he boldly asked the teacher if he could be partners with "someone less spoiled than a Caldwell". I was so used to our classmates fighting for my attention for the same reason that he didn't want to talk to me, I thought it was hilarious. Thankfully, our teacher didn't grant his request, and I was able to win him over with my sarcastic remarks about the other kids as we did the assignment together. We've been best friends ever since.

Adrian leans around me to answer before I get a chance to come up with an excuse. "He's been like this all day." Then he shifts his gaze to me. "Can you tell me what a single one of our meetings was about today?"

When I give him an unamused blank stare in response, he dramatically rolls his eyes and turns his attention back to Jordan. "I should have gotten him to agree to a raise or more vacation time or something while he was so distracted."

That finally gets me to speak. "Do you need a raise or more vacation time? What's going on?" *Why wouldn't Adrian tell me if something was wrong?*

"Calm down, you already pay me way more than any of your siblings' assistants make. I'm fine," he reassures me with a wave of his hand, but they have my full attention now.

"Beck, did something happen?" Jordan clearly won't let up. As an on-screen reporter for Chicago's largest news network, he shifts into full investigation mode anytime he thinks I'm hiding something. There's no chance he'll drop it.

Jordan originally applied for a journalist position—he'd be excellent at it, with his knack for getting people to open up—but his boss took one look at him and put him on camera instead.

Now, he's stuck doing fluff pieces. With his tall, athletic build, light brown skin, and gorgeous eyes, it's obvious why. He pulls in views just by being on-screen. They don't want him off-camera long enough to dig into anything serious. Whenever I point that out though, he just shrugs and says his big break will come eventually.

"Nothing bad happened," I admit, looking around to make sure that none of my family members are close enough to overhear. Our private seats are above the one hundred level at center ice, connected to the owner's suite behind us.

Oakley and his best friend, Parker, are on the opposite end of the second row. They're usually so absorbed in each other that I doubt they'll hear anything I say, but I wouldn't actually care. The five of us hang out all the time. Oak and I have always been close, and Parker is like his shadow.

The rest of my family must all be watching from inside the suite or networking in other ones by now. Although we all love the Werewolves, I'm by far the biggest actual hockey fan, so they're usually content to let us take the seats out here while they stay inside with the bar and food. "I have a date tomorrow, and I'm a little distracted by the whole thing. I don't think I've been on a real date since high school," I attempt to say casually and not like I'm kind of freaking out.

You'd think that I just admitted to a secret marriage with a woman by how shocked they both look.

Adrian grabs my arm, his voice coming out in a much higher pitch and volume than I think he intends. "You have a date, and *this* is the first I'm hearing of it?" His grip tightens as he goes on. "Who is it with? I thought that I knew every detail of your life! I feel so betrayed."

Shaking him off, I laugh at his theatrics. "His name is Cody, and he ran the seminar yesterday at work. You really should have come, A. He's very hot."

"What was the seminar about?" Jordan asks. He must finally be over his own shock.

"I couldn't tell you. I was too distracted by the man giving the presentation to care about the content. I don't think I've ever been more attracted to someone. All that I really remember was him flirting with me in front of everyone after asking us to stand on our chairs. Then he did a backflip off of his own chair before straddling it like he was starring in some kind of fully clothed Magic Mike show."

"Did he also ask you out in front of everyone? Is that why you agreed to a real date?" Jordan asks, continuing to look confused.

"Nope, believe it or not, I asked him out. After the day was over, he hung around to answer questions and talk to people about some class that he's hosting tomorrow. You'd think that he was a celebrity with how excited people were to talk to him. When everyone finally left him alone, we chatted and I tried to get him to go out with me to dinner, but he already had plans and suggested we go out and hookup after his class tomorrow."

"Wow! You *like* this guy," Adrian says excitedly. "I don't think I've ever seen you light up when you talk about someone until just now."

I roll my eyes again but don't disagree with him.

"I don't think that you need to be nervous if he already mentioned hooking up, sounds like he likes you too," Jordan points out.

"That's true."

The crowd groans, pulling our attention back to the game. A holding penalty was just called against one of our defensemen. With only three minutes left in the game, losing one of our players for the next two dramatically decreases our odds of winning.

Maybe we can hold them at a tie, go into overtime, and at least get one point for the season.

Our penalty kill unit takes the ice for the face off. Somehow, our center wins possession and passes the puck to the left winger, who breaks away toward their goal. The entire arena holds its breath as he charges down the ice. Near the net, he fakes right and flips the puck into the top-left corner.

Goal!

Werewolves take the lead with just over a minute left in the game.

Our goal song plays, and everyone jumps around scream-singing along. I love our fan base so much, I'll never get bored of being in this crowd. The joy is infectious and reminds me of Cody with his contagious smile and upbeat attitude.

Does Cody like hockey?

Focus. Stop thinking about the hot man. *Be present.*

We're all on the edge of our seats as the final minute counts down, and when the final buzzer sounds, the true celebration begins.

No one brings up Cody or my date again, but I can't stop thinking about him.

I'M PRETENDING like I'm my usual, confident, put-together self as I walk into the hotel for today's class. Like I *didn't* change my outfit five times while getting ready this morning.

I started in one of my usual designer black suits. I figured that I'd met Cody while we were both in suits, and he must have liked what he saw to agree to this date, I should stick with what works. But then I was worried about looking like a pretentious asshole wearing a fancy suit in a Saturday morning self-help workshop or whatever the fuck this class is.

My next attempt was too casual in a designer tracksuit. It probably costs more than most people's tuxes, but I have money and I like nice clothes, sue me. Back in the black formal suit, I thought that maybe a colored one would be more casual, but couldn't decide if that looked like I was trying too hard.

I finally landed on a pair of charcoal tailored chinos and a fitted black button-up with some wing-tipped black boots. It's one of those random warm days in early March, and if I don't have to deal with a coat all day, I'm happy to skip it. It'll probably snow again next week, so I'll enjoy it while I can.

I'd hoped to talk to Cody before the program began to confirm the details for this evening. I arrived at the hotel thirty minutes early, and even though they insisted on having us sign NDAs and turn our phones over as a part of the super fucking weird check-in process, I still figured that would leave us plenty of time.

Apparently, I underestimated his popularity.

Cody has a crowd around where he's standing at the front of the conference room, casually leaning against a podium in a hot as fuck fitted royal blue suit. He definitely doesn't look like he's trying too hard. His dress shirt has the top few buttons undone, and a silver necklace draws my attention to the light dusting of hair visible on his defined chest. My cock is already thickening as I picture ripping the rest of his buttons off tonight.

Fuck. It is way too early in the day for those thoughts. I don't know how I'm going to get through a whole day of staring at him without being hard the entire time.

I think of boobs and women, willing my dick to calm down as I reevaluate my plan of securing his attention before the class. There's no way all of those people will give us a moment alone.

I also don't want to be stuck in the back of the room all day, so I snag the last open seat that I can find in the first few rows. It's at the end of the third row near the center aisle, so my view of Cody should be unobstructed.

I still would have preferred to sit in the very front.

I'm not above asking people to give up their seat for me, but that might not go over as well when they don't work for me, and I'm not trying to start any drama before the class even begins, so this will have to do.

Looking around the room, I'm surprised by the number of people who have shown up to participate. The screen at the front of the room next to the podium reads "Individual Empowerment Program" with smaller text under that reading "a Kyla trademark developed by Viktor Kivela" so apparently that's what we've all signed up for.

I'll be the first to admit that I'm out of touch when it comes to the cost of things, and "expensive" to me might not be the same as the average person. I tend not to look at prices when I buy things, but even I was surprised when I heard how much this program was.

I've heard people complain about how expensive it is to go to a Werewolves game. But even if a couple bought first-level seats at center ice, brand new jerseys, meals, and beer for the entire game, it would cost less than one of these courses.

Looking at the crowd surrounding Cody, and even glancing around at the faces throughout the room staring at him, it's evident that most of the people are here to be around him. Not going to lie, that gives me a little ego boost.

You can all pay to spend time with him, but I'm going on a date with him later.

Granted, I paid to be here, too, but that's beside the point. While everyone else wants him, he wants me.

At least for tonight.

I wonder where Cody's from. I think he might have mentioned he flew into Chicago just for this. Maybe he's here often, and we could set up a regular hookup situation.

I know that I'm getting ahead of myself, but there's something about him that draws me in. Makes me want to wrap my arms around him and protect him from anything bad ever happening.

Even though he's taller than me and a little more built, he's just adorable, and I want to take care of him. *Which is a fucking weird thing for me to think about a practical stranger.*

There's no other way to describe how engaged he is with every single person that he talks to, though. His big eyes and the way he seems to be bouncing slightly on the balls of his feet like he's so excited that he can't stand still. *Adorable.*

The crowd around him disperses as he announces that it's

time to begin our program. I really do try to pay attention to whatever it is that he's saying, but when our eyes meet and his grin grows wider in response to seeing me, I start thinking about that mouth. Will he still be smiling later, looking up at me from his knees with his plump lips wrapped around my cock?

Fuck, I'm doing it again.

Maybe the screen is a safer focal point. There's a super cheesy picture of a diverse group of people with their arms thrown over each other's shoulders, all laughing like they're just so damn happy all the time. No one is *actually* that happy.

Except for maybe Cody. There's something about him that seems so genuine.

Most people who are all bubbly and have constant smiles make me feel like they're hiding something or trying to get something out of me by acting how they think I want them to.

Not Cody. For whatever reason, I actually think that his happiness is sincere.

After staring at the picture for a few more moments, I notice that everyone in it is wearing a matching necklace. The delicate chains are all different colors of metal, resting on their collarbone with a pendant dangling from it. The pendants look like mountain peaks—some with more peaks than others, some in different colors. A glance in Cody's direction confirms that it's the same one he's wearing.

It's probably a company thing, like how our HR is always trying to show off on our social media accounts how much fun it is to work for us. Their thing must be matching "friendship necklaces" to represent how close everyone is. Or maybe they sell them at these classes. A quick glance around the room doesn't show any merch tables, though, so I guess not.

They really should sell products with how many people Cody got to take the class. I bet he'd be great in sales.

To my extreme disappointment, there's no acrobatics or chair straddling to start off today's activities. He has us start by doing this strange handshake, if you can call it that, that's more like awkward hand holding with our neighbors. We have to keep our fingers spread apart so that we can interlock them with the other person's, but keep them extended straight so that they form a mountain or something. It's weird as fuck, but it has everyone laughing so I guess it's not the worst icebreaker.

I startle a little when Cody's upbeat voice is replaced by a woman, and I realize that we've moved on to watching videos. The person, I think they called themself a "coach", is talking about identifying your goals and playing to your strengths or some crap like that.

Looking at Cody is much more enjoyable. He probably watches these clips all the time, but he didn't pull out his phone or leave for a break. He looks utterly fascinated by whatever this lady is saying.

You'd think his team is in game seven of the Stanley Cup Finals with how closely he seems to be following the video, nodding along, a contented grin on his gorgeous face.

Adorable.

The videos seem to go on forever before Cody eventually tells us that it's time to break off into small groups for our working lunch.

They pulled this bullshit the other day at the office too. No one wants to work through lunch, I don't care what magic food you've catered, *let me have a real break, dammit.*

That also means there's no opportunity for me to talk to Cody before this thing is over. Given how much I've already built up this connection in my head, I'll be devastated if he has to cancel.

We're supposed to be talking about our goals with the ten or so people around us in a circle. I'm half listening, mostly watching Cody walk around and join the groups that seem to be struggling. Each interaction he has looks so genuine, like he really wants to hear whatever they have to say.

In between groups, he catches me staring at him, chuckling

when he sees that my attention is on him and not my group. He takes a few steps toward me before another group calls out for him, and he has to stop to help them.

He offers me an apologetic smile before giving them his full attention, and I can't even be disappointed that I'm not the one talking to him when he's just so damn nice.

When it's my turn to share with the group, I struggle to come up with an area in my life that isn't already perfect, so I blurt out that I'm single and let people assume what they want to about that.

I really have no issue with not being tied down to anyone. A few of my siblings are in serious relationships, and sure, it seems nice sometimes. I even used to think that was what I wanted, but I'm not convinced it's the path for me.

In high school, I was certain that my first real boyfriend and I would be together forever. Until Jordan overheard him bragging to his friends that he was only dating me because I paid for expensive dates and kept buying him presents. Jordan got suspended for punching him, and I was pissed that he didn't wait for me to confront the asshole with him. After that relationship ended, I found out how much fun I could have without commitments and have never looked back.

Since then, I've had a few too many guys find out my last name and try to be whatever version of themselves they think is perfect for me, only to turn nasty when I call things off. It's not even a true breakup when it was only a hook-up arrangement, but the drama has been very real. I meant what I told my friends the other day, I haven't gone on an actual date in over ten years. There's just something about Cody that makes all of this effort seem worth it.

Cody makes sure that everyone has had the opportunity to identify and share a goal with their groups before having us return our seats to the initial classroom setup that we began in. He goes back to the front of the room, setting up two chairs across from each other, angled out toward the audience, before sitting in one of them.

"You've all done a fantastic job here today identifying your individual personal goals and learning about some of the Kyla tools that you can use in your everyday life to help you achieve them."

He looks so fucking excited for everyone. I can't help but mirror his grin.

"This final activity will be the most challenging of today, but if you take it seriously and give it your all, it will also be the most rewarding."

That would sound kind of ominous coming from literally anyone but him. Cody makes it feel like he's about to introduce a summer camp game.

"I'd love for each of you to come up and sit across from me here." He gestures to the other chair. "While in your small groups, you've already identified what area of your life could use the most improvement. Now, I'd like each of you to share a goal with everyone about *how* you'd like to see that area improve."

Okay, that seems redundant with what we just did. But not any more challenging.

"Then, I'd like for you to reflect on your past," he continues. "It could be from your childhood or a more recent experience. Try to think about a memory that shaped this area of your life. Share that with me today so that we can shed its burden and begin building a new foundation for your better future," he says excitedly, flashing his giant smile at us.

People start clapping like he's just announced their team won the number one draft pick, and not like we're all about to trauma dump in front of an audience of strangers.

The back row "gets to" start, so I have some time to figure out what bullshit to say before it's my turn. I already told my group I was single, so I guess it has to be related to that.

Not awkward at all when I'm going on a date with the person running this.

Even though this New Age, self-help bullshit really isn't my thing, I can appreciate how passionate Cody is about it all. He really is damn good at his job. It's obvious from the way people leave the stage—lighter, happier, even when they were crying moments before. Cody never pressures anyone to share if they don't want to, and his empathy is evident in how gracefully he handles each person's experiences.

I'm so in awe of him that I don't even realize that it's somehow already my turn until the person next to me taps my shoulder.

I join Cody, cautiously lowering myself into the chair as I scramble to think of some random memory to share that he won't want to talk more about later, or be able to call me out on embellishing as we get to know each other.

I wait for Cody to prompt me as he did with the people before me, but I find that his eyes are locked on the intricate shading and lines of my tattoos. I must have folded up my sleeves as I was fidgeting, trying to think of something to share. His gaze seems darker, *maybe he has a thing for guys with ink.*

When he finally looks up at me, our eyes meet, and the moment seems to stretch on endlessly. The room around us fades away as I stare at this perfect man.

And then a throat clears, snapping us both back to reality. I remember where we are and shift in my seat before Cody chuckles, "Hey, Beck."

Fuuuck. Why did he call me that in front of all these people when I can't kiss him?

I've never asked anyone to call me Beck, but many of my closest friends and family do. It always makes me feel seen, like the person is interested in the real me and not the eldest Caldwell son and heir.

It's also really hot when he does it.

"So, what did you decide to focus on for your area of improvement?" he asks with a flirty grin.

After an awkward pause, I blurt out, "Well, my mother would love it if I found a nice man to settle down with." I swear I have no filter around him.

Cody's expression grows more amused. "Alright, let's take a moment to reflect. Close your eyes for me, and think about what experiences might prevent you from settling down with a nice man."

I'm so glad they took our phones at the beginning of the day and had us sign NDAs. At the time, I thought it was all overkill for a self-help class, but now I'm very grateful to avoid whatever potential PR nightmare my answer might cause.

I'm already this far in, so keeping my eyes closed, I continue with whatever pops into my head. "Growing up, I had a great life. A fantastic family, we all like each other and enjoy spending time together. My parents are still together and have one of those disgustingly sweet relationships where they're constantly all over each other and saying cheesy things. Anyone who looks at them knows they're still in love after the almost forty years they've been together," I say.

I never questioned if my family would accept me or treat me any differently for being gay. My coming out consisted of correcting my mom in the sixth grade when she asked if I had a crush on any of the girls at school, and I answered, "No, but the new boy is really cool. I think I like him."

She didn't have any sort of reaction. She just asked me to tell her more about him and reminded me that I was welcome to invite him over whenever I wanted. No one in my family ever asked me about girls again, and subtle rainbow decor seemed to appear throughout the house overnight.

The new kid did end up spending a lot of time with me that year, but he turned out to be straight and only wanted to be my friend so he could go to Werewolves games. Once the season ended, he completely ignored me. He wasn't the first or last to care more about my family connections than he did about me.

My family also didn't care when I started to cover myself with tattoos. I didn't get them as some big rebellion against the straight-laced corporate image my family presents to the world, like some people assume. I just really like the look of them and appreciate them as an art form and means of personal expression. My dad and I even have matching tattoos of our hockey team's logo on our triceps.

"I was always popular in school, being athletic with a lot of money helped, even if people only wanted to know me because of my last name," I continue, even though I'm not sure where I'm going with this. "And aside from not knowing if my friends only cared about getting to my family, I guess that I wasn't completely exempt from the struggles of growing up knowing that I'm gay. No one directly bullied me, but I still overheard 'gay' being used as a derogatory term. I heard what people said about the other out kids or even people that they thought might be gay. I knew everyone didn't accept same-sex relationships. Hell, same sex marriages weren't even legal until I was in my twenties."

At some point, I must have opened my eyes because I find myself searching the crowd for looks of disgust or judgment. I don't spot any, so I continue. "Maybe I internalized some of that, protecting myself from the criticism. I've always known I'm gay and that it wasn't something I had control over. But, I can't ever remember a time I fantasized about getting married or even living with a partner," I admit. Even with that first high school boyfriend, my thoughts of our future were more about prom or if we'd go to the same college, not anything beyond our teenage years.

As I say this, images of that life with Cody flash through my mind without permission. Cody waiting for me with dinner in my condo at the end of a long day. Us in matching jerseys at

Werewolves games. Sitting on a beach, enjoying a relaxing vacation, just the two of us.

What the fuck was that?

Cody interrupts those thoughts, his voice now calm and reassuring. "So you're saying that you think you might have subconsciously decided that if people were going to look down on same-sex relationships, you wouldn't want one. That you were protecting yourself by denying that you might actually want that type of future with someone?" He looks so supportive with his big puppy dog eyes looking right into my soul.

I thought that Jordan was good at getting people to open up, but Cody could give him a run for his money.

I have no idea if that's something I did. Those images with Cody were the first time I've ever considered it. But I numbly nod along because I have no idea what to say.

"Thank you so much for being brave enough to share that with me," he says in a soft tone. I'm not sure anyone else can hear it, and he places his hand on mine reassuringly. His touch sends a bolt of electricity up my arm. "I think you have a lot to reflect on as you consider your goals for the future. Don't be afraid to think about what will truly make you happy." He looks so fucking proud of me, that I don't even regret saying all of that.

A part of me might even be questioning if what I said had some truth in it.

The rest of the program flies by in a blur, and before I know it, Cody is talking about the other programs we can sign up for. A ton of people approach him after the class, and even more people go straight to the tables that have been set up off to the side to choose their next course.

I hang back for what feels like an hour as I wait for each person to get their moment with Cody. I can't even be mad about the delay, as everyone who talks to him seems to amplify his joy somehow while sharing in it themselves. Eventually, the last person leaves, and it's just the two of us.

"Hey, Beck! Did you still want to go out?" he questions, like that's not the entire reason I showed up today.

"Obviously." I wink and bump my shoulder with his. "I've been waiting all day to get you out of here."

He laughs as he shuts down his laptop and slips it into his bag.

"Can I help you do anything before we go?" I ask, even though looking around, it seems like everything that's left probably belongs to the hotel.

"Nope!" he replies with a big smile. "I'm all yours."

CHAPTER FOUR

Cody

Today was amazing. I absolutely love to teach entry-level programs like that. Watching people discover the benefits of Kyla's courses is such a privilege, and I hope to see some of them again in future classes.

I also love spending time with someone one-on-one after trying to split my attention between such a large crowd all day. I'm so glad that Beck suggested we hang out. He seems great.

His driver was waiting for us outside the hotel and took us straight to this awesome Italian restaurant. It's fancier than anywhere I'd choose for myself, and it's cool that Beck thought to show me something I'd never do on my own.

The restaurant is cozy, with red velvet-backed chairs and lots of leafy plants around, giving each table a private feel. The instrumental music floating throughout the space is so pure it makes me wonder if it's live, and soft lighting adds to the intimate vibe.

Beck is really polite, opening doors for me, asking which

chair I'd prefer, and pulling it out for me when we arrived at the table.

"Do you want to split a bottle of wine?" he asks.

"I don't know much about wine, but I'm up for anything," I reply with a shrug and a smile.

"I don't usually drink wine either, I'm more of a beer or whiskey kind of guy. But I thought maybe the occasion calls for it." He gives me a shy smile, and I nod.

"Yeah, it does fit the vibe," I agree.

Our waiter makes a big show of bringing the wine out and pouring some for Beck to sip and approve before he pours fuller glasses for each of us. Now we're both pretending to know anything about it other than the color.

"Only the finest reds have this... oaky aftertaste," Beck deadpans, swirling his glass.

If he hadn't already admitted to his lack of knowledge, I might have believed him. Instead, I crack up laughing at his serious expression and take a sip of my drink.

"Is a drink supposed to make you more thirsty?" I ask him skeptically. "I swear that my mouth grows drier with each sip." His poker face finally breaks as he joins in on my laughter.

"That's how they get you to buy more, I guess." He shrugs and smirks at me. "This is fun. I'm glad you agreed to go out with me tonight."

I smile back at him. "Me too."

"So, you got to hear my trauma dump today," he prompts, and I chuckle at his description of the workshop. "Tell me more about you."

"Well, I'm originally from California, but now I live in Montana when I'm not traveling for work."

"Why Montana, were you sick of being around other people? Was it too convenient to go to any store you could imagine?" he questions with a furrowed brow, and I chuckle.

"Why does everyone hate on Montana so much?" I tease. "It's gorgeous."

"It always sounded like the middle of nowhere to me. I've never been, so I'll have to take your word for it."

"Or you could visit." I'd love to show him around my city, or do some hiking around the mountains.

"Maybe I'll have a reason to now," he replies, and I smile at the idea of him visiting me.

"It's also where Kyla's headquarters are," I continue. "I went to school back in Cali, and I lived there for a bit after I graduated when I started as a local coach. Then I was promoted, so I got to move to Montana," I explain.

"So, what's your job title now?"

"I'm technically the VP of Recruitment and Retention for the company." His eyes widen a bit, so I rush to reassure him. "But it sounds fancier than it is, apparently, I have the highest recruiting numbers, like I get the most new people signed up for our programs." I think I'm rambling now, but I can't stop.

"I also have the highest retention rates for the coaches I train remaining with the company. I don't feel like I do anything special compared to the other amazing coaches. I just live my life and tell people how great the programs are, they're usually interested in the idea of improving their lives. It's not a difficult concept," I explain.

"I'm so sorry. I didn't mean to look so surprised. We haven't even gotten our food yet, and I've already offended you." His cheeks darken, and it's fascinating to see this confident man look embarrassed.

I laugh. "You didn't offend me, I promise. Even though my title puts me in the executive management team, my favorite days will always be the ones like today—running workshops and meeting new people. I do spend some time at our headquarters, but I also spend a good amount of time traveling to host the programs." I try to give him a genuine smile to show that I'm having a great time. His gaze drops to my mouth and lingers there.

"You have my new favorite smile," he says softly.

My cheeks heat, and I look back at my wine. "Thanks," I mumble.

The smile feels glued to my face, even as I feel my blush growing.

Must be the wine.

Not sure why else I'd suddenly feel so shy around Beck. That was a nice thing to say. He's a nice guy. No reason for me to be weird about it.

Luckily, our food arrives and interrupts my awkwardness. My grilled chicken and salad are both spectacular. The plating was also super fancy, and my friends all loved the picture I had to send to our group chat.

I'm having a great time, but still, there's something about Beck that makes me feel self-conscious.

Usually, I have no trouble talking with people I don't know well. I travel a lot, and I'm used to meeting people and spending time with them without there being this tension.

It's not a bad tension, though. It's actually kind of exciting and makes my heart race. I really want his approval, which sounds silly, even to me. It's almost like I'm the new kid at school again, and I want the popular boy to accept me.

My past doesn't define my future. If I want to be friends with Beck, I should be his friend. I don't have to be in my head about it. Besides, he was the one who suggested we hang out in the first place, no need for me to worry about his opinion of me.

As we continue to eat, I try to shake off whatever has me so in my head about him. "So, what do you do for work, Beck?"

He pauses with the fork raised halfway to his mouth, which twists into a grin. "Wait, you don't know who I am?" He sounds amused, like he doesn't believe me.

Someone's cocky.

"Well, I know that your name is Beck. We met at the Caldwell company, and judging by the driver and the fancy car that brought us here, you seem to be pretty loaded. I'm guessing you might be one of them," I answer honestly. "But I don't know enough about your family or the company to pretend that I know about your actual job."

"I'm guessing you're not a hockey fan then." He sounds disappointed. "And just when I thought you might be perfect." Then he winks at me.

My damn blush is back.

I laugh again. No one has made me laugh this much in a long time, and I love it. "I actually used to be really into hockey during college. One of my frat brothers was a big fan, and that got me hooked. But I can't say I've kept up with it recently," I admit guiltily. "Why, are you a hockey player or something? Why were you at the company headquarters that day then?"

"Not a hockey player," he replies quickly with a laugh, cutting off my rant. "But I am the current CEO of the Chicago Werewolves Hockey Team."

"Wow, what an awesome job!" I know that mine is the best job in the world for me, but as far as non-Kyla-related jobs go, that's gotta be a cool one.

"Yeah, I really do love it," he replies with a huge smile. "My family has owned the team since my great-grandfather purchased it, and I'm really glad I get to be the one taking over for my generation."

I ask him about his family and learn that he has four younger siblings, all brothers. His youngest brother is still pursuing his degree, but they all work for the family company in some way.

"That sounds amazing," I tell him. "Like the idyllic family I used to dream about as a kid. It's so cool that you're all so close and get to work together. I love that about my job too. A lot of people in the town I live in work for Kyla since our headquarters are there, so a lot of my work friends are also my neighbors."

Most of my friends left unfulfilling jobs to work for Kyla after taking our courses. It's always exciting to see someone pursue a more meaningful career—and it's even better when they're promoted to headquarters and we become neighbors too.

"What about your family? Are they still in California?" Beck asks.

"Yeah, but we're not as close as your family sounds," I admit, running my finger around the edge of the wine glass as I think about how to explain. "My parents are great people, always kind and verbally supportive of me. Everyone who meets them loves them, and kids growing up always told me how lucky I was to have them as my parents. They were very focused on their careers, so even though I'm sure that they would have loved to spend more time with me, it just wasn't possible," I explain.

"Mom was in a successful television show in her early twenties when she met my dad, one of the producers. They have great drive and ambition, constantly trying to find their next project. Mom was always off at auditions or memorizing scripts, and Dad was on location or pitching ideas to industry executives," I go on. While mom has always had to work really hard to earn her next role, my dad is actually one of those huge Hollywood names now. His stellar reputation and lack of scandals have meant everyone wants him involved in their movies. With all of the money he's earned, he's even started a charity that helps provide housing for families who can't afford it on their own.

"That sounds kind of lonely," Beck says. "Do you have any siblings?"

"No, sadly, it was just me. They were only married until I was three, and then their careers led them down different paths. I split my time evenly between them and was always jealous of the kids with one stable home. Or even the kids whose parents weren't together, but had siblings to navigate life with," I admit.

I've learned that jealousy can really hold you back in life. It festers and can lead to resentment, self-doubt, and feelings of inadequacy. The Kyla programs helped me understand that those negative emotions can be turned into tools—motivation to improve myself and my life.

Instead of focusing on what others have that I don't, I learned to look at the deeper emotion behind the jealousy. What was I missing? What did I need? Then, I could take positive steps toward achieving those things for myself.

And never in a way that would hurt someone else. I always teach that you don't need to bring others down to build yourself up.

As a child, I didn't understand my feelings of loneliness and isolation—I only knew the jealousy.

When I got older, I thought maybe finding the right woman to settle down with would fill the void in my life. But all my relationships fell flat. I didn't realize then that waiting for someone else to solve my problems was toxic behavior.

It wasn't until I attended my first Kyla class that everything clicked. That seminar was the turning point. I learned that if I ever want to commit to someone else, I need to be the best version of myself first. A healthy partnership is about supporting each other, not relying on someone else to fix everything.

Now, I've put in the work to build meaningful relationships with friends, neighbors, coworkers, and even new people I meet. Thanks to Kyla, I've created strong bonds and a sense of belonging I never experienced growing up.

Beck asks more about where I live and about the details of my job. He's such a good listener, and he seems really interested in everything I say. I almost wish that he didn't like his job so much because I think that he'd make a great coach.

"You should come out to the next retreat we're hosting!" I sit up straighter in my chair as the idea sparks my excitement. Even if he doesn't want to join the company officially, I know my boss would love to have a Caldwell there. More importantly, I'd love to hang out with him again.

"You can meet some of the people I work with and learn more about the programs," I add. The more I think about the idea, the more excited I become, bouncing a little in my seat. "I think we'd have a lot of fun!"

He looks like he's trying to hold in laughter at my enthusiasm. "You haven't even spent one night with me, and you're ready to plan a whole weekend away together?"

It doesn't seem like he hates the idea, and I can't stop nodding my head. I really do want him to come. "You should think about it."

He smirks at me. "Oh, trust me, I am."

By the time we finish our food and wine, Beck insists on paying for our meals.

I'm still buzzing from our conversation and the possibility of seeing him again. I really feel like we could be great friends. There's something about him that draws me in, and I decide I'm not ready for the night to end.

"Want to come back to the bar at my hotel?" I ask. I don't know any other bars around here, and I'm hoping he isn't done hanging out, either.

"That sounds great."

"You did not sneak a dog onto an NHL team's private flight," I say, laughing so hard my face hurts. I feel like I haven't stopped laughing since Beck and I arrived at the bar over an hour ago.

"Well, believe it or not, werewolves aren't real. And I wasn't sure where to get an actual wolf when I was only ten years old," Beck replies cockily.

"But you could get a dog that looked like a wolf?" I still can't tell if this is a true story, not with how good his poker face can be. "When you were only ten?"

"People will do strange things when you offer them a lot of money, even if you're still a kid. I was convinced we'd win our next game if we had a more realistic mascot to motivate the team," he explains, as though this is a totally rational story.

"What happened when they found the dog?"

"I could tell that my dad was amused, and a little impressed, but that he knew he needed to act like a parent and scold me." Beck looks proud of himself as I continue laughing. "Then the players took turns holding and petting the dog. One of them really bonded with him. He ended up adopting the dog and everything."

"That's adorable."

"It worked, too. They won the next game, so a few of the more superstitious guys insisted that the dog keep coming. My punishment was being in charge of him during the games for the rest of the season."

The bartender checks if we need anything, and we politely decline. Beck and I are sticking to water since he mentioned not wanting to drink too much, but the bartender's frequent visits seem excessive, given how little we're ordering.

"I think the bartender has a crush. He won't stop looking at you," I tease.

He's shorter than Beck, a smaller man with purple dyed hair and a nose ring. I could never pull that off, but he's rocking the look.

"Punk rock twinks aren't really my thing." He laughs. "What about you? What's your usual type?"

I think back to all the girls I've dated, considering their similarities. "I guess I tend to go for brunettes with blue eyes."

Beck seems to like that answer, his blue eyes gleaming as he grins at me. "That *is* a hot combination."

My phone startles me, making the special chiming noise that indicates a text message from Viktor.

"I'm so sorry. I try to stay off my phone when I'm with some-one, but that's my boss's alert tone."

VIKTOR

Five minute warning: full update on week requested.

CODY

Ready.

I LOOK up to find Beck glancing at me with disappointment. I show him the text as I explain. "I'm so sorry. I haven't had a chance to update my boss all week. He's so busy with everything that when he calls, the expectation is that you answer it."

"I get it. I just wish that we didn't have to cut our night short," he admits, standing up from the bar as I do.

"Me too. I can't remember the last time I had this much fun just talking with someone."

"Does that mean I'll get to see you again?" he asks as we exit the bar and head into the lobby.

"Let's exchange numbers and make it happen!" I can't explain why, but I feel like I need to make sure that this isn't the last time I see him. Beck tells me his number, and I send him a text so he has mine as well.

"A black cat emoji?" he questions.

"It was the first thing that popped into my head." I shrug. "You remind me of one, with your tattoos, dark hair, and clothes. Plus, you're quiet in big groups, like today. But one-on-one, you open up and show your true self. Don't worry—it's a compliment. I think black cats are cool," I add with a smile.

"That's funny. I keep thinking that your boundless energy and enthusiasm remind me of a golden retriever," he replies with a grin. "Also a compliment."

He winks, and I feel my cheeks heat again. *Seriously, am I getting a fever or something?*

We stop near the hotel exit, and I know that Viktor will call any minute, but the thought of saying goodbye fills me with anxiety.

He steps toward me, and I realize just how little space is left between us. He's staring at my mouth again, and I wonder if maybe he's struggling with the same thing I am—figuring out what to say to keep this moment from ending.

He must decide to go in for a goodbye hug instead because he reaches a hand toward my hip just as my phone goes off. We both jump back a little at the noise.

"I'm so sorry. I really do need to take this," I say quickly, giving Beck an apologetic look. "Thank you for such a great night."

Then I answer the phone. He looks just as disappointed as I feel as he leaves the hotel and I head back to my room.

At least we exchanged numbers. I'm determined that tonight won't be the last time I see him.

"So, how was Chicago? Any luck at the Caldwell Corporation?" Viktor asks.

"Yeah, the presentation went really well and our individual seminar was sold out today." I've already emailed him updates on recruitment information from the presentations that I put on during the week, but Viktor always prefers the connection that actual conversations allow.

I really admire that he takes the time to maintain such solid friendships with his employees. Most bosses would probably prefer all email correspondence, but Viktor and I talk at least once a week when I'm traveling, and every day if I'm in Montana. He's always asking about my day and who I've talked to and spent time with. He knows everything about my life, and I know that I'm super lucky to have a boss who cares so much about me.

"Any of the family interested?" he asks.

"Beck and I actually just got dinner after he came to today's program."

"That's great! His example could help inspire a lot of people to improve their lives with my programs."

"Yeah, he's awesome. And he seemed interested in joining our next retreat!" I add. I'm really excited about the idea and seeing him again.

"Do you think you can make that happen?"

"I don't know if he's free, but I'll definitely invite him!"

"Keep up the great work, Cody, you're helping so many people find happiness," he encourages. *Best boss ever.*

CHAPTER FIVE

Beckett

I should have kissed him.

The thought plays on repeat in my head like an annoying song that you can't stop hearing over and over again, even now, days later.

Another thirty seconds and I would have. We were standing so close. I knew we didn't have time, and a short kiss was the most I could hope for. I was already reaching for him because not touching him had felt impossible in that moment. Staring at his mouth, the anticipation growing as we leaned in closer.

And then his stupid boss ruined it.

I know I haven't been on many first dates, so I'm not the best judge, but I thought we had a pretty perfect one. Dinner was great, the conversation effortless, and we laughed so much. Everything just felt... right.

I can't remember ever wanting to just hang out with someone I'm this attracted to.

Sure, I wish we could have continued the night in his hotel

room, but I was still really pleased with how the night had gone. I need to see him again.

I've been trying to hold off on texting him, not wanting to seem too desperate. But as I sit in my office, completely ignoring the work in front of me, having this internal debate yet again, I decide a few days should be fine.

BECK

Hey Goldie

CODY

Goldie?

BECK

You're a big, muscular, golden retriever of a man. Goldie, duh.

GOLDIE

If you say so *Sunglasses emoji*

BECK

No need to pretend like you didn't sit up straighter, bouncing in your seat with a big smile on your face, all excited that I gave you a nickname.

GOLDIE

You caught me *winking emoji*

GOLDIE

Now you need a nickname...

GOLDIE

Hmmm, something with a black cat

GOLDIE

Salem!

GOLDIE

Like the cat in Sabrina the Teenage Witch

GOLDIE

That's fitting, you have spooky vibes

Even his rapid-fire, stream-of-consciousness texting style is adorable. It's like he's so excited that he can't wait to finish a complete thought, so he sends it as he goes.

SALEM

Haven't seen it…"Spooky vibes" in a good way?

GOLDIE

For sure a good thing!

GOLDIE

Growing up, I always wanted to be like the cool kids with dark hair, piercings, and tattoos.

GOLDIE

Spooky vibes haha all of the popular girls wanted to date them.

GOLDIE

I knew that I couldn't pull it off

SALEM

Does that look work on the popular boys too?

GOLDIE

Goldie laughed at "Does that look work on the popular boys too?"

SALEM

So, no tattoos for you?

GOLDIE

I still have a few! I just knew that I'd never pull off the badass look.

SALEM

Hopefully I'll get to see them soon *winking emoji*

GOLDIE

DOES THAT MEAN YOU'RE COMING TO THE CONFERENCE?!?

SALEM

That will probably be the easiest way to hook up, right? Can you send me the details?

GOLDIE

FUCK YEAH!

GOLDIE

What's the best email to forward the link to?

SALEM

Beckett.Caldwell@Werewolves.com

GOLDIE

SENT!

GOLDIE

I'm so excited!

SALEM

Ugh, why does it have to be in Florida?

GOLDIE

Please say you're actually coming and there isn't some important hockey game that weekend

SALEM

You already know me so well. That was the first thing I checked. It's before the playoffs start, no important hockey game. I'm officially booked.

GOLDIE

YAY! YAY! YAY!

SALEM

Can't wait to see you again.

GOLDIE

Goldie emphasized "Can't wait to see you again."

GOLDIE

Why does three weeks suddenly seem so far away?

SALEM

Salem laughed at "Why does three weeks suddenly seem so far away?"

BEFORE I CAN DO MORE than react to his message, my phone is snatched out of my hands.

"Who's Goldie?" Adrian asks. He's fast, already on the other side of my desk. Too far for me to reach to reclaim my phone.

"The guy I went out with on Saturday," I say casually.

I'm not hiding anything. It's not even a big deal.

The only reason that I'm so hung up on him is that I thought we were going to hook up, and it got delayed. I'm sure that once we do, I'll get him out of my system and move on. Like always.

Not that I typically wait weeks and travel out of state for a hookup, but I'm not looking too closely at those details right now.

Adrian folds himself into one of the chairs across from my desk and hands me back my phone, not bothering to actually read anything.

The fact I'm still texting the same man is out of character enough. Plus, Adrian knows I'll tell him whatever he wants to know.

"He must have been pretty great in bed for you to still be talking to him," Adrian says, and I roll my eyes. "And for you to have been looking all swoony when I first walked in here," he adds in a teasing voice.

"Swoony? Is that even a word?"

"You were definitely swoony. Big eyes, staring at your phone screen like it was your favorite thing in the world." He sounds smug. "You didn't even notice me come in!"

"Whatever."

"Soooo… tell me about it!" Adrian raises his brows and circles his hand dramatically in a *hurry up and spit it out* motion.

"Fiiiine…" I play along just as dramatically. "Our date was amazing." I'm trying to suppress the stupid smile on my face, but I know I'm failing. "We were laughing the whole time. He's so much fun to hang out with, and we never ran out of things to talk about."

"That's nice?" he says like it's a question. "But I asked about the sex, Beck, not his sense of humor." Adrian looks at me with concern, like he doesn't recognize me.

I throw my head back in frustration, rubbing my eyes with my hands as I groan. "I don't know, okay? His boss interrupted us with an important call, and we had to cut the night short."

"I'm sorry, Beck, that sucks." Adrian sounds bummed for me, which I appreciate.

"And now I can't stop thinking about him. Like, I'm worried that I'm actually losing my mind over this guy." Adrian laughs, but I'm only half joking. "A, I just agreed to go to a weekend retreat in fucking *Florida* so that I can see him again."

"But, you *hate* Florida," Adrian states, like I don't already know my own opinion.

I nod as I list off some of the reasons. "The humidity, the crowds, the families traveling, the sand." Then, I repeat myself slowly to really drive the point home. "Losing. My. Mind!"

"What's the retreat even for?"

"More of the self-help, New Age bullshit that he taught when he was here."

If possible, Adrian looks even more confused. "If you know that it's bullshit, then why do you keep going to the programs?"

"Because he's there, and I'm an idiot."

"You're clearly not an idiot." Adrian gestures around the fancy office like that proves I'm an intelligent, functioning adult.

Ignoring the fact that I mostly got my job because I was born into the right family.

"When it comes to Cody, it's like my brain just shuts off and hands the controls to my dick," I admit.

Adrian smirks, clearly amused as I keep going. "You should've heard the nonsense I spouted during that class, trying to impress him and act like I was taking it seriously. He's so good at his job, he even had me believing it for a minute."

"Do I even want to know?"

"He had me questioning if my lack of relationship resulted from some subconscious need to be accepted by society." I roll my eyes. "Not because I have no desire to spend extended amounts of time with the same person, don't trust anyone, and get bored easily."

Adrian is back to looking confused. "If you do want a relationship with this guy, that's not a bad thing. You know that, right?" he adds skeptically.

"Sure, but I don't want a relationship. I just want to hook up with him, and then I'll move on like I always do."

Adrian doesn't look convinced but drops the subject, returning to work. After about an hour of us reviewing things that I need to sign or approve for the team, he leaves to get to the Caldwell Center for tonight's game.

I'll meet him there later, but he likes to go early, claiming it's to check in with the players or staff—though I'm pretty sure it's just an excuse to check out the players in their suits. Not that anyone minds; they all love him.

When I finally check my phone again, I see that there are several missed texts from Cody, and I catch myself smiling down at it.

GOLDIE

I'm glad that you finally texted me

GOLDIE

I've been trying to hold off all week, worried that you'd think I was harassing you to spend money on the classes

GOLDIE

But I was bummed when we had to end the night early on Saturday

GOLDIE

At the risk of embarrassing myself, I had a really fun time hanging out with you. I'm glad that it wasn't a one time thing *smile emoji*

THE SMILE on my face grows with each new message that I read. This guy is just so fucking adorable. How could anyone not feel happier talking to him?

SALEM

Sorry for the delay, I got interrupted with work. That's not embarrassing. I really enjoyed our time together too and I'm looking forward to seeing you again. In the meantime, feel free to text me whenever you'd like, I know that you're not (only) after my money haha

GOLDIE

Hahaha, I guess I am happy that you'll be taking the classes with me

GOLDIE

But I'm definitely the most excited to get to hang out again

CHAPTER SIX

Cody

*L*ongest. Three weeks. Of my life.

Luckily, Beck gave me the go-ahead to text him, or I probably would've gone insane from the anticipation. I seriously have no idea what it is about him that makes me so excited to see him again, I just know that I am.

Everything else in my life has been just as great as usual.

I've been traveling a lot. The week after meeting Beck in Chicago, I was in Minneapolis teaching more classes. Then, I spent a week at home in Montana for meetings before heading to California for seminars. Now, I'm in Florida, eagerly anticipating his arrival.

I've met some great people since Chicago, too. And I always love my weeks at home with my coworkers and friends.

But for some reason, I've found myself thinking about Beck *a lot*.

I catch myself comparing the new people that I meet to him, wondering what he'd think about the classes I've been teaching, and wanting to share anything funny that happens with him.

Texting him has been really fun. At first, it was just memes and silly pictures we thought the other might like—or that reminded us of each other. Somewhere along the way, it shifted into actual conversations.

The first time that he called me instead of texting, I was shocked. I assumed it was a butt dial.

Instead, he explained it was intentional, that sometimes work keeps him busy and makes texting hard, but he can still chat while getting things done. And he didn't want me to feel neglected by his slower replies.

He's always so thoughtful.

Getting to know Beck and learning more about his interests and life has been amazing. He's so funny, his dark humor and sarcasm never cease to entertain me.

I feel like I've known him for years. I know all about his siblings and his friends. I'm now practically an expert on the Chicago Werewolves and am very excited that they've officially secured a spot in the playoffs, which begin in two weeks. I'd love to go to a game with him. To see first hand if he gets excited when they score, nervous if they're losing, or if he tries to play it cool as their owner.

I dismiss that thought as soon as I have it. I'm really glad that Beck wants to be friends, but realistically, this will be mostly a texting friendship.

We live in different parts of the country, and both have super busy jobs that we love. I know that his demanding life will probably prevent it from becoming a common occurrence, but I'm so excited that he decided to come this weekend.

I can't imagine where my life would be today if I hadn't found my way into a Kyla program. During my senior year of college, my fraternity brother's mom had signed him up for it, but he'd really wanted to go to a sorority formal that weekend instead. He asked if I was interested, since the class was already paid for, and agreeing to go was probably the best decision I've ever made.

After that first class, something in me clicked into place, and I knew I needed to continue taking them. My grades improved, my relationships improved, and I felt a sense of purpose in a way I never had before. Sure, I was already going to a fancy college for a business degree, but I had no real ambition or idea of what to do after graduation.

I am the man I am today because of what I've learned in these programs. When the opportunity to join the Kyla team was presented to me after graduation, I didn't hesitate to accept the challenge. I work hard to do the team and our founder justice every day, striving to improve people's lives the same way that mine has been.

I always love these retreats. It's a chance to reconnect with friends from over the years and to learn from Kyla's senior leaders. This weekend, at least thirty coaches I've personally trained will be here, plus some of my closest friends from management.

But if I'm being completely honest, I'm probably the most excited to see Beck again.

When my Uber pulls up to the venue, I spot Beck leaning casually against the building, absorbed in his phone. Excitement courses through me as I grab my bag and head straight for him.

He doesn't notice me approach, so I lean in close and whisper in his ear, "Just who I was hoping to see."

In the next moment, Beck spins to pin me against the wall with his forearm horizontal, digging into my chest, holding me in place. Damn, he's strong. Not many people could hold me down so easily.

He's panting, and his pupils are blown as he looks up at me with an expression of anger and confusion. Then, it melts into relief as he recognizes me and smiles.

"Holy shit, Cody, you fucking scared me. You can't surprise someone from a big city like that."

"I didn't expect you to attack me. I thought I'd get a little jump or a laugh or something." I smile back at him, but it's hesitant.

Beck is still holding me against the wall, and as our eyes meet, I'm suddenly very aware of how his hard body is pressed up against mine.

My cheeks heat as I realize that's not the only place blood has rushed to. I finally give him a little shove to get him off of me before he realizes that my dick is hard.

Apparently, I like being manhandled?

I've never been with a girl who's tried anything like that before. And I've never really played any contact sports where I would be that close to other guys.

I've obviously never been with a man sexually. I'm straight.

Right?

Yeah, I'd know if I was into dudes by now, I'm almost thirty years old.

Definitely straight. I just wasn't expecting that, and it got my adrenaline going and my blood pumping.

Totally a thing.

Beck clearly has no idea what tangent my brain just went on, and a laugh seems to force its way out of him. He has a great laugh, and hearing it instantly brings my smile back full force.

"Well, that wasn't how I expected our reunion to go," he says when he finally stops laughing.

Nodding, I gesture toward the front entrance, where I see a few more people heading in. "Should we act like responsible adults and go get checked in?"

"Yeah, I figured I'd wait for you since this was my first time, and I didn't know if there was a special system."

For some reason, hearing that he waited for me makes my chest feel lighter.

"We can go to the front desk and check in with the hotel employees. Then, there are usually a few different Kyla tables set up with name tags and itineraries for the weekend, depending on your rank in the company."

He looks at me a little skeptically as I say that part, so I rush to clarify. "Not a ton of people who are new to the programs want to jump right into the retreat weekends. They tend to be more for coaches to learn from the company executives about how they can improve their own courses or learn new materials for themselves before going out to teach them to people."

"So it's okay that I'm here, though, right?" he asks, still looking unsure.

"Definitely!" I assure him. "Viktor loves when people want to join retreats, especially people who are already so successful on their own, like you. We've had CEOs and politicians come to these retreats, they can skip the middleman and learn from the people actually creating the material. The coaching system is great for helping to make Kyla more accessible for everyone by coming to them, but learning from Viktor himself is something that I wish everyone could experience," I add with enthusiasm.

Beck finally looks convinced, visibly relaxing as he picks up his own bags to follow me inside.

We've arrived toward the end of the check-in period, and there's only one person ahead of us in line. We approach the desk together, but I gesture for Beck to give his information first.

Then the woman looks at me expectantly to also give my info like we're together.

"Sorry, I should have hung back. We're booked separately." I flash her a big smile. Her cheeks darken a little, and she looks at her computer and then back at us again, her expression growing more concerned.

"I'm so sorry." Her friendly demeanor has been replaced, and she's in full customer service apology mode. "It seems we've overbooked this weekend. I think there was an error with our system because we only have one open room left on the property."

I glance at Beck, who gives me a questioning look.

The venue consists of the main building with hotel-style rooms, where I'd planned to stay, and cabins near the lake used for team-building and bonding activities. The cabins are typically reserved for couples or high-level executives like Viktor.

My job title might qualify me for one, but I've never bothered —it seems unnecessary when I'm used to regular hotel rooms.

"The opening is a studio-style suite," she continues. "It's a cabin, so more spacious than a hotel room in the tower here would be, but unfortunately, there's only one bed."

Beck raises an eyebrow at me, clearly wondering how I want to handle this.

"Would you be okay sharing a room?" I ask. "If you want your own space, I'm sure I could ask around and find someone else to crash with. I know most of the people here."

I don't want him to think that I don't want to share with him, though, so I backtrack. "But I was also really looking forward to spending time with you this weekend, so a sleepover could be fun! No pressure. Either way, I'm sure we can hang out." I really do try to sound casual as I ramble on, but I can't stop some of my excitement about the idea from showing in my tone.

Beck grins at me indulgently. "If you're okay with it, I think that a sleepover with you could be very fun." He winks and turns back to the woman checking us in. "That will be fine with us both, thanks."

After giving her my info so that she can combine our reservations into one, we each get a key and head toward the only Kyla welcome table that still has someone sitting at it with papers.

The young man behind the table perks up as we approach. "Hi, Cody!"

I recognize him from a program in Vermont and smile back. I'm pretty sure his name was Justin. "Hi, Justin! Good to see you again."

"Oh my god, you remember me?" He's so excited. *Nailed it.*

"Of course. How's Vermont?" I always try to connect with everyone I meet, and moments like this, where someone feels seen and special, make the effort worth it.

It doesn't cost me anything to be kind. Why wouldn't I be?

"It's great! I just graduated, so now I'm able to work for Kyla full time. I love it so much!" he replies.

"Congrats! Hopefully I'll see you in Montana working at our headquarters soon."

He nods eagerly at the idea. It's a big deal to be promoted to corporate headquarters, and it's a goal for many in the company. Everyone who works there raves about the community, so even those who've never visited understand how special it is.

Once we get our welcome materials, Beck and I head out toward the cabin.

"I didn't even think to ask beforehand, will we have similar schedules this weekend, or will you be working a lot?" Beck asks as we arrive at our door.

"I probably should have asked if you had any special interests in the smaller classes. I could still change your schedule if you do, but I went ahead and matched yours up with mine so that we could hang out all weekend," I admit with a laugh.

"Sounds perfect," he agrees.

Luckily, he looks genuinely happy and *not* like I'm being a clingy weirdo. *Small victories.*

Opening our door reveals a nice studio-style, open-concept space. There's a small kitchen just ahead, with a stove, microwave, and even a full-sized fridge. Off to the right, where the space opens up a bit more, there's a round table with chairs for four. Behind that is the bedroom area. The bed looks smaller than the one I have at home, so it must be a queen or even a full.

When she'd referred to the cabin as a suite, I assumed there would be a couch of some sort, but the seating area beyond the table only has two plush armchairs facing a television. There's a desk pushed against the wall to the right of the bed, and a door to the left of the bed must lead to a bathroom behind the kitchen.

Looking around, I realize there's nowhere else to even volunteer to sleep to avoid sharing the bed. I glance at Beck to see if he seems annoyed or upset by the lack of options, but he just sets his bag down at the foot of the bed and smirks at me. "I call the side closer to the bathroom."

"That's fine," I agree with a laugh. If he doesn't care about sharing, then I won't either. It's no big deal. I'm not sure why I've even given it this much thought. *No need to be this nervous.*

"I'm going to shower off my day of travel before the welcome dinner if you don't mind me using it first?" Beck asks, and I nod for him to go ahead.

This weekend is going to be great. I just need to stop over-thinking everything with Beck.

He obviously wants to be my friend. He's here to spend time with me. He didn't hesitate about us sharing the room... or the bed.

My old feelings of loneliness from moving around so much as a kid and never having consistent friends have no place here. I'm going to have fun with my friend.

So why am I so nervous?

CHAPTER SEVEN

Beckett

The welcome dinner is fine, I guess.

I'm at Cody's table with a bunch of the Kyla executives. They seem like friendly people, but I'm really only interested in talking to Cody.

"So tell us about yourself," the woman across from me prompts.

"I'm Beckett," I answer flatly.

She laughs, and the man next to her tries to get more out of me. "What do you do, Beckett?"

"I'm in management." I know I should probably put in some effort so that Cody doesn't think I'm an asshole, but when I glance his way, he's biting his lip like he's trying to suppress a smile in response to my attitude.

I'm so distracted by his lips, wishing that I could be the one digging my teeth into them, that I don't notice the man's follow-up question until someone loudly clears their throat and he obviously repeats himself. "What type of company do you work for?"

"Hockey." I smile at him to try to cover up how rude I know I'm being, but I'm sure it looks as fake as it feels.

Cody bursts out laughing, and I smirk at him. After a few more one-word responses to their questions, they give up and leave us alone. They probably all think I'm a jerk, but I don't care. I really did attempt to be polite. It's just so hard when the hottest man I've ever seen is sitting right next to me.

Speaking of hard, Cody's muscles when I had him pinned to the wall this morning felt even bigger than I'd fantasized about after only seeing him in suits.

He was dressed more casually when we got here, in shorts and a T-shirt. After I got over the initial fight or flight response to his up close and personal greeting, I wanted to drop to my knees right there in front of the hotel and address the obvious erection he'd gotten after I manhandled him.

If he's as into that as I suspect, he'll be so much fun to boss around in bed. He's always so energetic and eager to please. I bet he'd love to have me take control while I make him feel amazing.

I've found that a lot of guys who are bigger than me, both in height and muscles, have fallen into the more dominant role when it comes to sex in their previous relationships. It can be so fun to be the first one to throw them around a little or order them to do things.

I don't *need* it to enjoy myself or anything. I'm sure that Cody and I can have a *lot* of fun with whatever we do, but I definitely enjoy taking the lead. I can't wait to get him back to our room. It's all that I can think about as these people go on and on about how amazing our weekend will be.

I know that mine will be, but not because of this silly company or the classes that I'll have to sit through.

There have been a few speakers during this dinner, welcoming everyone and getting them excited. They all hype up the company and employees, but especially the CEO. The number of times I've heard "Viktor is so amazing" or "Viktor is so smart" or "Did you hear about this great thing Viktor did?" or "Have you gotten to speak with Viktor yet? *Because I have*" today, is wild. It's like they're all in love with him. Honestly, if Cody wasn't right there agreeing with how "special he is" and how "lucky we all are that he's here this weekend" I'd think all of these people were groupies trying to sleep with the lead singer in their favorite band, not employees talking about their boss at a company retreat.

Imagine my disappointment when he finally takes the stage and is just a normal-looking guy. A little on the plain side, if I'm being honest. He's tall with light blonde hair, smile lines, and freckles covering his face. He's got an average build, probably late forties or early fifties if I had to guess. I wouldn't think twice if I passed him on the street.

"Thank you all for being here this weekend," he greets everyone in a calm voice, like he's teaching a yoga class. "I am so excited for you all to learn from our latest courses and can't wait to hear about how each of you has improved your lives since we last spoke. I know that we're all eager to move onto the cocktail hour, so I'll save my lectures for my seminar tomorrow. Dinner is over, the bar is officially open. Grab a drink, socialize, and relax before our big day tomorrow!"

Finally.

I want to follow Cody's lead on drinking tonight, so I wait for him to order first. I figured that we could still have a drink or two before sobering up in time to have the real fun in our room. I want him to remember every moment, and I never want my partners to make alcohol-inspired decisions in bed. Consent is sexy. He ordered water, though, so we must be on the same page.

If I thought Cody was popular during the class I took in Chicago, he had nothing on this Viktor guy. He has a full-on receiving line set up so that everyone can say hello and have a moment with him.

I'd rather not. But of course, Cody joins the line.

I follow him and watch as every single person greets Viktor with what looks like a very intimate hug that lasts way too long for my comfort.

After Cody's super long hug that definitely didn't make me jealous and Cody's enthusiastic greeting with him, Viktor gives me a much shorter one. Still overly enthusiastic for a stranger, but better than the borderline groping some people got. I couldn't imagine doing that with my employees—it's just weird.

I truly can't understand the hype around this guy. Everyone talks about him like he's the second coming, but he's just… boring.

"We're so happy that you could join us this weekend," he tells me with way too much eye contact. "I'm always honored when successful people like yourself take an interest in my courses."

Successful for having the right last name, maybe. "Happy to be here." I give him a tight smile, but I'm way too preoccupied to actually care. My brain, and my dick, are both focused solely on what happens next, knowing Cody and I are about to share that tiny bed.

"Always great to see you, Cody. I'm looking forward to your presentation tomorrow," Viktor says before finally excusing us. I think we're free, but Cody gets stopped every few steps by someone who's either a "great friend" or a devoted fan. It's cute seeing how much everyone loves him and how he remembers little details about their lives, but I can't help wishing we could get back to the cabin already.

When I notice that some people are leaving for the night, I suggest we do the same. Cody is eager to go along with that plan, and he looks so fucking cute, practically skipping to our cabin. I'm glad that we're both excited for tonight.

WHEN WE REACH OUR DOOR, Cody uses the key and steps inside to hold it open for me. Hoping to recreate our hot moment from when I arrived and had him up against a wall, I step in past him before closing the door and place my palms on his chest to back him up against it.

"I've been waiting for this all day," I admit as I raise my hand to cup his jaw. My other hand goes to his waist as I step closer, eliminating the space between our bodies. I meet his eyes, expecting to find him as lust drunk as I feel, and even though his breathing is heavy and his pupils are blown, I notice some confusion mixed in.

"What's wrong?" I ask, taking a small step back as I stroke my thumb along his cheek.

"What… what's happening right now?" His voice cracks, and he sounds so genuinely perplexed that I drop both hands and take a much bigger step back before answering.

"I was going to kiss you?" I sound like I'm asking a question even though that had definitely been my plan. "Was that not okay? Is… is that a hard limit for you or something?"

"Hard limit?… Kiss me?" Cody mutters, and his expression is one of such shock that I kind of want to laugh, except now my face probably matches his because *what the hell is going on?*

"Did you change your mind about wanting to hook up?" I ask as gently as I can, trying not to sound too disappointed because I don't know what else to say.

"Change my mind about hooking up?" Cody asks, still mumbling.

"Yeah, I know you were the one to suggest a hook up after I asked you on our date, but if you don't want to do that anymore, that's okay. I won't pretend that I'm not bummed because I mean, look at you," I can't help checking him out again. "You're the sexiest man I've ever met," I say with a laugh. "But, consent is also very important. I didn't mean to pressure you into anything by agreeing to share a room," I ramble, hoping that he'll snap out of his confused state to stop me and explain what's happening.

"You think I'm the sexiest man you've ever met?" *Why does he sound so shocked?* Has he not looked in a mirror recently? At least he finally meets my gaze for this question.

"Easily. Have you seen yourself?" I laugh again, gesturing my hand in his direction because I don't know what else to do at this point. We're both still standing about an arm's length apart, staring at each other with confusion.

"Wait. Our date? We went on a date? Like a romantic one?" His tone elevates a little with each question, and my heart sinks.

Fuck.

I really hope there's a better explanation than the conclusion I'm jumping to. But as the reality of his confusion sinks in, I can only think of one question, and I know that I have to ask.

"Cody, are you straight?"

CHAPTER EIGHT

Cody

"Cody, are you straight?" Beck asks, sounding so disappointed.

The truth is, until this morning, I'd never once questioned it. I've always considered myself an ally of the queer community—fully supportive and open-minded. *But being part of it?* That's never been something I thought applied to me.

I'm twenty-eight years old, and I've exclusively dated and slept with women. Being straight seemed like an obvious part of who I am.

I've always been able to identify if a man is attractive, but I've never looked at one and thought, "I really want to see him naked".

Until maybe now.

As I had that thought, it was quickly followed by, "I wonder what Beck looks like naked" and my dick is definitely a part of this conversation. It's been thickening since he slammed the door and backed me into it.

I did have a frat brother who's gay who used to talk about his hookups very openly, and they always sounded really hot, but talking about sex is always hot, right? It doesn't matter if it's with a girl or a guy. *That doesn't sound very straight either. Huh.*

Beck is still staring at me, waiting for an answer I'm not sure I can give him. "I thought I was," I finally choke out.

He somehow looks even more confused. "You thought you were straight?" he clarifies.

I nod stupidly as I continue to think about Beck and all the nerves I've had around him today. All of the excitement about seeing him again, and how much I've enjoyed talking to him over the last few weeks. Was that just normal friendship stuff... or is something else happening here?

He said that he asked me on a date. And now that I think about it... okay, yeah, that dinner at that fancy restaurant could have totally been a date. And the way we were smiling and laughing the whole time...

Fuck. *Are we dating?*

Am I so oblivious that I didn't even realize I've been dating a man?

More importantly, why does the thought of dating Beck make my stomach all fluttery? *Do I want to be dating him?*

All of these thoughts and questions fly through my head as he slowly takes a seat at the dining table. I'm way too hyped up right now as I think through all of this to sit down, but I go to the table and hold on to the back of one of the other chairs.

"So, does that mean you were questioning your sexuality?" he finally asks, sounding a little hurt as he continues, avoiding looking my way as he stares down at the table. "Was I an experiment, and now that the moment is here, you've confirmed that you're straight?"

"What? No!" I sit down next to him and take his hand, needing him to hear and see me as I say, "The opposite, I think."

That gets him to look up, and he hasn't pulled his hand away, so I think that's a good sign that I haven't completely offended him. "What's the opposite of that? You were gay until you went out with me, and now I've ruined men for you? Awesome. That's a real confidence boost."

Fuck. I'm somehow continuing to make this worse.

"No! Not that! I've always thought that I was straight. Up until today, actually," I admit. I wish that I could explain this better so that he wouldn't still look so disappointed and confused. "But now that I know you want to kiss me and that we went on a date, I'm reevaluating the feelings I've been having around you and about you. I'm realizing that I'm an idiot," I say with a laugh.

"You're not the idiot," Beck scoffs as he stands abruptly. He starts pacing the room, running his hands through his hair.

"I can't believe I almost kissed you when you're straight," he mutters, his voice thick with disbelief. "I really thought you were flirting with me that first day. I thought you were checking me out."

I stay silent, unsure of what to say as he shakes his head. His voice rises slightly as he continues, "I even thought you were implying *I* was your type—dark hair, blue eyes—when we were joking about that bartender." He drops his hands to his sides, looking utterly defeated.

"And now I'm trying to put the blame on you for all of this," he says, his voice breaking. "God, I'm such an asshole. I'm so sorry."

He sounds so distressed that I can barely stand it.

I know that I'm not doing a good job of expressing myself right now with words, but I really want him to understand what I'm feeling.

Before I can think about what I'm doing, I'm out of my chair, grabbing the back of his neck, and crashing my lips to his. He's frozen for a moment before giving into the kiss, opening up for me. His lips are softer than I expected, and the rough scrape of his stubble is surprisingly hot.

I tease his lips with my tongue, wanting him to give in entirely. With a moan, he tangles his fingers in my hair, pulling just a bit until I give an echoing moan, and he finally fights me for control. His tongue is in my mouth, exploring and making my head spin.

There's no denying that I'm kissing a man as we both attempt to eliminate the space between our hard bodies, grabbing onto each other desperately. The firm muscles of his back and arms are hot as hell.

Why have I never kissed a man before?

I bite his lower lip before sucking it between mine, and I love how rough we're being. I seriously don't know if my dick has ever been this hard from just a kiss. I try to grind my aching cock into him to get some sort of friction, but he pulls away with a gasp.

"What are you doing?" I ask desperately.

"What am *I* doing?" he echoes, still sounding so confused. Can't we move on from that part and agree that we should be kissing? "What are *you* doing?"

"Trying to kiss you, *duh*," I say with some amusement that our answers have swapped in so little time.

"Cody, you just told me you woke up this morning thinking you're straight, and now you're making out with me like it's no big deal!" His voice wavers between incredulity and amusement, like he can't decide whether to laugh or question everything. "Shouldn't you be freaking out?"

"Do you want me to freak out?" I genuinely ask. "If I need to have some sort of sexual identity crisis before we can get back to kissing, just let me know. I'll make it quick." I give him a cheeky grin.

"I don't *want* you to freak out," he says, ignoring my kissing suggestion, still looking amused but concerned. "But, I also don't want you to change your mind tomorrow and wish we hadn't done anything. I don't want you to feel like I pressured you at all, in any way."

I smile even bigger at him. He really is such a great guy. No wonder I like him this much.

"Beck, I thought that I was straight because I'd never wanted to kiss a man before today. Right now, I'd very much like to be kissing a man. Specifically you. So, I must not be as straight as I'd previously assumed," I shrug. "Seems pretty simple to me."

I'm sure that for many people, this situation would lead to a more significant moment of self-reflection or a possible identity crisis, but I'm not feeling any distress over this.

"Kyla has taught me to just accept things as I learn them about myself, to not let them hold me back from my future happiness. Kissing you made me very happy, Beck," I tell him. I know that my smile is obnoxious at this point, but I can't help it. "You didn't pressure me to do anything I didn't want to do other than stop," I tease and quirk my brow.

He finally gives me a small smile in return. "This is so not how I thought tonight was going to go," he chuckles.

"Me neither," I agree and join in laughing. "Can we get back to kissing now?" I ask hopefully, stepping closer to him and placing my hands on his hips.

He grabs my hands to remove my hold, squeezing them in his own before meeting my gaze. "As much as I'd love to continue kissing you and so much more, believe me, I really want to." He takes a deep breath, then goes on. "We need to stop."

I feel my smile drop, and I know my face isn't hiding any of my disappointment right now.

"Or at least pause. We need some ground rules," he continues, and I perk up at the pause clarification. That means we can start again.

Yes, please.

"What ground rules?" I ask, trying to hurry him along.

"Like, if you're really sure that you want to do this, what *this* even means?" he says, sounding like he still expects me to back out.

No fucking way.

When I get excited about something, I can't focus on anything else. And I'm very excited about the idea of making out with Beck again.

"I'm very sure," I agree, trying to sound confident and calm, but I think I'm too eager.

"So what does that mean to you, Cody?" he looks at me expectantly like it's my turn to talk. "Do you want to kiss for a while, get used to the idea of making out with a man, and then go to sleep?"

That does sound nice, but based on how hard my dick still is, I'm not sure it will be enough.

"Beck, I just want *you*. That's all I can think about right now," I admit.

"Cody, I'm trying to be a good guy here. Act responsibly. But you're making it very difficult not to throw myself at you."

"So throw yourself at me," I agree enthusiastically. I might not have done anything sexual with a man before, but as I imagine what hooking up with him might look like, each image is hotter than the last. I definitely want to have sex with Beck.

Beck lets out a frustrated groan, pulling at his hair before spinning and plopping back into a seat at the table. He gestures to the seat next to him for me to sit down, so I do.

"Cody, my previous partners have all been men very comfortable having sex with other men well before they met me."

I look down, suddenly worried that my lack of experience will be a deal breaker.

"Cody, look at me," he says in a firm tone that has me immediately doing what he asked. He waits for our eyes to meet before continuing. "There's nothing wrong with being curious or realizing that your attraction isn't what you'd previously thought," he tries to reassure me. "I'm simply explaining my own lack of experience with this specific situation."

He pauses briefly, making sure I'm following his train of thought. "I feel like we need to clearly discuss what you would and would not be comfortable with doing. If you do want to go any farther than the kissing, which I think you have already confirmed you enjoy."

"Yes, very much," I enthusiastically agree.

Beck lets out another small laugh before trying to relax his smile. "There are a lot of things that you have never done before. Or at least never done with a guy," he begins, and I nod because I feel like we've already gone over that. "I just want to make sure you won't freak out if I touch your cock or pull out my own. That you won't run for the door," he adds.

Hearing him say 'cock' makes my own twitch in response.

He really is the best, going over consent like this. Everyone should probably be more focused on it the way he is.

"My dick has been hard since you backed me into the door," I admit. "Even during this entire, confusing conversation, it has not lost interest in touching you, or you touching it."

He's starting to look a little more hopeful, so I continue. "I can't promise exactly how I'll react to every situation because, as we've established, it will all be new for me. But I trust you. I know you won't do anything I don't want."

"Of course, I wouldn't. But, if you want me to stop at any point, you need to be comfortable telling me that," he says with conviction, determined for me to believe him, which I obviously do.

I get up and walk to where he's sitting, grab his hand, and pull him up to stand with me. Still holding that hand, I place my other on his jaw, meeting his eyes with a playful smile. "Beck, I'd really like to kiss you now. If that's all that you think I can handle tonight, then I want to spend the night making out like teenagers," I say with a smirk.

He looks like he's trying so hard not to smile as he bites his bottom lip, and ugh, I want to be the one doing that. "But, if you can trust me to know my own limits, then I'd like to do more than just make out," I add.

His gaze drops to my mouth for only a moment before his lips return to mine.

Finally.

The desperation between us is electric. We're both frantic, grabbing and trying to pull the other closer, hands roaming, exploring the other's body with urgency. His hands find my ass and squeeze. My mind is racing with ideas of what he might want to do with it and what I want to do with his. *Does he ever bottom? Will he want me to right away?*

This could be what he was trying to talk about before we jumped in.

Then he grinds his hard erection against mine, and it feels so good that all other thoughts disappear. I feel like I've won the lottery. Some sort of sex lottery where my prize is Beck showing me everything that I've been missing out on by not being with men.

I can't wait.

CHAPTER NINE

Beckett

Kissing Cody is even hotter than I'd hoped it would be. He really is enthusiastic about everything that he does, and making out with me is no exception. My whole body heats as our tongues tangle and we explore each other's mouths, teeth nipping and hands roaming over hair and hard muscles. He's pulling me closer as if trying to fuse us together, and I want everything he's giving me.

His hard dick is rubbing against mine, and even through our pants, it's making my head spin. I want to tear his clothes off, pin him onto the table, and show him the wonders of his prostate.

But that might be a little much for his first time with a man.

I know he said he's not freaking out, so I shouldn't be holding back completely, but jumping from thinking you're straight to a dick in your ass on the same day is a bit extreme.

He hasn't flinched at any of this, and he didn't hesitate when I mentioned taking our cocks out earlier. Maybe I can escalate things a little and ease him into it. Starting small, I trail wet kisses down his jaw and neck while unbuttoning his shirt. He eagerly helps me shrug it off, already working the buttons on mine.

Once our shirts are gone, he tangles his fingers in my hair, holding my head to him like he's afraid I'll stop kissing across his pecs. His muscles are insane, big, and defined in a way that makes it obvious he loves working out, but not in a bodybuilder, "does he use steroids?" kind of way. I move down to one of his peaked nipples, running my tongue over the pink tip before sucking it into my mouth. He whimpers, and my dick twitches in response.

"Holy fuck, do that again!" He sounds desperate, and I move to repeat the motion on his other side.

I'm not sure if he's even aware that his hips are thrusting forward, and I decide to see how he feels about me touching him. I unbutton his pants, careful not to put pressure on the very obvious bulge tenting them, before sliding my hand inside to cup his erection through his boxer briefs.

He makes another high-pitched noise at the contact. "Oh god. Yes," he pants, his thoughts spilling out between gasps. "More of that. Please touch my dick," he adds, and I smile as I work my mouth back up to his neck. Then I hook my thumbs into the back of his underwear and push them down with his pants.

I knew that Cody would have a great dick after seeing the bulge in his shorts this morning, and my mouth starts watering as I take in the size of him. He's a big guy and is definitely proportionate; his thick cock is straining toward his defined abs and the angry pink head is already shiny with precum. I spit in my hand before wrapping it around him and glance up to see a look of awe on his face.

Cody crashes his lips back to mine as I give him a few firm strokes, and he fumbles with the waistband of my pants as I continue to work his erection.

He hasn't taken his hands off of me this entire time, and I know that he's fully aware that a man is touching his dick— there's no mistaking my muscular frame for anything else. But

I'm still a little hesitant to show him all of me. What if, when he sees my achingly hard cock, he realizes this isn't what he wants after all? What if he realizes he prefers women?

Pulling back, I try to give him an out. "You don't have to—"

"Beck, please let me see your dick," his tone is pleading, not hesitant or shy. "I know that you're the first man I've been with, and you're worried about me, but I'm fucking fantastic right now, and I'd really like it if I wasn't the only one with my cock out." He gives me a reassuring smile.

I nod as my nerves ease, and he wastes no time removing the rest of my clothes, leaving us standing naked in the kitchen. His expression is full of fascination, and his eyes are glued to my cock. Cody reaches out his hand and gently grasps it, his thumb tracing a vein, making me shiver.

"I'm sure that you've played with your own before. I promise you won't break it." I smirk at him, and my comment must give him a confidence boost. He grips me more firmly, moving with a small twist from the base up to where he smears precum over the swollen tip.

"Fuck, this is so hot," he says absentmindedly, like he doesn't even mean for me to hear.

"If you think that's hot, wait until I have your dick in my mouth," I tease, mostly just wanting to see how he'll react, not really expecting us to go that far.

His gaze snaps back to mine. "Is that an option? Please tell me that it's an option." He's giving me the biggest puppy dog eyes, practically begging for me to agree.

Fuck, how is he so adorable and so sexy at the same time? He could get me to agree to anything with that look.

I drop to my knees, and before I can even wrap my mouth around his wide tip, he's rambling like he can't possibly keep his thoughts to himself. "I'm definitely not straight. This is so fucking hot, and you haven't even used your mouth yet."

He's speaking so quickly that I can barely understand the

string of words. "Just the image of you on your knees for me. Jesus, I'm not going to last long. Don't make fun of me if I blow the second I'm in your mouth. Fuuuuuu—"

His final curse turns into a deep moan as I interrupt his rambling by grabbing the base of his cock and guiding him into my mouth, taking him as deeply as I can. He grips the back of my head with both hands as I work my way up and down his dick, going a little deeper with each pass. I run my tongue over the sensitive area just below the head, and he whimpers. I can't get enough of all the sounds he's making.

Not wanting this to end too quickly, I ease up, giving lighter strokes and moving my mouth to his full balls. "Fuck, yes. Play with them. That feels amazing," he groans, his voice thick with need and desire.

I've never considered that I might have a praise kink, but his constant encouragement is really doing it for me. "Are you always this bossy?" I tease before returning my attention to his heavy sac.

"I'll be whatever you want me to be if you keep doing that," he says on a dreamy exhale.

Inspired by his enthusiasm, I pull away from his balls, wet my finger, and proceed to swallow his cock. Deciding to push my luck, I trail my hand between his legs, seeking his tight hole. I don't press in. Just tap it a few times to gauge his reaction.

"Fuck! I'm going to—"

Hot, thick cum shoots down my throat, and I continue to swallow around him, wanting it all. When his dick finally finishes twitching, I make sure I've had every drop before pulling back and smiling up at him, licking my lips.

"Fuck, you're so hot. Shit, sorry I didn't have much warning there." He looks down at me, his expression full of awe.

"No need to apologize. That was great."

When I stand, I'm surprised that Cody tries to pull me in for a kiss. "Wait, I still have the taste of your cum in my mouth," I chuckle.

His eyes grow darker as he goes in for a desperate kiss, licking all around the inside of my mouth and moaning before he finally pulls away. "That's sexy as fuck."

"You swear a lot when you're turned on," I comment, smirking as he laughs.

"You going to punish me for it?" he asks, but there's a teasing challenge in his tone. The look he gives me tells me that he doesn't hate the idea.

This man continues to surprise me with how perfect he is.

"Don't tempt me with a good time," I tease back as I start to stroke my own aching cock. After all of that, I'm so close already. "Can I come on you?" I ask. I probably should go take care of this in the shower or something, but Cody is so hot, and the look of hunger still in his gaze as he watches me touch myself emboldens me to stay right here.

"You don't want me to blow you?" he asks, sounding disappointed.

My cock twitches at the idea, and I know I won't last long enough to attempt his first blow job. "No time, I'm right there," I manage to grunt out, my voice sounding deep and tortured as I feel the orgasm building in the base of my spine.

Cody scrambles to his knees in front of me as he says, "Come on my face."

Then he opens his mouth, relaxing his tongue out like he's ready to catch my load, and I am dead.

Dead.

Cody kneeling before me with his hands resting on his thighs, gazing up at me with his mouth open, waiting to taste me, his cheeks still flushed, looking wrecked from his own release, has to be the single hottest thing that I'll ever see in my life.

My stomach muscles clench, and waves of pleasure crash

through me, my orgasm hitting harder than ever before. My entire body feels like it's buzzing, overwhelmed by the euphoric sensation. My release goes on and on, thick ropes of cum covering Cody's face and tongue as my dick somehow isn't done.

Did I think him kneeling there was the hottest thing ever? Because clearly, this takes the cake.

I must still be in some sort of post-orgasm haze because I have no control over my hand as it raises to his cheek to collect my release that's missed his mouth before shoving two cum covered digits past his full lips and in a deep voice growling, "Suck."

Cody whimpers again, eagerly sucking and swirling his tongue around my fingers like he's desperate to taste every drop. Holding his gaze, I stroke his cheek with my other hand before softly praising him. "Good boy."

His eyes flash as the words light him up. This man is truly perfect. *How am I going to give him up after this weekend?*

I dismiss the thought as quickly as it comes. No need to worry about silly things like if I'll see him again while he's still right in front of me.

"I've always been a big fan of facials, but being on the receiving end was way hotter than I expected," Cody says casually, making me chuckle.

"Let's go take a shower and get cleaned up," I suggest as I help him back up to his feet.

"Together?" he questions, his eyebrows practically in his hair as he gives me those pleading eyes again.

"If that's okay with you," I tease because he's obviously excited by the idea.

"Being bi is awesome." Cody's got a huge smile as he practically skips into the bathroom, leaving me with an excellent view of his ass.

Maybe I'll sign up for another one of these weekends. Just to give him the full experience of being with a man. No harm in that.

It doesn't have to mean anything.

And maybe if I lie to myself enough, it will start to sound more convincing.

CHAPTER TEN

Cody

Being bi really is awesome. Last night with Beck was the hottest sex of my life, and there wasn't even penetration. I'm not sure if being with men is always that amazing or if it's specific to him, but that was the best release I've ever had.

I wanted to continue our fun in the shower, but I think that Beck was worried about me freaking out. He insisted on taking care of me, washing my hair and body, taking his time massaging and exploring. When I tried to touch his cock, he swatted me away with a warning glare saying there was no way that he'd come again after his orgasm drained him and that we didn't need to overdo it on the first night.

I think he meant for it to be intimidating, but his glare was pretty hot.

He had a point, though. I didn't realize how exhausted I was and quickly fell asleep with Beck wrapped around me in our bed. I'd never been the little spoon before, and it was everything. I felt so content and peaceful with his muscular body holding me safe in his arms.

I'm so glad that we get to share a room this weekend. Hopefully, tonight, Beck can continue to show me everything that I've been missing out on while assuming I was straight.

Unfortunately, this morning started with sunrise yoga, leaving no time to fool around before the full day.

I might have spent the entire time checking out Beck's muscles as he bent and stretched. How have I never realized how sexy a man's body can be? I also spent the entire class trying—and probably failing—to hide my half-hard cock. *Oh well.*

Now, we're at a buffet-style breakfast in the venue's main restaurant before today's programs officially begin. The seating is designed to encourage socializing, which means no private tables for couples.

Not that Beck and I are a couple.

At least, I'm pretty sure we're not. I know that we went on one date, but I think that was just a way to hang out and hook up.

...Right?

So, I'm, like, seventy percent sure that we're not *actually* dating.

"Are you my boyfriend?" I ask, just in case.

Beck freezes, then starts coughing, choking on whatever food he just tried to swallow.

We're sitting with some of my friends, and luckily, after brief introductions, they've been mostly happy to let us chat among ourselves. I don't think anyone heard my question, but I wouldn't care if they did. I have nothing to hide. Kyla is very supportive of all types of love and relationships, and there are plenty of LGBTQIA+ identifying members at the company.

We have programs specifically created to help people struggling with their own identity, as well as courses to encourage better allies in the community. Even the courses for "enlightened relationships" that are designed to help people strengthen their relationships and marriages, examine the history of marriage itself, including for same-sex couples. They look at the ramifications of the legal definitions of marriage and how these have impacted society, communities, and individual relationships over time and in our world today.

I've heard from many of the LGBTQIA+ members of our community in Montana that our city feels like a paradise of acceptance compared to their previous towns.

Beck finally stops coughing, and I'm pulled back from my racing thoughts as he gives me a bewildered expression. "I'm not your boyfriend," he finally gets out. "I haven't been anyone's boyfriend since I was sixteen," he adds, still looking very concerned by my question.

"Cool, I just wanted to clarify since you said we went on that date, and I've realized that we've been talking a lot more than I talk to my other friends," I add casually.

I wasn't trying to say I *want* Beck to be my boyfriend, but I also don't completely hate the idea if we're being perfectly honest.

Still, that feels like a big decision, and it's not like we live near each other.

Beck's shoulders visibly relax, and he lets out a big exhale. "Sorry, I didn't mean for that to sound like such a horrible option. I've just never seriously dated anyone, and the thought of it at all sounds so absurd to me that I couldn't help but freak out a little."

I meet his gaze with a smirk. "Don't worry, I wasn't too offended. I know that anyone would be lucky to be my boyfriend," I wink.

I expect him to laugh or tease me back, but Beck just gives me a soft smile and says, "They would."

My heart rate picks up at his words, and my stomach feels all fluttery. I'm worried that I might like Beck more than he likes me. I'm not ready for things to go back to how they were before yesterday. The idea of not being able to kiss him again makes my chest tight with anxiety.

If I'm about to have a freakout, that's what it'll be about.

"I know that we don't have time for this conversation now," I begin, wanting to get this out before my thoughts spiral all day when I should focus on learning.

And not the kind of learning I hope Beck has planned for tonight.

"But I just want to put it out there that I'm so happy about what happened last night and that I really hope it can happen again tonight," I say, flashing him my biggest smile. I want him to understand how sincere I am—that I have absolutely zero regrets.

Well, other than not having his cock in my mouth yet. Sure, swallowing his load and sucking his cum-covered fingers had been hot as hell, but I'd *really* like to blow him.

And when he touched my hole, my whole body felt alive. Nerve endings I didn't know existed were overwhelmed with the pleasant sensation caused by his pressure. I definitely want him to do that again, and if I enjoyed just his finger touching me there, I can't even imagine how it would feel to have him inside me.

I know that we still have more to talk about regarding preferences, but I'll be happy to do whatever Beck wants me to. When he called me a "good boy" last night, it was like a jolt of pleasure went through my spine and straight to my cock.

I've always been happy to go along with what my partner wants as far as sex goes, their pleasure turning me on, but no one has ever called me that before. I really hope that he does it again.

Beck smirks and glances down at the obvious bulge in my slacks. "You're going to need to stop thinking about whatever is causing *that* before you have to lecture today."

"Maybe signing us up for the same schedule was a dumb idea," I admit. Isn't it bad for you to have an erection all day?

"Nah, I'm glad we'll get to spend the day together," Beck says casually before his eyes widen like he didn't actually mean to say that out loud.

"Somebody likes me," I sing, bumping our shoulders together.

"You're alright," he grunts back, rolling his eyes.

"I'm 'the sexiest man you've ever seen' *remember*," I tease, unable to resist.

He shoves my shoulder, and it only makes my smile grow even wider. He finally laughs and shakes his head like he doesn't know what to do with me.

"Obviously you're really hot too," I concede, "if you've made me realize I'm into men." That gets him to return my smile just as our Vice President of Operations speaks into a microphone, announcing that the day's events are set to begin shortly.

I'm so excited for today. The schedule is packed with presentations about the latest Kyla programs and team-building activities hosted by the venue. Attendees can pick sessions that interest them most or align with their future teaching goals. For those not in classes, there's a variety of activities like a ropes course, kayaking, tennis, pickleball, golf, and even dance classes. The focus is on keeping both our minds and bodies active while fostering team connections.

Viktor emphasizes that happiness and success stem from taking care of yourself first. That's why Kyla provides full-time access to top dietitians, nutritionists, personal trainers, and sports medicine professionals. At the corporate headquarters, meals and daily group fitness activities are offered to all employees, and these perks are extended to the local community as well. Viktor believes in uplifting everyone because, as he says, "A village is only as happy as its least happy member."

"So, what's this first class about?" Beck asks me, looking at a printout of his schedule for the day.

"It's a new one that our VP of Finance has created about maximizing the value of your money. I'm really excited about it! Howard is one of my best friends, and he always helps me when I have questions about money." I've always admired when people get to teach about their passions and expertise.

Personally, I've been fortunate never to stress much about finances. With both of my parents finding success in Hollywood, money was rarely a concern. My mom even set aside earnings from the commercials and modeling gigs I did as a kid into an investment account. As part of their divorce settlement, my parents also funded a college account that ended up with more than I ever needed for school. The investments paid off, and by the time I graduated, I had more financial security than most people ever dream of.

If I ever have questions about taxes or finances, though, Howard or Viktor are happy to help. I really am so lucky to have such supportive friends.

Beck doesn't look as thrilled about attending this program as I am, but he probably also has people who help him with his money. You never know when you might learn something important, though, so hopefully, he'll get into it.

He jokes about the class of mine that he took being a 'trauma dump', but he seemed happy to be there and eager to take another. I think he just needs time to warm up to things since he's generally more guarded about his emotions.

After we finish breakfast, I take Beck's hand and lead him toward the theater. He looks momentarily surprised but lets me guide him, chuckling softly. I flash him a wide grin as we find seats near the front.

"How are you always so peppy?" he whispers as Howard walks onto the stage.

"Is there something wrong with being happy?" I tease with another grin as I turn toward him.

He looks equally annoyed and amused with me, and I love it. He really is hot when he's all scowly.

CHAPTER ELEVEN

Beckett

I've been in the corporate world for a long time now. At thirty-two, I've been working for my family's company for half of my life, and I know all about the cheesy bullshit buzzwords that HR departments like to throw around about "company culture" and "high-performance mindsets".

But something about these Kyla programs is setting off little alarm bells in the back of my mind.

Admittedly, I've been highly distracted during Cody's classes. I can't focus on more than what I want to do to him tonight when he's standing in front of me, flashing that gorgeous smile or flexing those insane muscles.

Now that he isn't teaching the classes, though, I can't ignore the fact that something feels… off.

I know that I'm generally a pessimistic and suspicious person by nature. But I'd like to think that over the years, I've honed a pretty good ability to spot a scam. Nothing in the classes so far has been *super* concerning, where I could point to a specific thing that was said and just call bullshit, but I can't help this nagging feeling that I'm starting to have about this company.

It started in the first class this morning when Cody's buddy, Howard, was teaching. A lot of his investment recommendations and strategies were solid. I could tell he's probably great at his job with the company's finances, but every once in a while, there would be a comment about how everyone could use their earnings to participate in more Kyla programs or invest in the stock portfolios run by the Kyla financial specialists. He also mentioned using earnings to cover the fees associated with things in Montana, like the company fitness center or meal plan.

Wouldn't those things be a job perk for free?

Aren't the majority of the people here this weekend employees who would be getting paid to be here? Not the other way around. I know my fee for this weekend was astronomical, but I assumed it was because they were making an exception, letting me crash the event intended for employees.

If everyone had to pay to be here, then that raises some significant concerns for me over the legitimacy of their business plans, and really, the company as a whole. I know that they're a pretty large company that's involved with a ton of big names in both business and entertainment, with quite a few celebrities and politicians taking their classes, but something isn't sitting right with me.

It continued in the other classes, too. Except for the program that Cody led on not letting your worries and fears hold you back from success and happiness—I really did try to pay attention to his class today and not just gawk at him the entire time, and I definitely didn't get any of the weird vibes from anything he said.

All of this is running through my head as I watch Cody get strapped into a harness for the ropes course that we're apparently doing before lunch. I've never done one, and I'm not a huge fan of heights, but I also want to spend time with Cody.

Risk breaking my neck or spend a few hours apart? You'd think it would be an easy decision, but clearly, my dick is back in charge because here I am, risking life and limb.

Not that I'm complaining about the view—the harness outlining Cody's ass is giving me some ideas. It reminds me of a jock strap, and now I can't help but wonder if he owns one.

"Your turn, Beck!" He sounds so fucking happy as he gets out of the way for me to get into my harness, he's practically jumping up and down as he shifts, clearly too excited to stand still. His endless enthusiasm continues to amuse me and, luckily, distracts me from focusing on what we're actually doing here.

Once everyone in the group is strapped in, one of the employees walks us through the process. She explains the two heavy clips attached to our harnesses, each clip is secured to a giant wire, and they're color-coded with a chunky plastic "key" that unlocks them. Only one clip can be opened at a time as we move from section to section.

In theory, it sounds safe. But in reality, this whole thing is looking more intimidating than I thought it would be. I was picturing something much lower to the ground, and I sure as shit wasn't imagining that I'd be unlocking and reattaching my fucking harness myself.

What the hell have I gotten myself into?

She reassures us that there's staff on the ground throughout the course to help answer any questions and help us if needed. Apparently, they even allow children to do this.

I obviously don't have any children, but that seems like a poor parenting decision to me.

We're all given helmets and are directed to staircases that lead to different points in the course. Cody grabs my hand and drags me toward what must be the tallest one, *of course.* We end up on a small wooden platform built into a tree at least fifteen feet off the ground, and there are plenty of sections even higher that it seems we'll make our way up to.

In front of us, there's a bridge straight out of a fairytale movie. A bunch of planks of wood that are way too far apart at inconsistent distances are held together by some very questionable-looking rope. It looks like it's been there for hundreds of years and no one has bothered with repairs.

This would be the part in those movies where the heroes need to cross the bridge and fight an evil dragon to save a princess on the other side.

I'd make a terrible movie hero. I'm way too spoiled and way too afraid of heights to help any princess. Or prince, which I'd obviously prefer.

Cody, on the other hand, looks like he could be filming his own superhero action film. He effortlessly crosses the bridge, keeping his balance as if he's walking on solid ground. When the gaps become too wide, he jumps across easily, the workout clothes that we changed into showing off each flex of his muscles as he moves.

"What are you waiting for?" He turns back toward me and flashes that fucking smile again, the one that I knew could get me to do anything—I just didn't realize he'd be using that power against me so soon into our relationship with this stupid ropes course.

Not that we're in a relationship. Obviously not. I just meant I haven't known him long enough to endure this kind of torture.

"Just mentally preparing to save the prince," I blurt out. Apparently, my fear has eliminated any filter I have, deciding that I should go with the most random thoughts possible.

He bursts out laughing. "Does that make you a knight in shining armor?"

I glare back at him, crossing my arms. "I'm trying to psych myself up to risk my life. I don't need you to make fun of me."

"Should I pretend to be a prince in distress?" he teases, and I smirk back at him.

"If you want to role-play, I'd rather wait until we're alone," I respond in a cheesy, suggestive tone. His eyes grow comically large, and it's my turn to laugh.

As much fun as shout-flirting with him is across this bridge, I really would rather be near him. I take a deep breath and try to convince myself that this is easy, nothing to worry about. I double-check that my clips are secure.

Logically, I know that I'm safe. If I do fall, my harness will catch me.

But logic doesn't slow down my rapid heartbeat.

I cling to the railings of the bridge with a death grip as I take my first steps onto it. The plank of wood immediately moves away from the platform that my other foot is still balanced on, shifting me into a wider stance. I quickly bring the other foot forward so I can stand on the moving board, gripping the swaying rope railings for dear life.

One down, another fifteen or so to go.

How did Cody make this look so easy?

I glance up at him, and he looks so proud of me for that one step, that I decide to go for the next one. Then I kind of blackout until I'm on the platform with Cody, and he wraps his arms around me in a big bear hug.

I immediately sink into the embrace, appreciating how secure I feel in his arms after being so unsteady on the bridge.

"You did amazing," he encourages after pulling back. "Wasn't it exhilarating?"

"Wait, wait. I wasn't done." I pull him back in, not ready for the hug to end. Or to continue this stupid course.

Cody laughs, giving me a tight squeeze before he steps over to the next obstacle. This one involves a rock wall.

Great. Let's go even higher. *Just what I wanted.*

Cody's already clipping in, and I decide to focus on the bright side of the situation: at least I get to watch him climb. And what a sight it is.

I'm probably drooling, but the course is big enough that we have some space to ourselves, and no one can call me out on it.

Before long, Cody is at the top of the wall, kneeling over the side of what I assume is another platform.

I don't want to give myself more time to freak out before I begin, so I grab onto a rock and begin my ascent. Thankfully, the wall that the stones are attached to doesn't move, and I get to the top without incident.

Between the humid Florida air and the surprising amount of strength this climb demands, I'm sweating when I reach the top. At least wearing all black hides how much effort this actually took.

Cody helps pull me up into a standing position, and I'm confused by the lack of obstacles in front of us. "Are we supposed to climb back down now?"

"It's a zip line." He chuckles, gesturing to the platform about fifty feet ahead and slightly below us. He tugs on his cords, making sure that the clips are secure, and squats down a bit like he's preparing to jump.

"No fucking way, absolutely not," I say as I grab Cody's arm, preventing him from leaping and abandoning me up here.

He returns to his full height and looks down at me with concern. "What's wrong?" Then, his expression shifts as he seems to understand. "I'm so sorry, Beck, are you afraid of heights?" He looks so apologetic, and I hate that I'm the reason his gorgeous smile is gone. "I should have asked what activities you wanted to do instead of assuming," he continues.

"To be fair, I saw it on the schedule. I could have said something," I grumble.

"Is there a reason that you didn't?"

Groaning, I rest my head back against the tree our platform is built on and cover my face with my hands. "I wanted to spend time with you and didn't want you to think I'm a coward," I mumble through my hands.

He peels them away from my face, still holding onto them as he meets my gaze with a small smile. "I could never think you're a coward, Beck," he says so earnestly, and my heart starts to race for new reasons.

Whatever connection we have seems way too intense for the few weeks I've known him. Especially since so much of that time has been apart. He looks at me with such adoration and fondness, and I really want to deserve that look from such an amazing man.

"Okay, I'm ready. Let's jump." I try to sound confident, but it comes out as defeated.

"Beck, I'm sure that we can climb down. You don't have to do this."

"No, I know." I take another deep breath. "But I want to prove to myself that it's okay to do scary things," I say.

Totally only talking about the zip line.

It's not at all about the feelings I'm having for him. *No scary feelings happening over here.*

"Do you still want me to go first? Maybe it will help to see how safe it is," he offers.

"Only if you promise to catch me if I fall," I wink at him while I gesture for him to go ahead.

He's laughing as he leans back a bit, squatting down with both hands holding the cords attached to the clips, and jumps right off the platform. His laughter turns into loud whoops as he descends onto the next platform, and I have no control over my smile at his pure, unfiltered joy.

When I'm sure that he's finished and it's my turn, I tug my clips to triple-check I'm secure. I look across the space to Cody, and even with the distance between us, I feel a strange sense of peace wash over me as our eyes lock.

And I jump.

Even I'm surprised at the loud laugh that escapes from my mouth as I begin to free-fall. Then my harness catches me, jerking me slightly as it does, and I start hysterically laughing as adrenaline courses through my veins, and I zip toward Cody.

For some reason, in this heightened state of fear and exhilaration, my brain decides it's fucking hilarious that I'm literally falling because of him. As if I wasn't already worried that I'm falling for him in other ways.

I land awkwardly, stumbling a bit, but Cody is there to help steady me with his strong arms and megawatt smile. I really do feel like I could do anything if he were there to support me.

Still riding the high of my adrenaline rush, I grab his face in my hands and pull him down to capture his bottom lip between mine before pushing my tongue into his mouth, desperate for him. For a moment, he kisses me back just as passionately, and I forget where we are.

Too quickly, he's stepping back. "I don't want to have to finish this with an erection," he explains, chuckling.

"Too late for me," I grumble, glancing down. When I look back at him, he's biting his lip, obviously trying to suppress his amusement, but when I smirk, he gives up and we both end up in another fit of laughter.

I MANAGED to keep it together for the rest of the course, even if my knees were still a little shaky from the zip line. After a quick break to shower and change back into less casual clothes, we sat through a lunch featuring more key speakers. I'd like to say I was a model student and learned a lot, but I don't think I could even confidently say what they were about. I can only take so much of this self-help bullshit before completely spacing out if Cody isn't the one teaching.

Now, for the main event, we have a program run by Viktor himself. "Today we will be talking about a topic you all know is near and dear to my heart. The very idea that inspired our company name of 'Kyla'," he takes a dramatic pause, smiling and making obvious eye contact with people in the audience before continuing. "We're here to talk about improving our community by embracing the adage 'it takes a village'."

I raise a brow, aiming a questioning look at Cody. "Kyla means Village in Finnish. That's where his ancestors are from," he whispers.

"You all know how important I believe it is to put in the work to improve yourself, to achieve your dreams," Viktor goes on. "We have countless workshops and seminars to help empower people to do just that. But all of it is completely pointless if we don't use our success to help others. Our programs give you the knowledge and tools to find your personalized version of happiness, but no one can truly do it on their own. Where would you be without your Kyla village? Without the coaches who gave you these skills? What life would you be living if you'd never attended your first Kyla seminar?"

I certainly wouldn't be in fucking Florida. But, I also wouldn't have met Cody, so I obviously wouldn't wish for that.

"If you put good into the world, good will come back to you. This room is full of executives, high-ranking members of Kyla, and some of our best coaches. I am honored to have each and every one of you as a member of my village. It's especially important that we remember the power we hold. The tools and knowledge offered in Kyla programming can change people's lives for the better. *You* have the ability to help people. To make others happy. Are you doing everything you can to improve your village? To help those around you?"

I'm definitely improving Cody's weekend if last night was anything to go by.

I get lost in my head daydreaming about last night, but I'm fairly confident the rest of his monologue is just more cheesy, inspirational stuff about helping the people around you and how great his programs are.

Honestly, I've never really been a churchgoer, but it reminds me of the few times I've had to sit through a service for a friend's wedding or gone to a funeral.

Viktor spends some time comparing the company and its culture to a traditional village. Again, nothing he says is blatantly problematic, but little comments about Linna—the town where they all live in Montana—stand out to me. He describes how much time everyone spends together and all the activities they do that don't sound remotely work-related.

When Cody talked about his friends and his city, I assumed his enthusiasm for literally everything bled into his descriptions. But the way Viktor describes it, Linna sounds less like a small Montana city and more like some utopian society.

I keep meaning to ask Cody about it, but every time I look at him, rational thought becomes much more difficult, and all I can think about is what we'll do back in our room tonight.

I was definitely a little nervous this morning that he'd try to rationalize what happened last night as a fluke and go back to insisting he's straight.

The golden retriever of a man couldn't seem to contain his excitement about doing it again, though.

I think I'm starting to believe he really is that relaxed, that he's fully embracing his new sexual identity in less than a day, with no doubts or hesitation.

I'd still be more reserved about advancing things physically so quickly if we had more time. With tonight being our last planned night together, I've been debating how far might be too far to take things. Obviously, I don't want to pressure him into doing anything that he doesn't want to do or that he'll regret. But if tonight could be the last night I ever get with him, I also want to make the most of it.

Still, there's a lot we can explore without needing to do everything in one night. And if I never see him again, that's fine. *Totally fine.*

Cody seems like the type of person who stays friends with his hookups. He'll probably continue to send me funny texts and memes until we eventually grow apart, and I'll look back on this whole experience fondly. No big deal.

I'm not getting attached to his warm hazel eyes or the way the left side of his mouth quirks a little higher than the right when something amuses him. Or to his laugh and how deep and full it always sounds, like he's never holding any part of his joy back.

Nope. No attachment here.

Okay, fine, I don't think I can fuck him.

If he's even ready to try bottoming, I don't think that I could go through with it and then just leave him tomorrow. And there's no way that I could be vulnerable enough to let him fuck me and not feel more than I already do.

I've never felt like this before, and I don't want to examine what it means.

It doesn't matter anyway. Cody is obsessed with his job and his friends, and I have no intention of abandoning my perfect job and family to move to the fucking middle of nowhere Montana of all places.

So, tonight, we'll fool around a bit more, and I'll let him have some fun with his first man. Then tomorrow, we can go our separate ways, and I'm sure that the next man he's attracted to can show him the rest.

There's a sharp pain in my chest at the thought of him with another man, but I don't see another outcome here. So, I need to accept it and have fun with Cody while I can.

The fantasies I'm having of kidnapping him and locking him in my condo as some sort of sexy, muscular houseboy are definitely unrealistic. And completely inappropriate. *Right?*

But what if I—*Fuck,* I need to stop thinking of ways that I could trick him into coming back to Chicago with me.

We finally sit down for dinner, and I'm so distracted by how small the portion is on my plate that I almost miss the announcement.

"Viktor, we're all so grateful that you could join us this weekend. Your presence always elevates the experience of a Kyla retreat," a woman on stage says into a microphone. "We'll now be showcasing some of our members' talents while you eat, so sit back, relax, and enjoy the entertainment!"

What follows is a bizarre mix of what feels like a corporate talent show and a pep rally. Groups perform skits, show off their "talents," and do these weird cheers about how amazing the company and its different programs are. It's painful. Honestly, I wouldn't wish this on my worst enemy.

"I'm next!" Cody whispers before getting up to join the executive management team's routine. He stands front and center, leading a cheer with the same enthusiasm he applies to everything else. Thankfully, theirs was one of the least cringe-worthy performances.

It had absolutely nothing to do with how hot he looked clapping with his muscular arms above his head, or how adorable he is when he's excited about something.

Nope. Theirs was genuinely better, and I'm sticking with that answer.

Viktor finally gets on stage, which I'm praying to whoever will listen means we're done. "Thank you all for another fantastic day. Each and every one of you should be proud of yourself for the work you put in, and the investment that you made for your future success and happiness. I only wish that we didn't have to say goodbye so soon."

Like he's not the one who needs them all back to work on Monday.

"I know that many of you will be joining me back in Linna, but for those who don't work at our headquarters *yet*." He pauses with a dramatic wink and everyone in the room laughs like he's so fucking funny. "Don't forget that your work is just as important! You have just as much potential to change lives as anyone else in this room. Put that good into the world, and know it will come back to you. Do the work to help improve your village, I am so fortunate to have you all in mine, and I can't wait until our paths cross again. I wish you all success and happiness in each of your days. Goodnight!"

He bows, intertwining his extended fingers in front of him in the weird mountain pose we had to do in my first Kyla session as he does so. I wish that we could sneak out after that, but of course, we have to repeat the weird reception line from last night. There's groping hugs, and everyone is just as excited to see him and say goodbye since so many people are leaving first thing tomorrow.

When it's finally our turn, I can't seem to force my expression into anything even resembling a polite smile. Viktor seems unfazed, grabbing my hand as he speaks. "Beckett, it has been such a pleasure to have you with us. I hope you've learned something this weekend that you can use to achieve even greater success and happiness. Be sure to spread the word, and if you or any of your family would be interested in furthering your Kyla journey, don't hesitate to reach out to me directly. Cody can pass on my contact information." He flashes a huge smile my way, giving my hand a squeeze.

"I'm sure Cody can answer any of my questions. He's the one who got me here, right?" I point out, pulling my hand away.

"Cody is such a fantastic asset to our team," Viktor says, nodding like he's agreeing to what I said, even though I meant it as more of a dig at him.

"I'm just happy that I get to help so many people," Cody adds, also not picking up on my intended slight.

When we finally wrap things up and say goodbye, Cody takes my hand as he practically jogs away, dragging me back to our cabin.

"Someone's eager," I tease, stepping up behind him as he

attempts to unlock the door with the old-fashioned key they gave us. I put my hands on his hips, dragging his ass back, grinding my hardening cock into him. He whimpers impatiently, finally getting the door open before spinning in my hold so that we're facing each other, chests pressed together as he rubs his large bulge against mine.

He cups my face with both hands as he leans down to kiss me, and his soft lips against my own send a shiver of pleasure down my spine. Then his tongue is in my mouth, and I pull back to bite his bottom lip before sucking it. Kissing him is addicting. I'd happily stay here all night and enjoy every moment.

But I know we both want more, so I back him into the cabin, kicking the door shut behind me before pulling away from his hold. Cody's lips try to chase mine, but I stop him with a finger to them.

He looks devastated by the distance between us, so I rush to reassure him with a smirk. "I was just going to suggest that we make it further into the cabin before we attack each other tonight." His answering smile lights up the entire room, and I wish that I could take a picture, be able to revisit the proof of how happy he looks in this moment.

But this is just a hookup. So I grab his hand and tug him toward the bed.

CHAPTER TWELVE

Cody

The bed sounds like an amazing idea. Kicking off my shoes, I shed my clothes as quickly as possible. Once I'm naked, I sit on the edge of the bed and watch as Beck strips for me in a slow, deliberate tease. He's smirking at me the entire time as I fidget, too excited to sit still. My cock is already rock hard at the thought of touching him again, and his show is making me squirm with the building anticipation.

All day, I couldn't get the image of Beck on his knees for me out of my mind. I know I'm technically bigger than him, but the way he carries himself makes him seem so much larger and more dominating. I've never been with someone like that, and I'm really into it.

Seeing him be so vulnerable *for me* was exhilarating.

Beck has this general air of "I truly don't give a fuck" with almost everything. I don't think he does it consciously, but he acts as though he expects everyone to respect him already, to want to impress him.

Or maybe I just want to impress him.

I noticed it the first day I saw him at his company—the way his employee handed over their seat without question, how so many people followed his example in the exercises. It made sense there, where he's the boss, but this weekend, I was surprised to see how little his attitude changed around strangers. Even with the Kyla higher-ups, who can be pretty intimidating, Beck acted like they needed to earn his notice.

He's never acted like that with me, though.

Somehow, I've done something to hold his attention. Whenever I looked at him today, he was already studying me. It's intoxicating to be the sole focus of such a self-assured man. Every time he looks at me, it makes me feel invincible.

Now, seeing the evidence of his arousal as he stalks toward me, I know I'm playing a dangerous game. I could quickly get addicted to this feeling, and I'm not sure if this thing between us will end after this weekend.

And that terrifies me.

Beck has been honest about his lack of serious relationships in the past. During the program, he'd talked about his family wanting him to settle down, but I don't know if he's ready for that.

Not to mention the fact that we live in different states, both with demanding careers that keep us constantly on the move.

But I refuse to borrow tomorrow's troubles today. Instead, I decide to stay present and enjoy this moment. I'm sitting on the edge of a bed naked with a very sexy, also very naked, Beck standing in front of me. I spread my legs so that he can walk into the space between them and lean up to meet his kiss.

It's a soft, slow kiss. Nothing like the frantic and desperate ones from yesterday. I grab onto his hips, letting my hands explore the firm curves of his ass as his tongue teases my lips, tasting me.

Before I lose myself entirely in the feel of him, I pull back, and he stands back to his full height with a quirked brow. From my position on the low bed, I'm perfectly in line with his swollen cock, and I can't help but stare, completely fascinated.

It's long and thick, not quite as big as mine, but I've been in enough gym locker rooms to know that he has a big dick.

And now that I've had *that* thought, I realize straight guys probably wouldn't notice or remember other men's cocks well enough to know what qualifies as a "big dick".

Obliviousness has always been a personal quirk of mine. Social cues, flirting, or being hit on always go right over my head, or so I've been told. But missing the fact that I'm attracted to men? That has to take the crown on my list of oblivious moments.

Looking at Beck now, though, naked and in front of me, I know for a fact that he's the sexiest thing I've ever seen. His defined muscles, the ink that covers his arms and chest in a complicated patchwork of images and shading, accentuating every curve of his physique. Then there are his ink-free, defined abs, with a light dusting of hair leading down to his enticing cock. I am one hundred percent not straight.

The urge to touch him is overwhelming. Before I even realize what I'm doing, my hand reaches out, wrapping around his rock-hard erection.

Obviously, I know what my dick feels like, but there's something so incredibly hot about the opposing sensations of how soft he feels in my callused hands as I stroke up his shaft and how hard he is.

For me.

I love being able to see the physical proof of what I'm doing to him.

Beck lets out a low hum of appreciation as I continue to move my hand up and down, adding a slight twist as I get to the angry pink head. I realize I should probably focus more on how this feels for him, rather than just the weight of him in my grip, so I spit in my hand before returning to the motion.

I glance up to catch the look of complete awe on his face. "How do you look so excited to be jerking me off when yesterday you were straight?"

"Well, I obviously wasn't straight. I was just oblivious to how amazing other people's cocks could be."

"Mine," he corrects in a possessive growl. "How amazing *my* cock could be."

I love that he doesn't like the idea of me with other men. I know that we have no real chance at a future, but right here, in this moment, I can let myself pretend. Pretend that Beck's the only one I'll ever need again.

"Yes," I agree on an exhale, looking up at him between my lashes. "Your cock is it for me." I'm surprised by how hot that line of thinking is, how turned on I am by the idea of him owning me in that way.

He must like it too because he grabs a fistful of my hair, yanking my head back up to look at him after my gaze had wandered back south. "Say it again," he demands. "Say my cock is the only cock for you, that you're mine."

It might feel a little intense for the second time we've hooked up, but something about the idea feels right. It settles something inside of me. So even if I know deep down it won't be real, the words feel true as I speak them on a breathy exhale. "I'm yours."

Our gazes lock for an endless moment before he leans down to meet my mouth in a claiming kiss. He tries to pull me up to stand, but I'm determined to taste him.

I push him away. "Dammit, Beck, stop distracting me! I want to blow you," I complain. I've always wondered what it was like for the women I've been with, and after how hot last night was with him finishing on my face, I'm even more excited to be on this side of things.

His eyes shine with amusement as he holds up his hands in mock surrender. "Don't let me stop you."

Shifting my focus back to his cock, I grip the base firmly in my hand before looking up at him again. "I'm probably not going to be very good at this. Believe it or not, I've never had a dick in my mouth," I tease, trying not to get too in my head about my lack of experience.

He chuckles and mocks a shocked expression. "You mean straight guys don't give their friends blowjobs? Porn has completely lied to me!" His tone of fake outrage makes me laugh, the tension in my chest easing as I let the humor ground me for a moment.

But I quickly shake it off, mentally scolding myself to focus. As much as I love how comfortable we already are with each other—how effortlessly we shift from dominating to playful—I want to make this good for him. Sex should be fun, and this? *This definitely is.*

I decide to just go for it, trying to remember what felt good last night when our positions were reversed. I wrap my lips around just the head at first, running my tongue over the tip as I lightly suck. The salty flavor is heady, and I instantly want to earn more.

Beck lets out a low hum of approval, and I love what his praise does to me.

Feeling emboldened, I try to take him deep into my mouth, but when his head bumps the back of my throat and I gag, I realize I might have been a little too enthusiastic.

Pulling back just a bit, I use my hand to work what doesn't fit into my mouth and explore the rest with my tongue as I bob my head up and down. He seems to like it when I run my tongue over the sensitive spot just below the crown, and I give it a lot of attention as my other hand comes up to play with his balls.

His hands are back in my hair, not controlling my movements at all, and I can tell that he's holding himself back, allowing me to remain in control. His firm grip reminds me that this powerful man is being driven crazy by me and what I'm doing to him.

I fucking love it.

I don't think I've ever realized how much power you could feel while you're the one choking on a cock. But I feel invincible in this moment as I hear his uncontrolled moans of pleasure.

"That's it, baby. Fuck, you look so sexy swallowing my cock," he praises, and his words give me even more confidence. I love hearing how much he's enjoying this.

"That feels amazing. I never want another man to know how amazing your mouth feels," he adds.

And honestly, I don't want that either.

"You look so happy, blissed out like you were made to have my dick between your full lips." He's stroking my cheek now. Between his firm grip on my hair and the gentle touch on my cheek, for probably the first time in my life, I feel cherished. I never want this feeling to end.

"Fuck," Beck says, letting out a deep moan. "You're such a good boy for me."

My cock is painfully hard and I can't wait any longer, desperately stroking myself as I continue to devour him.

"Don't you dare come," he warns, and my hand instantly freezes. "Your load is mine," he continues, and I whimper around him. "I'm so close, if you don't want to swallow, then pull back and let me come all over your gorgeous face."

As much as I fucking *loved* having his release cover me yesterday, how claimed it made me feel to have his cum on me, there's no way that's happening tonight. I need to taste him more than I need my next breath.

"Then I'm going to swallow down your needy cock while I play with your tight hole. Would you like that?" he asks.

I nod as I try to take him even deeper, wanting him to know how desperate I am to swallow his release. His grip in my hair tightens, and his cock thickens even further. His words become frantic as hot cum shoots down my throat and I think I hear "baby" and "perfect" in between his incoherent ramblings. I desperately swallow, not wanting to lose any, but some ends up spilling from my mouth as his cock continues to twitch.

He's still stroking my cheek as I lick his softening dick clean. Actually, I think he's rubbing his release in, marking me with it. *Holy fuck, that's hot.* I want to be covered in his cum as often as I can, marked by this man in any possible way.

"You're perfect," he whispers, and I feel like I could come from his words alone.

Before I can process it, Beck drops to his knees between my legs where I'm still sitting on the edge of the bed. As much as I want him to do all of the things he promised, blowing him was way too hot, and I'm honestly surprised that I didn't finish already. As soon as his lips wrap around my cock, trying to swallow as much off me as he can in one go, I'm a goner, shooting into his mouth.

My vision blurs as my body convulses around him, the pleasure so intense that it's almost painful. When it finally subsides, I'm panting, and my arms are wrapped around Beck. He pulls off with a cocky grin, wiping the corner of his mouth before arrogantly saying, "Good boy."

"Fuck off," I laugh and playfully shove him.

He's laughing too as he tackles me fully onto the bed before kissing me senseless. We lay there for a while, making out and enjoying the feeling of being together.

Eventually, Beck is the one to pull away. "We have to be up pretty early for our flights tomorrow," he says regretfully.

I feel like our little bubble of bliss is bursting as reality comes crashing in. The truth is that we don't have any plans to do this again. That we live so far away. That Beck probably doesn't even care to see me again now that we've hooked up. He doesn't do relationships and has never wanted one.

"Yeah, I guess we should pack or something," I admit, feeling defeated.

"Or we could stay cuddled up in bed and set our alarms for a little earlier," he murmurs into my neck before kissing me there. The embers of hope I thought had burned out flare to life in my chest at his suggestion.

He maneuvers us so that he's under me, and I snuggle into his embrace. He wraps his arms around me, resting my head on his heart. The rapid beats match my own as I drift to sleep, fantasizing about a world where we board the same plane in the morning, to the same city, where we go to the same home.

Together.

CHAPTER THIRTEEN

Beckett

Whoever invented the default phone alarm is at the top of my shit list today. That obnoxious fucking noise woke us up way too early, interrupting the fantastic dirty dream I was having about Cody.

At some point in the night, we must have switched positions. I woke up spooning him, with my morning wood nestled between the perfect round globes of his ass. He was grinding back into me in his sleep, and I can't believe I had the self-restraint to roll away from him.

Last night we forgot to actually set our alarms earlier to fit in more cuddling, so we had to scramble to pack before the rideshare arrived to take us to the airport.

Pretty sure we mixed up some of the clothes we'd left thrown around the cabin after two nights of stripping without care, but I'm secretly hoping that I ended up with something of his.

I'm not ready to say goodbye.

Not at all.

The ride to the airport was quiet, but I couldn't stop myself from grabbing his hand. He held tight for the entire trip like he also didn't want to leave me.

I know all of that "mine" stuff we said yesterday was just hot, in-the-moment sex talk, but a part of me really wishes that it could be real.

I'm so fucked.

I kept telling myself that I'd be fine after we hooked up. I thought scratching the itch would get him out of my system so I could move on.

I don't do more. I've never wanted more.

But now that I know what it's like to have him, how am I supposed to just stop wanting to be with him all the time? Those stupid visions I had of a future with him are clearer than ever.

"United Flight UA 425 is now boarding to Chicago. Priority boarding, please make your way to the gate," a woman's voice says over the speakers.

We got through security quickly with both of us having TSA PreCheck, and our gates are in the same terminal, so we haven't had to split up yet, but the conversation has been limited to pointless small talk—like neither one of us knows how to address this inevitable goodbye.

I turn toward Cody, placing a soft kiss on the corner of his mouth before quickly pulling away. I intend to say a quick goodbye before going to drown my sorrows on the flight home, but my brain seems to malfunction somewhere between what I'm planning to say and what comes out.

"I want to see you again," I blurt out.

Cody's whole face lights up at the suggestion. "Really?" he sounds so hopeful that I know this can't be goodbye for us.

"Yeah, I don't know when, but I'd like to," I admit more confidently.

"I'd love that!" He sounds relieved, and I start to mentally comb through my schedule for the next few months, determined to remember an opening.

Nothing comes to mind, but I continue. "The end of hockey season is unpredictable. We're actually in the playoffs for once, and hopefully we'll make it all the way. So, we could still be playing in two months, or it could be over in four games."

He looks hesitant, but I go on. "We can keep talking—texting and calling like before. I don't want to make any promises and risk disappointing each other, but when hockey season is over, I should be able to get some time away. We've got great management and coaching staff, so other than the draft itself, I shouldn't have too many commitments. If you still want to, we'll find time then," I promise, earning his gorgeous smile.

"Okay." Cody nods enthusiastically, back to looking like his usual excited self and not the kicked puppy he had been all morning.

I grab his shirt and pull him to me, planting one more firm kiss on his lips before backing away toward my gate. "See you soon, Goldie," I promise.

"See you soon, Salem." His giant grin makes the knot that had been growing in my stomach all morning finally shrink.

I might not know how I'll make it happen yet, but no matter what it takes, I'm confident that I will see Cody again.

GOLDIE

*Photo of mountains in the distance overlooking
a small town*

GOLDIE

Home. I told you Montana is pretty!

GOLDIE

I hope that you had a good flight!

GOLDIE

Jealous that yours was direct.

GOLDIE

But my seat neighbors were really nice so the
time flew by

SALEM

You would be the person who befriends your
"seat neighbors." Adorable. Meanwhile, I've
never in my life thought to talk to the person next
to me on a plane. Glad you enjoyed yourself. I
caught up on some sleep and am headed to my
grandparents house for family dinner. Montana is
very pretty, but the view of the Chicago skyline
against Lake Michigan will always be my favorite.

SALEM

*Photo of countless skyscrapers reflecting back
the large body of water across the busy road
with a large pier visible*

GOLDIE

There you go again, sounding like a dream family
from the sitcoms I loved watching as a kid. Tell
them I say hi!

GOLDIE

Or don't

GOLDIE

That's probably super weird

GOLDIE

IDK why I said that, your family obviously
wouldn't know who I am.

SALEM

> Deep breaths, baby, you're not super weird. Only a little bit *winking emoji*. And they actually do know who you are. I told my brother Oakley about you when I was explaining my sudden need to visit Florida, a place that I've complained about incessantly in the past. My family doesn't really have secrets, so if you tell one person, it's assumed to be family knowledge within hours. Even if I don't mention you myself, I'd bet that someone will ask about you in the first five minutes.

GOLDIE

Wow, I love that! My grandparents had all passed away before I could really remember them, that's so cool that you guys are all so close.

GOLDIE

Have fun at your dinner!

SALEM

> Yeah, I'm really lucky. I wish that you could have had that growing up too.

SALEM

Two minutes.

GOLDIE

???

SALEM

> It took less than two minutes for my mom to ask about you by name.

GOLDIE

THAT'S AMAZING

GOLDIE

Tell Susan I say hello!

SALEM

Did you just look up my mom so you could also address her by name?

GOLDIE

Maybe

GOLDIE

Was that endearing or creepy?

SALEM

Adorable. She says "Hello Cody".

GOLDIE

Giant smile emoji

GOLDIE

Was that all she said, or are you paraphrasing?

SALEM

The parts about wishing that she could meet the nice young man who has me jet-setting across the country and actually smiling as I talk about Florida seemed unnecessary. *winking emoji*

GOLDIE

Your mom sounds awesome!

SALEM

She is, and now the grandparents are scolding me for only staring at my phone. I'll talk to you later.

I PUT the phone back in my pocket, ignoring the buzzing that indicates at least three more messages from Cody. His back-to-back messaging really is cute. *Fuck.* Everything he does is endearing.

How am I supposed to go months without seeing him again?

"So, Beck, does this mean you finally have a boyfriend?" Oakley teases me.

"Haha, very funny." I smack him on the side of his head, and he sticks his tongue out at me like we're children again. He's always been the closest to me, both in age and in friendship. We both like to give the other shit, but I'd do anything for him, and I know that he'd do the same for me.

"So, where's your better half?" I ask him.

"He's out back playing fetch with Spot," he answers, not having to ask who I'm referring to. Our whole family has referred to Oakley's best friend, Parker, as his better half for years. His dad passed away when we were kids, and even though they'd been close before it happened, they've been inseparable ever since.

"Is he *your* boyfriend yet?" I tease, knowing full well they both identify as straight. With how much they dote on each other and constantly find reasons to touch, though, it's no wonder people often assume they're a couple.

"Haha, very funny," he repeats my words. "But, we *are* dating these awesome girls we met in our building," he says, perking up. Then he tells us about how they kept running into the girls at the gym in their building, how they are also roommates and lifelong best friends, and how the four of them have been going on double dates and hanging out all together.

Oakley keeps emphasizing how great it is to be able to all go on dates together so he doesn't lose time with Parker. I exchange a skeptical look with my youngest brother, Lincoln, who mutters something under his breath about everyone loving the closets in their building.

I chuckle but shake my head, I'm happy for Oakley and his very codependent best friend. Maybe this will be the perfect situation for them to find someone serious.

His relationships in the past have all fallen apart, usually because the girls don't understand why a wealthy thirty-year-old man would choose to have a roommate, or they complain about how they feel neglected with the amount of time he spends with Parker. I know that Oakley gets anxious about Parker's diabetes, and that he's more comfortable knowing Parker isn't alone for extended amounts of time, but I've also wondered if it might be more than that.

Oakley's always insisted that the right woman for him wouldn't care about how close he and Parker are. He's always wanted a big family with lots of kids and the white picket fence in the suburbs, and I've always hoped for that future for him.

Does Cody want kids? I don't think I've ever even thought about having them. I've never slept with anyone who could get pregnant, so luckily, I've never had to worry about accidentally becoming a dad.

But now, for the first time, I'm beginning to realize I want more with someone–with Cody.

That realization shouldn't shock me, but it does. My brother teased me earlier about having a boyfriend, and for the first time, I wish he were right. It's evident to me now that I want to be in a relationship with Cody, but no matter how much I want a future with him, I don't see how it could work in the long term.

Even if we agreed to be exclusive—which I want to do but am too afraid to ask in case we aren't on the same page—how often would we realistically see each other?

Cody works a lot of weekends, so even if I flew to wherever he was on my days off, we'd only get a few hours together at most. And even if I signed up for the programs he's teaching, his schedule wouldn't allow for much time together. His first class proved that—they even worked through lunch for fuck's sake. And neither of us is looking to change our career. There's no way I could step back from the Werewolves—not when I've spent my entire life dreaming about this role. I've worked my ass off for the last seventeen years to learn all of the ins and outs that keep the team, arena, and league running smoothly.

I know how much the Werewolves mean to the city because they mean so much to me. I don't know who I'd be without Werewolves hockey.

And Cody is so important to Kyla. It was apparent during the retreat that he's well-respected in the company. The other executives clearly rely on him to keep the business as successful as it is. During the class that Cody taught at the retreat, one of his buddies mentioned that recruitment and retention rates more than triple in any area Cody visits to run programs compared to their other coaches. He's not just a good employee, he's essential to their success.

He also obviously loves Linna and all of his friends there. How could he possibly leave that? Kyla was his first job right out of college. What would he even do if he came here?

Feeling discouraged, I try to focus on spending time with my family. We have a great night, and I manage to stay off my phone despite my thoughts constantly shifting back to Cody. I even delay my departure by helping my grandma with the dishes and packing up the leftover food she always manages to have, despite having a full house for dinner. When they practically kick me out, saying I need to get back to the city, I finally get into my car and pull out my phone.

GOLDIE

Talk to you later!

GOLDIE

Maybe call me while you drive home so that you
can tell me more about your perfect family, I
want to know everything!

GOLDIE

I mean, if you want.

GOLDIE

> Not trying to sound like a total clinger here, I'm
> casual and not at all needy *sunglasses emoji*

GOLDIE

> Hope you're having fun, call me later if you want
> —but no pressure!

I'M STILL LAUGHING as I hit the call button at the top of my screen, and he answers on the first ring. "Totally casual," I tease.

"Yup! That's me," he agrees before snickering. "Sorry, texting is so hard when I can't tell if I'm annoying someone. I like to see people's expressions so I can gauge if I'm being too much."

"Cody, I don't think it's possible for you to annoy me," I admit sincerely. "Or anyone, for that matter, but if it's easier for you, I'm happy to video call or at least call whenever we're both available if that's your preference."

"That sounds great," he agrees. I can hear the smile in his words and the relief in his tone. I hate that he ever worries about what others think of him. Especially when, from what I've seen, everyone who meets him adores him.

"So tell me more about your family!" he eagerly prompts, as if he really wants to know all of the mundane details. And not because we're "The Caldwells," but because they're important to me.

I know I shouldn't risk further heartbreak by sharing these parts of myself with Cody—not when I'm just starting to admit the power he has over me. The thought of saying goodbye for real feels like it might actually break me.

But I want him to have these parts of me.

Even though my head is arguing against it, my heart wants him to have all of me.

CHAPTER FOURTEEN

Cody

Beck and I have been talking nonstop. We're both super busy, but we still manage to find time to text: good mornings, updates about our daily plans, and sending funny memes throughout the day. If we're alone, even when working, we tend to have the other on the phone or video call—both of us prefer the company.

Even though Beck might seem like the loner type if you don't know him, I've realized that he initiates contact just as often as I do. My chest always feels a little lighter when I see his name lighting up my screen, and it makes me happy to know that I'm not bothering him with my constant texts and calls.

The Werewolves killed it in the first round of the playoffs, advancing in only four games. I was able to watch all of the games even with my busy schedule—I wanted to know what I'm talking about when Beck and I caught up. Their captain was on fire and scored at least two points in each game, not counting his assists. I might have been out of the loop with hockey stats recently, but even I know how great that is.

Great for the city of Chicago and its hockey fans, but not so great for me.

Does it make me a bad person to admit that a small, selfish part of me was hoping they'd have lost right away so I could see Beck sooner? I want his team to do well, but the playoffs can last months, and I'm not very patient.

These past three weeks have felt endless.

But, I just got some news that has me grinning like an idiot as I hit the video call button under Beck's name. I'm so excited that I catch myself muttering, "pick up, pick up, pick up" under my breath until his handsome face fills my screen.

"Hey, sexy," he says in greeting. We've been very flirty while talking these last few weeks, but neither of us has brought up our hookups or explicitly said that we want it to happen again.

"Guess whaaat?" I sing, bouncing in my seat at my desk.

"You just quit your job and decided to become my houseboy?" he asks playfully, and it's so far from what I was expecting that I freeze.

"Your *what*?"

"Nothing," he laughs. "Just getting frustrated by the situation and wishing I could see you."

"That's why I called!" I'm back to bouncing in my seat. "I just got my schedule for the next month and I'll be back in Chicago in two weeks!"

"Thank fuck," he exhales, sounding as relieved as I feel. "I was starting to worry that I'd have to hire you again just to see you before June."

"Lucky for you, someone at your company must have given a good recommendation because another company reached out specifically requesting to have *me* come do the same seminar for them.

"It's a quick trip because I was already scheduled earlier in the week in South Carolina, so I won't get in until late Thursday night and need to travel back to Montana on Sunday. I'll be pretty booked during the work day, and I do have to run another program on Saturday, but in the evenings, I'm all yours!" The smile on my face feels permanent as I think about what we might get up to during my visit.

"I can't wait." He looks amused by my enthusiasm, but his smile matches mine. "I have to run to a meeting about the logistics of streaming the away games in the stadium to a full crowd during the rest of the playoffs, but I didn't want to ignore your call."

"I'm glad I caught you. I'll send over the details of my trip, and we can figure out a plan! Have fun at your meeting." I blow him a kiss and he laughs a "goodbye" before we hang up.

I send over all of the details before getting back to my work for the day, feeling a renewed sense of energy now that I know when I'll see Beck again.

My heart is still racing and my muscles ache as I leave the kickboxing class that was held at the Kyla gym for our morning workout. Pretty much everyone in town participates in some sort of group fitness activity. It's one of the ways that we can keep up with the healthy mind and body routine that the Kyla nutritionists and doctors have created under Viktor's guidance.

Viktor is always so disappointed when someone tries to skip out on exercise, so he's created accountability programs with financial incentives to help motivate everyone to attend classes at least five times a week. I love working out and would do it anyway, but it's also nice not to lose money.

The gym offers a great selection of activities to choose from: hiking, swimming, yoga, dance, spin classes, you name it. If you want there to be an activity and it isn't offered, you can even suggest it for them to add.

I love that I get to start my day with exercise to wake me up; I always feel more energized after the intense workouts. The classes are pretty early to ensure that everyone has time to participate before they need to work, and it's so cool that I get to see my friends first thing.

My best friend, Nick, one of the personal trainers at the gym, recommends which classes I should take, and they're always so much fun. Now that this morning's class is finished, I'm meeting up with him so he can let me know what other classes he'll be running while I'm in town and so we can catch up.

We meet at the coffee shop next to the gym, and after I grab our drinks, I join him in one of the booths near the front of the store.

"Hey man, it's been too long!" Nick says with a big smile. He's like me in that we're both usually upbeat and energetic. Nick is about my height and super fit from all the work he does at the gym. He's also got really pretty eyes. Actually, he's hot, now that I think about it.

"What's that look for?" he asks in a teasing tone.

I'm unsure what look I'm giving him, so I just go for honesty. "I didn't realize how hot you are." He starts choking on the sip he'd just taken, and I can't help but laugh. "Sorry. That was probably random, but I have a lot to catch you up on."

So I tell him how I met Beck, that he thought I was flirting with him, and how we actually went on a date, but I thought we were just hanging out like I always do with people I meet while traveling. Nick purses his lips as I talk, amusement shining in his eyes, but he doesn't interrupt, so I go on. "We kept in touch, and I invited him to the Florida retreat. They were overbooked, so we ended up sharing a room." His eyes go wide, and I chuckle. "He went to kiss me, and I was shocked because I'm oblivious and didn't recognize the tension between us until he explained it." It all sounds so strange when I say it aloud.

"We ended up hooking up, and I realized that I'm bi. Now I'm looking at everything with this new perspective, and I feel like an idiot for not realizing it sooner."

Nick is obviously trying not to laugh.

"Go ahead," I say with a grin. "It's funny."

He bursts out laughing, and it takes a minute before he can calm down enough to say anything. "Congratulations on realizing that you're bi," he begins.

"Thank you!" I say earnestly.

"And thank you for thinking I'm hot," he teases. "If I'm being honest, though," he continues, and I frown, unsure where this could be going. "I've always assumed that you were into both men and women," he admits with a shrug.

"Wait, really? Why?" *Do I give off some secret bi vibe that I didn't know about?*

"You unintentionally flirt with everyone," he says like it's obvious.

Which it's *not.* Sure, I flirt with Beck, and in the past I've flirted with the girls I wanted to hook up with, but definitely not *everyone.* My face must express my confusion because Nick laughs again before he continues.

"Cody, you're constantly giving people flirty grins, casually touching, asking about details of their life that most people would forget. You use a lot of eye contact..." he trails off.

"None of that is flirting," I insist. "It's just being nice! I'm nice."

"You're very nice," he reassures me. "But most people aren't. So when you're your normal nice self, I think that some people confuse that for interest."

"Huh." *I'm not sure how to react to that.*

"I'd bet that most of the people here have you specifically in mind as a potential partner when they commit to having an 'enlightened relationship'. Both the men and the women," Nick adds.

There are very popular programs run here in Linna that Viktor teaches on modern relationships that focus on avoiding the capitalistic downfalls of relationships in popular society today. So many people are with their partners because they feel trapped in the relationship financially or legally. People care more about their image—competing with other couples for likes online or with the neighbors for the best date night or the newest, shiniest car. Basically, people waste time and money ignoring their desires and needs to fit the mold of what society tells them a relationship should look like instead of supporting and empowering their partner.

I've never taken one of these programs because I haven't been in a serious enough relationship to consider learning more than the basics that Viktor has shared with me. I've never been against being in a serious relationship the way that Beck seems to be. I just haven't felt drawn to someone enough to put in the effort, with how much I travel and would be away from them.

Still, I know enough about the enlightened relationship idea to understand what Nick means. After the workshops, some couples decide they'd benefit from less traditional views on monogamy or from redefining what their relationship looks like. In fact, many people here choose to remain emotionally committed to their partner, living with them and maintaining their marriage or relationship while pursuing physical connections or even additional emotional and physical relationships outside of that initial pairing.

A lot of people also explore their sexuality for the first time as a result, which I've always thought was cool.

The concept of enlightened relationships reminds me of the swingers' parties I've seen in movies. Personally, I've never understood the appeal, but I'm glad that they all feel comfortable pursuing what makes them happy.

"I really doubt that," I say as I try to focus back on the conversation, and Nick gives me an indulgent grin. "Anywaaay," I say, drawing out the word, hoping to move on. "I haven't been able to stop thinking about this guy," I admit.

"When will you see him again?" Nick asks excitedly.

"That's the problem." I slouch in my seat, throwing my head back with a frustrated groan. "He's super busy with his job until the hockey team he works for is done for the season, but we don't know when that will be because they made the playoffs," I explain.

"Bad timing."

"Luckily, I'll be back in Chicago for a couple of days soon, but even then, I'll see him for maybe a few hours," I continue. "At least he has a lot of money, and his family is well known, so Viktor was eager to meet him in Florida. I've already talked to him about having Beck come here over the summer and started the visitor approval process with Kyla."

"Smart," Nick agrees, nodding. "What about video calls?"

"Oh yeah, we video call all the time. We both like to have it up while we're working or doing stuff around the house so that we can spend time hanging out."

"I meant like naked video calls," he clarifies with a laugh, and I feel my cheeks heating.

"No, not those kinds of calls," I say as I let out a nervous chuckle.

"Well, you should, especially if you're not seeing other people while you talk to him."

"I'm not, but I guess I don't know if he is," I admit as I realize I really don't want him to see anyone else. Just thinking about the possibility makes me angry, *and I'm never angry.*

"Sounds like you need to talk to your man," Nick points out unhelpfully, and I grunt in agreement.

I SHOULD PROBABLY BE GOING to bed since I have an early yoga class in the morning and could really use the sleep. Instead, I'm lying in bed with a bottle of lube, some tissues, and my laptop open to a porn site, feeling like a nervous teenager.

Since my weekend in Florida with Beck, I've been jerking off to the memories of us together at least daily. But now that I know I'll see him soon, combined with my conversation earlier about sexy video calls, I can't stop fantasizing about what else Beck and I could explore in the bedroom.

And I realized today that my fantasies about sex with another man are seriously lacking. I know porn isn't exactly a reliable source for realistic expectations—not that I have anything against it or the people in the industry. But I'm a visual learner, and surely the positions have to be somewhat accurate.

Why am I so nervous?

To ease into it, I search for a couple I've liked to watch in the past. It's a man and a woman who are together in real life. I've always preferred it when there's an actual connection between the actors. I try to watch like I usually would to see where my eyes land, and it doesn't take long to acknowledge I'm definitely watching the man just as much as the woman. I notice his muscles and his swollen cock, and realize these are details I've paid attention to in their other videos.

Interesting. Definitely attracted to both people.

If there was ever a question about whether I'm bi or just into Beck, my growing erection while thinking about the man on my screen has erased it.

Feeling a bit more confident, I decide to search for what I logged on intending to watch, so I go back to the category selection and click on *gay.* I'm not sure what to look for, so I scroll, noticing a wide variety of body types and titles—some of which honestly intimidate me.

Finally, I stumbled across a video labeled "Real Life Couple, Frotting and Anal."

Not sure what "frotting" means, but in the still image of the video, one of the guys has dark shorter hair like Beck, so I click on it.

The video starts with them making out, and I can appreciate that they're a real couple—their chemistry is obvious, and they look completely at ease with each other.

My cock is definitely getting excited.

They're standing naked beside a bed when the smaller of the two—the one who looks like a fake Beck—takes his hand and lines up both of their erections, wrapping them together in his grip as they thrust up into it.

My cock twitches, very intrigued by this new-to-me position that I'm guessing might be *frotting.*

What else have I been missing out on by limiting my sexual experiences to women?

On the screen, the larger man pulls away and crawls onto the bed with his plump ass in the air, and the fake Beck crawls up behind him, massaging his cheeks before leaning in and licking his hole.

Damn, I've never even considered what that would feel like, but the sounds coming from the men make me think they're both really enjoying it. I loved it when Beck teased my hole with his wet finger. I bet his tongue would feel amazing.

Fake Beck is really going at it now, making out with his hole and fucking his tongue into it. When he starts to add a finger to stretch him, I realize that my cock is leaking and decide that I've waited long enough.

Spreading my legs, I bend my knees and let them fall apart as I lie back on pillows so that I'm propped up. I grab some lube and spread it up and down my aching erection with a few firm strokes. It feels incredible with how horny the video has made me, and I decide to be a little more adventurous.

I add some more lube to the fingers on my right hand and switch my left hand to grip my shaft, still working it as I explore. With my right hand, I reach down to tease my taint before moving further to tap my tight hole with a single digit. Immediately the pressure on the opening has my cock twitching, more precum weeping from the angry head.

I squeeze the base in an attempt to hold off my orgasm and moan as I add pressure, not yet breaching the hole. My hips thrust up involuntarily in response to the sensation. Pleasure is building at the base of my spine, and I know that I won't last much longer, but I want more. I slowly increase the pressure until my finger is knuckle-deep while my other hand works up and down my rock-hard cock.

The sensation is unlike anything I've felt before, a fullness that seems a little forbidden while also feeling so fucking *right*. I'm overwhelmed by the desire to keep going, to seek more, go deeper, to be filled. I imagine that it's Beck's finger inside of me, that he's stretching me out for his use, so that he can fit his thick cock inside of me. *I want it.* As much as I'd like to keep going, the thought of Beck filling me in that way is too much, and I can't hold back my release. I curl in on myself as my muscles tighten, and thick ropes of cum cover my abs and chest, some even landing on my chin. My entire body seems to buzz as I continue to writhe in pleasure.

When I finally come down from the high of my orgasm and get cleaned up, I think more about the couple I'd been watching and the fantasy of Beck that had taken over. Even now, when I'm more clear-headed, I definitely want to know what it feels like to have Beck inside of me.

I'd love to top him, too, but the idea of being filled by him, of him fucking me until I can't think straight, has me practically salivating.

I really hope he's into that.

I think back to the way he pushed his cum covered fingers into my mouth after he finished on my face, the possessive way he smeared his release against my skin as if claiming me. The thought of his release filling me sends a shiver down my spine—

what would it feel like to have him mark me from the inside with his cum?

I've always been negative, but I think I'll get tested before I go to Chicago again. Just in case.

Would Beck be interested in being exclusive so we can skip condoms?

And how the fuck am I supposed to bring that up without sounding like I'm asking for a relationship?

A relationship that he's never wanted.

CHAPTER FIFTEEN

Beck

My mood instantly lifts as I see Cody's name light up my phone screen, requesting a video call. I'm the last person still stuck at the office, here way too late reviewing some final things that need my approval before tomorrow in preparation for our first game in the second round of the playoffs.

The players had a few days off between rounds because they won the first in four, and other teams ended up playing all seven games, but things seem busier than ever for the back office.

I smile as I answer, and his sexy face comes into view. "Hey, Goldie," I greet him with a wink. He's been blushing when I call him that, and I love watching his cheeks darken because of me.

"Hey," he says softly, glancing away from the camera.

"What has you looking all shy and bashful?" I tease. He's usually so confident.

"Who, me? Nothing, who's shy? I'm not shy."

"Oh my god, I was teasing," I chuckle as I attempt to reassure him. "But I've never seen you like this. What's up?"

He rolls his lips between his teeth, glancing up at me between his lashes. "I wanted to ask you something, but I'm worried about your answer," he admits. "And I don't want to push you or make you uncomfortable. It's just that I can't stop thinking about it, and I don't know if I even want to know your answer—"

"Cody," I interrupt him, unable to hold back a smile at how endearing he is when he's nervous.

"Yeah?"

"Take a deep breath," I demand, and my cock twitches when he follows my command without hesitation. "Ask me," I say in the same tone. "I don't want you to ever be afraid to talk to me."

He finally relaxes, looking reassured by my answer. His shoulders rise with the deep breath he takes before continuing. "I was wondering if you're seeing other people?" He says it like a question, even though he didn't technically ask one.

My heart starts to race as my thoughts fly, trying to determine why he's asking and what he wants my answer to be. *Is he seeing other people?* I fucking hope not. My stomach drops at the idea of him touching another man. Or a woman.

Apparently, I don't just want to be his first man—I want to be the *only* man he's been with.

I certainly don't want to be with anyone else. Is that why he's asking? Is there a chance he's feeling as jealous as I am? Or did he hook up with someone and feel the need to tell me before his visit next week?

Fuck. This is why I don't do relationships. How do people put up with these feelings?

Thankfully, I'm pulled from my spiral as he continues. "I was thinking that it might be nice if we could maybe not use condoms if the time comes, and I didn't want to wait until we were in the moment in case you needed to get tested, but then I started thinking about how long it's been since Florida, and I haven't wanted to hook up with anyone else, but we also didn't make any promises, and I know that you don't do rela-tionships…"

Each word makes the smile on my face grow wider. I feel like I could float away with how relieved I am by his nervous rambling.

"I have no desire to see anyone else," I reassure him.

"Really?" He sits up straighter and beams. "I mean, cool, yeah, that's good." He tries and fails to sound casual.

"You're so fucking adorable," I tell him, and he preens, shim-mying his shoulders and rolling his eyes playfully. "I was tested two weeks ago, and I haven't been with anyone else either," I inform him.

"So, no condoms?" he asks hopefully.

"No condoms," I agree. Then I force myself to ask, "Are you alone?" before I tell him what I'm really thinking.

"Yeah, I'm home for the night."

"Good, then I can tell you how hard I am at the thought of claiming you with nothing between us. I can't wait to mark you as mine, to fill your virgin hole with my release." My voice is like gravel as I cup my growing erection through my suit pants.

He lets out a desperate whimper before nodding. "I really want that."

My heart races at his admission. I thought he'd need more time before he considered bottoming. "You want me to fuck you?" I clarify, needing to hear him say it. Because a part of me still doesn't believe that this man went from straight to needy bottom in two seconds. But my big, bi, adorable man is still nodding adamantly, like the idea of me topping him would make him even happier.

Not *my man* like my boyfriend, I just meant…well, I'm not sure. *I guess we did just agree to be exclusive.*

Now is not the time for this commitment panic, so I force those thoughts to the back of my mind as he continues.

"I might have watched some gay porn," he mutters softly, pulling me right back to the moment.

"And?" I prompt when he doesn't continue.

"And… I kept focusing on the bottom, how blissed out they look. I liked it when you teased me while you were blowing me, I want to know what it would feel like to have you inside of me."

"Fuck, Goldie," I groan, quickly opening and shoving my pants down enough to pull out my aching cock.

I had my phone propped up on my desk so that he could only see my upper half, so I quickly adjust the angle and back up enough that he can see my hand moving up and down my hard dick, smearing the precum that's already leaking from the swollen head.

He repositions his phone so I can see him strip down before sitting back on the edge of his couch. The silver necklace he always wears seems to glow against his tan skin, drawing my attention to the defined muscles of his chest. Then he spits in his hand and starts to work his perfect cock, pulling my attention there. It really is impressive—long and thick, with a few prominent veins running up the shaft.

I wish I was there in person so that I could attempt to swallow it down again, but I know that my self-restraint will be nonexistent when I do see him again if he's offering me his ass.

"Did you see anything else you want to try?" I ask, my voice husky as I spit into my hand, wishing it was his mouth wrapped around me.

His blissed-out expression makes it seem like he's struggling to focus. "Umm, there was this one thing."

"Tell me," I encourage.

He gets out a few words at a time as he struggles to answer while visibly approaching his release. "While the top was prepping the bottom, he used his mouth before adding fingers."

"I can't wait to eat your ass, baby," I quickly respond. "I'll worship your hole with my tongue like a starving man finally allowed salvation. Then I'll fuck you with it to open you up for me. I'll take my time stretching you out, adding fingers until you're desperate for my cock," I promise.

"Oh, fuck, Beck!" He shouts my name out in a cry of ecstasy as I watch cum paint his chest and abs, spurring my own orgasm. I ride out the waves of pleasure, ignoring my now-stained shirt.

When I eventually calm down, I see he's still staring dreamily at me, his release shining on his exposed muscles. "Good boys don't waste cum," I warn him.

He looks confused for a moment before I see his eyes darken and his full lips twist into an amused smirk. "What do you want me to do with it, sir?" he asks, and my dick stirs, already wanting another round. His teeth are digging into his bottom lip now, no doubt trying to stop a huge smile as he blinks at me expectantly.

Fuck me, what did I do to deserve this perfect man's attention? "Clean it up with two fingers, and then I want you to pretend it's my cock you're licking clean," I instruct.

He nods eagerly, doing precisely what I said, taking his time to really make a show of it before holding my gaze as he licks and sucks his fingers clean.

"Good boy," I praise when he finally pulls off with a *pop*. "That was hotter than any porn I've ever seen. I wish I'd been recording somehow," I say offhandedly.

"Do you want me to send you videos when I get myself off?" he offers, sounding very into the idea.

"You'd do that?"

"That sounds hot, knowing that you could watch me whenever you wanted. I already told you that I trust you," he adds with a smile.

"Fuck, you're perfect," I say, still somewhat in shock about his offer.

He laughs and grabs his phone as he finally stands from the couch.

I remove my shirt and use it to wipe up the rest of my mess.

Cody must have taken his phone with him to get dressed because I'm watching him pull on loose gray sweats in what appears to be his closet.

When we're both settled and focused back on the phone, he's giving me a shy smile. "Well, that was fun," he says cheekily.

"It really was," I agree.

"I miss you," he admits, and his cheesy grin falls into a much softer smile.

A knot forms in my chest at his words. "Miss you too."

I don't know what we're doing. Neither of us is in a position to compromise our career for the other. I've never been in a real relationship, and now that I think I want one, it seems impossible. But at the same time, I know we're not ready to say goodbye.

"I get to see you next week, though!" Cody adds, no doubt trying to lighten the mood.

"Thank fuck."

Cody goes on to update me about his day, telling me about all of his friends that he saw and the presentations that he gave. I swear he could describe the most boring day and still make it sound like the best time.

I love that about him. How eternally happy he is.

I tell him about my day too, and then we talk about our plans for the rest of the week.

At some point, Cody moves to lie down in bed, his phone propped on the pillow beside him. His eyelids are growing heavy, and after the third yawn, I know I should say goodnight, but I can't bring myself to end the call.

"Go to sleep," I tell him, and when he starts to protest, I add, "I'll stay on the line, but you need to rest."

With a contented smile, he nods, eyes already closed. "Night, Beck," he whispers.

"Goodnight, baby," I say so quietly that I don't think he hears. The term keeps slipping out without much thought, but looking at his peaceful expression, grinning even in sleep, it feels right.

After finding an old Werewolves t-shirt in the closet of my office, I settle back into work, reviewing everything I need to do before tomorrow. By the time I finish, it's nearly one a.m. I leave the physical copies on Adrian's desk with a note explaining I might be a little late in the morning and head back to my condo. I'm glad I drove today, even though it's only a few blocks away. I hate walking when it's this late, and I'm happy that I don't need to bother anyone else to drive me at this hour.

I keep the video call with Cody up the entire time, carrying his beautiful sleeping face with me as I prepare for bed. When I finally get under my covers, I plug in my phone so that it's lying next to me on another pillow.

With my eyes closed, the sound of his soft, steady breaths fills the room, pulling me back to the weekend I spent with him, curled in my arms. I can't remember ever sleeping that soundly.

When I wake up the next morning to that god-awful alarm tone, Cody's face is no longer filling my screen. I'm hit with a surprising wave of disappointment at the realization before I see a text from him.

GOLDIE

Waking up next to your sleeping face is my new favorite thing.

GOLDIE

Sorry I had to end the call. I had a sunrise hike this morning and knew I'd lose signal eventually.

GOLDIE

Wanted you to at least wake up to a text and not a dropped call.

GOLDIE

Thanks for last night. Can't wait to spend the night with you again in person!

CHAPTER SIXTEEN

Cody

I'm buzzing with excitement as I approach the Caldwell Center for Saturday's game.

As Beck put it, the "Hockey Gods" weren't on our side this weekend. Chicago faced Buffalo in the second series, winning both games in New York. We hoped for a sweep back in Chicago, but Buffalo won games three and four. That meant Beck was still in New York for game five when I arrived in Chicago on Thursday night—and I still haven't seen him.

Then, to make it worse for our timing, a network issue forced back-to-back games, so the teams stayed in New York overnight and didn't land here until after I was already at work today. But at least they managed to scrape by with a win last night.

Now, the Werewolves are fighting to close out the series with a win tonight. If they lose, they'll have to head back to New York for game seven.

And I thought my work travel was crazy! These hockey schedules make mine look like a walk in the park in comparison.

On the bright side, Beck invited me to watch tonight's game

with him! I'm so excited to see him in person again. He told me to go to gate six and a half to check in and give my name. I thought he was joking at first about the "half" thing, but apparently, it's real.

When I walk up to the gate, an intimidating man in a suit asks for my ticket.

"I don't have one. I'm so sorry, my friend said to give my name. It's Cody Richardson," I rush to explain when he seems annoyed by my lack of ticket. At the mention of my name, though, he perks up.

"Richardson is here for Mr. Caldwell," he says into the headset he's wearing.

Moments later, a short man with stylish blonde hair appears from behind him. He's wearing a Werewolves jersey that's slim fit to his small frame and tight black pants that make his butt look great when he steps in front of me to flash his badge at the man I was talking to.

"No need to call anyone, he's with me!" the man says excitedly.

"Go ahead," the security guy confirms, waving me toward the metal detectors that lead inside.

After I'm cleared by security, I stick my hand out to introduce myself to my new friend, who apparently knows who I am and is very happy that I'm here, but my words are cut off before I can even begin.

"Cody, it's so great to meet you!" he squeals, practically jumping into a hug. He's much shorter than me, so the height of the hug is a little awkward, but I quickly lean down to adjust to his size and hug him back firmly.

I'm still confused as to why we're hugging, but ever since I learned that the princesses at theme parks aren't allowed to end a hug first, I've decided to follow suit. You never know when someone else needs that connection. I'd hate to cut it off and leave them feeling neglected.

When he finally pulls back, he leads me toward the elevators in the lobby we've entered.

"It's great to meet you, too?" I say the end like a question, hoping he'll also introduce himself.

"Oh shit, sorry! I forgot you don't actually know me. Beck's been talking about you so much that I feel like we're already friends," he explains. "I'm Adrian, his best friend slash assistant, in that order."

"Oh, I do know you! Beck's talked about you too," I confirm. "It's great to put a face to the name." I smile brightly at him as we board the elevator up to the 100-level suites. I had no idea that this would be such a fancy experience, but I probably should have assumed with Beck's family being the owners.

We exit into a long hallway with numbered doors on one side that must lead to the suites. There's another member of security standing there to recheck tickets, but they wave us through when they see Adrian.

"Beck is going to be so bummed that I got to you before him," Adrian says with an evil grin. He heads into the suite labeled 01, and I immediately smile at the loud laughter filling the space. It's full of at least twenty people of varying ages.

Oh my god, do I get to meet Beck's sitcom family?

As soon as I step into the room, I see Beck across the space and our eyes lock. It's like everything else fades away, and it's just us in the room. I'm sure that my smile is bordering on obnoxious, but I'm just so excited to be in the same place after weeks of endless texts and video calls across state lines. We've gotten into the habit of falling asleep with our video call still going, and every morning I feel so lucky that I get to wake up to his sleeping face.

We both rush toward each other, and I wrap him up in a huge hug, lifting him slightly off the ground. He squeezes me back just as tightly, and we're both laughing by the time I lower him to the floor. He steps back, and I realize that the rest of the room has gone silent.

"I never thought I'd see the day," says a man who looks like a slightly shorter and younger version of Beck. "My scary big bro, laughing and smiling while he hugs his *date.* Definitely wasn't on my bingo card."

His tone is teasing, and he holds out his hand with a laugh, "You must be Cody. This guy hasn't shut up about you for weeks." He pats Beck on the back with his other hand as we shake ours. "I'm Lincoln, his youngest and favorite brother. Thank fuck you're here. I was starting to worry that Beck was going to disappear in the middle of the night and ditch the playoffs to go see you," he says, actually sounding relieved.

After Lincoln steps away, I find a line of people waiting to be introduced to me. The whole family is here. I meet Beck's three other brothers, Oakley, Harrison, and Dominic, then his grandparents, his other best friend, Jordan, and even some of his brothers' friends who seem just as close to him as his actual family members.

Finally, an attractive, slightly older couple approaches with warm smiles on their faces. The woman ignores my outstretched hand and pulls me in for a tight hug. While she squeezes me, she goes up on her tiptoes and whispers, "Thank you," into my ear. "I don't think he's ever been this happy," she continues. "I know the situation isn't perfect, but it's like something's settled in him since he met you. He doesn't seem to be so on edge." She steps back and takes both of my hands in hers, giving them a tight squeeze before letting go. "I'm Beck's mom, Susan, and this is his dad, Greg. We're so excited to finally meet you."

"Great to meet you, son," his dad says as he takes my hand and uses it to pull me in for a one-armed, back-slap, guy hug that makes me laugh.

I knew that I'd love his family from everything Beck's told me and how he always talks of them with such fondness. I wasn't expecting to meet them today, though, and I certainly wouldn't have expected this warm of a welcome when Beck and I aren't even dating.

My parents are nice people, but they're always so busy that I only get to talk to them every few weeks for quick hellos and updates. I know they both love me and want me to be happy, but I can't imagine my mom being so genuinely excited to meet someone I've only been talking to for a few weeks. I've told her about Beck, but I doubt she'll remember his name the next time we catch up.

I'm surprised by how emotional this warm welcome has made me. I've always craved this sense of family and belonging. It feels like a cruel joke from the universe to tie everything I've ever wanted to Beck, knowing there's no realistic way for us to be together.

Even if I wanted to leave Kyla... I don't think I actually can with the ways that I've tied myself to the company. I've been trying not to focus on that, though. Who knows if Beck even wants a relationship anyway? No use stressing over a possibility that doesn't exist.

It makes me so happy to hear his family talk about the positive changes in Beck since meeting me, but for all I know, that could have been from the programs he's taken with Kyla, not because of our *situation*.

He's told me that he's never wanted a relationship. Just because we've agreed to be exclusive doesn't mean he suddenly wants us to be together for the rest of our lives or anything.

I've found some good friends through Kyla, but most of what we talk about is related to work in one way or another. Nick is probably my best friend in Linna, but I can't imagine him meeting my parents or me his. Most of the people in our town have moved there for Kyla, so we're away from our extended families and don't see them much. Now that I think about it, other than a few people who have had to cut contact with their toxic family members, I can't think of any of my friends ever really talking about their families.

Adrian and Jordan fit in with Beck's family seamlessly, as do his siblings' friends. The only people here who look slightly out of place are the two attractive girls sitting on an armchair in the corner. Beck's brother, Oakley, explained that one of the girls is his girlfriend, and the other is dating his best friend, Parker. They look so comfortable with each other that I wonder if they're sisters—one is sitting on the other's lap, both laughing at something on the phone they're looking at.

Maybe I need to make more of an effort with my friends, to learn more about them outside of Kyla and work-related topics. It's just hard when so much of our time in Montana is structured, and so many of us travel for the programs.

"I grabbed us some food," Beck says, interrupting my thoughts as he comes up beside me. He places his hand on my lower back and hands me a plate of delicious-looking fruits and veggies. "I've noticed you tend to go for the clean stuff, so I grabbed the healthiest-looking options. If you want to watch warm-ups, we can go sit in the balcony seats."

"Thanks! That would be awesome," I agree, trying to shake off my jealous thoughts about how amazing Beck's family and friends seem. Instead, focusing on how sweet it was of him to notice the kinds of foods I like to eat.

He leads us to the door at the back of the large suite. We pass a full bar with a bartender, a private bathroom, couches, tables, and more food than this group could possibly eat in one night. Through the door is a balcony with two stadium-style rows of plush seating. Adrian and Jordan are already in the front row, and I follow Beck toward them. Beck has me sit next to Jordan while he sits on my other side.

They all include me like an old friend, not someone they met less than an hour ago, and it makes my chest feel like it could burst with how grateful I am to be so welcomed.

We spend the warmups with them pointing out specific players and telling me more about their positions, stats, and even personal lives.

"So, do you have favorite players when you personally know them all?" I question the group.

Beck gives me a very serious look as he answers. "No, with my position, it is imperative that I remain impartial to specific players and focus on the team's success as a whole." His tone is flat, but at the last second, he winks, and I know he's fucking with me.

"Bell," Jordan coughs the star rookie's last name in answer, and we all laugh.

"I have a favorite!" Adrian declares, and Beck and Jordan snicker and start making kissing noises.

"Are you dating a player or something?" I ask based on their responses.

"Ugh, I wish!" Adrian deflates a bit. "I don't know of any out players on the team. There are a couple in the league, but their reception has been pretty mixed."

"You'd think that with an out CEO of the team, if anyone wanted to come out, they would," Jordan adds.

"It's not that simple," Beck argues, sounding defeated. "No one's buying a ticket to see me here, and it's not my name on the jersey they're paying hundreds of dollars to buy. Even with Chicago being a fairly accepting city, the Midwest isn't always as kind. A lot of the rural states west of us don't have an NHL team, so they root for the Werewolves.

"Plus, hockey players tend to be a superstitious group. I wouldn't be surprised if there are guys in the league who'd love to come out but don't want to risk it affecting their game at all."

"That's sad," I respond, thinking about how easy it was for me to embrace being bi. Apparently, my closest friend thought that I was already out. I can't imagine how hard it must be for people who are forced to deny who they truly are.

Beck nods. "I've been trying to think of ways to improve the situation, and I've dropped some pretty blatant hints to our guys that there's no need to hide anything from our staff, even if they had something about their personal life they didn't want fans to know. So far, though, no one's said anything."

"Back to meee," Adrian cuts in, making us all laugh. "My favorite player is the sexy as fuck captain, Hudson Roy," he says with a dreamy sigh. "Sadly, he's not only straight but he's married to a super pretty blonde woman who's literally an ex-model."

"You're super pretty and blonde," I point out, trying to cheer him up.

"I *am* super pretty and blonde. Thank you for reminding me," he sits up straighter with a big smile. "I knew I was going to like you, Cody."

Beck's friends really are amazing.

After warmups, we head back into the suite for more snacks and to hang out with the rest of the family. Oakley and Parker are super funny, and they keep finishing each other's sentences. It's obvious with the way they move around each other and do small things like grab the other a refill or toss the other's empty plate that they care about each other and have been best friends for a really long time.

We cram as many people as we can onto the balcony for the start of the game, and when the Werewolves quickly score, it's the coolest thing I've ever experienced at a professional sports game. The crowd explodes, people sing along to their goal song, others wildly clap, and there's a lot of howling, which I think is supposed to resemble a wolf.

It's incredible to witness such a display of excitement and unity amongst thousands of people, all brought together by their love for this team. I've only been to Chicago a few times for work, and the trips were always quick, but this city is quickly becoming one of my favorite places.

The game itself is a blur of excitement. The Werewolves score twice more in the second before Buffalo gets one past our goalie.

Yep, *our* goalie... I'm a die-hard Werewolves fan now, so I'm claiming it.

Buffalo scores again at the start of the third, and things get pretty tense for a while with Chicago only having a one-goal lead. Luckily, Buffalo pulls their goalie too early in an attempt to tie the game, and Roy is able to send it into their empty net, securing the W for the Werewolves and advancing them to the next round of the playoffs.

CHAPTER SEVENTEEN

Beckett

I'm fucked.

Tonight was perfect. My team won, we're going to the semifinals—closer to the cup than we've been in years. It was a home win, too, which is always more fun to experience.

And Cody was there.

He was with my family and friends, fitting in like he's always been part of our lives. Sitting next to me, laughing, smiling, looking at me like I'm something special—it made me so damn happy.

And I. Am. Fucked.

Because how am I supposed to give that up? How do I bring him back to my place, where he wants me to be his first, and then say goodbye tomorrow with no idea when I'll see him again?

My feelings for Cody have already far surpassed anything I've ever felt for anyone else. I've never wanted something real.

There was always this nagging fear that someone would be more interested in my last name than in me. But Cody? He wanted to get to know my family because they matter to me, not because of money or influence.

I know that if I fuck him tonight—if I truly know what it feels like to be inside of him instead of just fantasizing about it—I will be a complete goner for this man.

I'm scared I'll wake up tomorrow and insist on flying back to Montana with him, abandon everything I've built here to be with him.

The fear that I'll have to choose between Cody and my life in Chicago is constant, and even on a night when hockey, my job, and my family and friends were all such positives, I'm afraid that I don't know what my answer would be.

We're not even really together; we're exclusive, but he hasn't asked to be my boyfriend. He hasn't talked about wanting more or a future between us. I don't think it's necessarily that he doesn't want those things, but we're both just so stuck with work that any future feels so unlikely.

I can't get the images from tonight out of my head. Cody hugging my parents. Cody joking around with Oakley and Parker. The look on Adrian's face when Cody told him that he was pretty.

I want more of that.

I want him at all of the home games. I want him at family dinners at my grandparents' house, chasing their dog around the backyard with Parker. I want the feeling of his hand in mine, like it is right now, as we enter my building and are greeted by the doorman.

But I can't ask Cody to give up his whole life to fit into mine. Even if he does seem to fit so perfectly.

He loves his job, his town, and his friends. I could never ask him to give up what makes him happy.

Maybe when I visit Linna, I'll figure out a solution that works for both of us.

For now, though, I need to protect myself without hurting

Cody. I know that he wanted me to fuck him tonight, but I don't think I could stop myself from blurting out my feelings for him if I did. That, or I might end up tying him to the bed and not letting him leave tomorrow. That's probably not the solution. *Not yet, anyway.*

Maybe I can distract him with other new fun things.

We can still hook up, keep it casual for now, and I'll just ignore the feelings of impending dread that arise when I think about how long it will be before I see Cody again after tonight.

CHAPTER EIGHTEEN

Cody

Beck's condo is incredible, easily the fanciest building I've ever stepped foot in. There's marble and chandeliers everywhere, a sleek modern aesthetic complemented by intricate moldings and ornate furniture that I'd expect in an older building. Not to mention the doorman and multiple security guards in the lobby. Beck scanned us into the private penthouse elevator, and even though it took us right to his floor, it felt like the ride lasted forever.

There's tension between us right now, and I can't tell if it's the *I need you naked* kind or something else, especially with how quiet he's being.

He keeps giving me very heated glances like he wants to devour me, but then he looks away just as quickly like he's holding something back. I know that the distance between us has been a stressor, but I'm hoping that he'll feel more comfortable once we can finally touch each other.

The elevator opens into a decent-sized entryway, and we step through into a gorgeous state-of-the-art kitchen. Everything is dark and sleek—black cabinets and black quartz counters, with dark walls and furniture. It all feels cozy in the large space, and it seems to fit Beck's vibe perfectly.

There are huge floor-to-ceiling windows on the far side of the room looking out over the lit-up skyline and the vast, dark expanse of what must be Lake Michigan.

We both pause in the large open-concept living room, full of pictures of his family and friends, and he turns to face me. Without saying anything, the tension breaks, and we collide into each other's embrace—a tangle of desperate kisses and groping hands.

My blood had been rushing south since the elevator ride in anticipation of finally being alone together, and my cock is now aching to break free of my pants. I grind into Beck as I kiss down his jaw and neck, wanting to taste every inch of him.

He pushes me toward the deep sectional that's taking up most of the room, stripping me down and forcing me back until I'm completely naked and falling onto it with a laugh.

I twist to get comfortable, lying back like I would on a bed, propping myself up with some pillows. Beck quickly sheds his clothes and grabs a bottle of lube from the end table, tossing it next to me. I quirk a brow at its location.

"I like to be prepared," he says with a smirk. The bottle looks pretty full, though, like maybe he prepared specifically for my visit.

Beck is unbelievably hot as he crawls up the couch until he's on his hands and knees above me, trapping me under him.

"Hey, Goldie." His tone is practically a growl with how low his lust-drunk voice sounds.

I let out an embarrassing whimper and attempt to pull him down onto me fully. Our rock-hard cocks rub together and even that feels spectacular.

I thrust my hips up into him, desperate for more, but Beck lowers his weight to sit back and straddle me. He's sitting up at the perfect angle to line up our erections, and he grabs the bottle of lube. Beck gives himself a few rough strokes, slicking his cock, then does the same to mine. His firm grip feels so unbelievably good, I could fall apart right now if I'm not careful.

Then he blows my fucking mind when he wraps his hand around us both.

I gasp as he moves his fist up and down, twisting and squeezing with just the right amount of pressure. But the really mind-blowing part is how amazing it feels to have our cocks rubbing together. The swollen heads bumping and dragging against each other as we both thrust our hips, fucking up into the warm, wet channel his hand creates has me desperate for release already.

"Who knew that other dicks could be so fun?" I manage to get out after a needy moan.

"I've always known," he says with a smug grin.

"Well, thanks for sharing," I tease. He continues to work us both, and the sight is so fucking hot. I try to take in every detail of our cocks rubbing together, knowing how often I'll want to remember exactly what it looks like when we're not in the same city again. Beck's movements feel so good, and I've been so desperate for us to be together again, that I'm worried I won't last much longer. "Fuck, Beck, I'm seriously so close already. This feels amazing."

"Come for me." His voice has that growly undertone, and there's no mistaking his words as anything other than the command that they are.

"I don't want this to be over yet," I say with an edge of panic. *I really wanted him to fuck me tonight.*

Beck looks at me indulgently before he continues, picking up the pace of his movements and making it really difficult for me to even focus on what he's saying. "I won't last either, we've been apart for too long. Come for me. Paint our bodies in your release. I'm right behind you."

"I want as many rounds as possible before tomorrow," I insist, still trying to hold back. How is it possible to already be craving more of him, even though he's right here, making me feel incredible?

"Baby, I need you to be a good boy and come for me," he says in that deep, commanding tone.

His term of endearment, combined with the demand and potential for praise, makes me lose all hope of prolonging this orgasm. I let out a strangled cry, my muscles tense, and my cock jerks, cum shooting all over my abs and chest as waves of pleasure crash violently through me.

Beck's release mixes with my own as he follows me over the edge, moaning out my name as his body shudders over mine.

He collapses next to me on the deep-set couch, taking a few moments to catch his breath before repositioning us so that I rest my head on his chest. His fingers play with our cum, mixing it together even more before scooping it up to bring it to my mouth for me to lick off. I love tasting him. Earning his release always gives me such a feeling of accomplishment, and knowing how much he loves to see me finish it all is hot as hell.

"Good boy," he whispers when I've licked it all up. His praise fulfills me in a way that I've never experienced before. It's a high that I want to continue to earn over and over again.

Eventually, I shift to look up at him, smiling and not saying anything, just taking in the moment.

"How was that?" he finally asks with a cocky grin.

"Obviously amazing."

"You're amazing," he whispers, squeezing me tighter to him. I close my eyes, cuddling in closer, and pretend like we have all of the time in the world.

LAST NIGHT WAS SPECTACULAR, even if Beck didn't fuck me.

Eventually, he got up from the couch to get some damp towels to clean us up with before we made our way to his super fancy bathroom. If I thought the one in the hotel during my last trip to Chicago was extravagant, it had nothing on this one.

Everything was black marble, from the long counter with a built-in vanity to the sleek sinks that looked like sculpted bowls resting on the surface. There was a clawfoot soaking tub in the center of the room and a huge jacuzzi tub that looked like it could fit four people built in against the wall. The shower had all of the bells and whistles from the hotel, with a crazy amount of shower heads and benches, and there was even an attached sauna and steam room!

We ended up in the shower together, washing and finding any excuse to run our hands and mouths all over each other. By the time we stepped out, we were both painfully hard and desperate again. Beck wasted no time dropping to his knees and taking my cock to the back of his throat. Even though I'd just cum on the couch not even an hour before, I didn't last long at all. When Beck started teasing my rim with his finger, I couldn't hold back and quickly shot down his throat. My lack of stamina would be more embarrassing if Beck didn't seem to be having the same problem.

It was so fucking hot that I needed to have a turn myself. My blowjob skills could definitely use some work, but I think my enthusiasm makes up for my inexperience. Beck didn't last long either, and we hopped back into the shower for a quick clean-up before climbing into his bed.

I packed my usual sleep pants but decided against them and ended up curled in Beck's arms, both of us naked.

Now, I'm still wrapped in his arms as my alarm rings, but Beck has me trapped with how tight his hold is, and I can't quite reach my phone to silence it.

"Shut uuuup," he draws out the word and groans loudly,

blindly swinging his arm in the general direction of the phone. I don't think he's even opened his eyes yet.

"Sorry, Beck, but I've got to head out for my flight soon," I whisper.

"Okay," he agrees, holding me tighter instead of letting go. He thrusts his hips into me, causing his hard morning wood to rub against my ass, and now it's my turn to moan.

He'd seemed so eager to fuck me when we talked on the phone, but then last night, it was like he was so desperate for me that he couldn't possibly slow down to actually get that far. At least, that's what I'm telling myself because I'm not sure why he wouldn't want to take things further.

Everything we did was amazing, I just wish I knew what was going through his head. *Was there another reason he didn't want to top me?*

"Come on, I should really order a ride share so I'm not late. I never know how long it'll take them to get here," I say, finally stretching far enough to reach the phone and turn off the alarm. I try to encourage him to let go of me without success.

"No rideshare," Beck says with a deep sleepy tone that makes my cock thicken.

"Um, is there a better option?" I ask, willing my dick to calm down because we really don't have time for anything.

"I'm driving you to the airport," he says, like I should have already known.

"Oh, that would be great!"

I'm a little surprised by the offer, with how in my head I've been about what's going on between us. Driving me to the airport feels like a boyfriend move. Meeting the family was obviously a big deal, but with Beck, it felt natural—his family is so close with him, and all his friends are practically an extension of that.

But Beck also has money. The kind of money where he's got *people* for everything. A driver took us home from the game last night, just like someone chauffeured us to dinner on my previous trip. He even had an employee come to my hotel yesterday to take my bag here so I wouldn't have to bring it to the game. He's got people for everything, I'd kind of assumed he never drove himself.

So his offer feels significant.

"No driver this morning?" I clarify with a teasing tone, trying to keep things light. I don't want him to second guess his offer if he knows I'm kind of freaking out about it.

"Nah, I want you all to myself when I have to say goodbye," he responds possessively. He leans over to give me a quick kiss on the cheek and a tight squeeze before finally releasing me from his grip.

Not my boyfriend. We're not dating. He doesn't do relationships. This is just a fling while I have his attention. I repeat the statements over and over in my head, trying to ground myself as my heart soars at his answer.

Maybe he'd agree to come to Linna for the *entire* hockey offseason. Viktor seemed okay with the idea when I suggested we show him around headquarters. It's not a long-term solution, but the summer together would be better than nothing.

Beck grabs my suitcase—*not my boyfriend, not my boyfriend*—and we take the elevator straight down to a parking garage. I've never been a car guy, but the shiny black one we get into looks pretty fancy. It only fits the two of us, with a huge touchscreen display in the front, and it's really loud as Beck guides it out onto the busy streets of the city.

Beck rests his right hand on my thigh, squeezing it, and I place my hand on top of his. We sit in comfortable silence, and I'm soaking in the moment while we're still in the same place and can casually touch each other. We pull up to park right in front of a coffee shop, and I look at Beck with a raised brow. "This isn't O'Hare."

"You don't need to be at the airport for at least another hour and a half, we have time for coffee. Or are you that eager to leave me?" he teases as he pays for the parking.

"Definitely not." I wish I didn't have to leave so soon, but Viktor scheduled a meeting this evening, and I'm hoping to talk to him more about Beck coming for the summer.

That is, if Beck wants to.

"Would you, maybe, want to come stay with me when the hockey season ends?" I ask as we walk in, sounding far less confident than I'd like to be. I'm nervous to even ask, afraid he'll brush off the suggestion, or worse, tell me it's been fun while it lasted, but he actually drove me himself today for privacy while he ends things.

He turns to face me with a hopeful smile as we get in line, which I take as a good sign as he considers his answer.

"I'm not sure how long I can realistically be gone. I'll definitely need to be here the week of the draft," he trails off, and I can't seem to stand still, my leg bouncing as I wait for him to finish.

"But I think I could get away for a while, especially after that," he says, reaching out for my hand and giving it a squeeze. I grip it tighter, lacing our fingers together so we're properly holding hands.

"So, is that a yes?" I can't keep the excitement out of my tone, and he chuckles.

"Yes, I'd love to," he admits with a smirk, and I feel like I could run a marathon with all the excitement now coursing through my veins.

"Oh my god, I can't wait! I'll talk to Viktor tonight about getting you approved as a temporary visitor, and I can show you around headquarters and the town!" He gives me a slightly confused look at that, but I'm rambling now and can't seem to slow down as my excitement grows. "Oh, you can meet Nick and all of my other friends, and you'll love how pretty it is! We can go hiking and kayaking. It'll be the best summer!"

He looks amused, and it's our turn to order, so we step up and both ask for plain black coffees. Beck insists on paying, and we move to the pickup counter.

"Wait, is this where we first met?" I ask as I finally look around the coffee shop.

"Uh, yeah. I thought it would be nice to come back here, together this time." He looks down, shifting his weight like he's nervous. He tries to pull his hand away, but I tighten my grip. "Now I'm wondering if that was weird and maybe we should pretend like it's just about wanting coffee…" he trails off when he looks back at my giant smile.

"Oh my god, Beck! Is this a sentimental date?" I tease, loving the idea that the man currently glaring at me as he clearly tries to suppress a smile, wanted to take me back to where it all began. He might not want a relationship, but I think he'd make a pretty great boyfriend. *Again, that's not what he is, even if this is totally a date.*

"Don't make it weirder," he grumbles with a laugh as they call out our names. We grab our drinks and find a place to sit, still holding hands across the table like neither of us is ready to break the connection.

"So is this our second date, or did last night count?" I ask, continuing to tease him.

"Last night probably counted," he admits, rolling his eyes before he relaxes into a more serious expression. "I'm sorry I didn't warn you about meeting everyone. I was just so excited to have you at a game, I didn't even think to offer a different seating arrangement."

"It was perfect!" I insist. "They're truly spectacular, Beck. It was such an honor to meet the people who are important to you."

I spend some time gushing about how much fun I had yesterday and how incredible it was to meet his family and friends as we drink our coffees. His eyes soften as I talk about them, and I feel guilty for asking him to leave them all for so long. But I try not to dwell on that and think about how lucky I am that he's choosing to spend the summer with me. My chest feels ready to burst with how special it makes me feel.

This important, amazing, sweet man wants to not only spend his free time with me, but he's putting in a lot of effort and going out of his way to do so.

I've always wanted to feel important to someone in that way. My parents were so busy in their lives and careers that I never had that growing up. Whenever I imagined my future partner, I'd fantasize about them making our relationship a priority. I'd think about how amazing it would be to find someone who just wanted to spend time together and made it happen.

Sure, in the past, I'd always pictured a woman, but that's only because I didn't think of expanding my options. Now, when picturing a future, I desperately want that person to be Beck. I just need to figure out if that's something he could want, too.

I think I'd do anything at this point to make that happen. But now isn't the time for that conversation.

We reluctantly leave when our drinks are empty, and I ask Beck more about his brothers on our drive to the airport. Now that I've met them all, I want to know even more about his family, his childhood stories, what their relationships are like now, and if he thinks they liked me.

When we arrive, I expect Beck to pull up to the departure drop-off lane, but he surprises me and heads into the short-term parking garage. He insists on carrying my bag for me and walking me all the way inside. I only have a carry-on and checked in online, so I can head right to security, but we both linger near the line's entrance.

"Thank you for coming," he says softly. "I had a really great time having you there with all of my people. I'm glad they got to meet you, even if it meant I had to share you for a few hours." I didn't think it was possible, but I swear his cheeks darken. This broody man is actually blushing. *Because of me.*

I'm not sure how he feels about airport PDA, but I can't possibly stop myself after seeing that. I cup his jaw with my hand, tilting his face up for a kiss. I mean for it to be a tame kiss good-bye, but it's like the moment our mouths meet, I lose all control, pushing my tongue into his mouth and pulling him closer.

He responds with equal passion, trying to take control of the kiss. By the time someone coughs loudly near us, and we break apart, we're both panting, and my dick is straining against my zipper.

We both burst out laughing, and eventually I take my bag. "I'll see you soon then?" I ask hopefully, not wanting to say goodbye.

"See you soon," he agrees with a smile.

I really hope it feels soon.

The flight back is good but uneventful, the people around me are all super nice and help to distract me from how sad I am to be leaving Beck. I try to focus on the positives—that he agreed to come for the summer, and I go into my meeting with Viktor excited to make that happen.

It takes some convincing on my part to get him to approve Beck's extended stay. Viktor's a very private person and is always nervous about having people who don't work for Kyla come to the headquarters. I think he's worried about someone stealing his ideas or poaching his employees or something.

But Beck wouldn't do that.

I think it helps that Viktor met Beck in Florida, so he already knows him and the interest he's taken in Kyla's programs. He knows Beck isn't trying to compete with him or anything. Viktor loves it when influential people show interest in Kyla and typically jumps at the chance to use photos of them taking the courses or even just hanging out with him for promotional purposes, so I'm surprised he hesitates to grant the approval.

He asks me some questions about Beck's intentions, including whether I thought Beck was trying to convince me to leave Kyla to work for him. I explain that Beck and I don't talk about the details of our jobs, and that I don't think he'd want me to work for him, and Viktor seems relieved. He also asks how I think Beck might react to the town, the people, and our routines here. I assure him that Beck would love it—because who wouldn't? *They seem like silly questions to me.*

Eventually, Viktor agrees that Beck's influence could benefit the company and approves him as a temporary visitor.

The following day, I'm back in the coffee shop waiting for Nick, excited to update him on how my trip went. He slides into the booth across from me with a giant grin on his face. "Well, how's your man?"

"Ha ha, sadly he's still not *my* anything," I admit. "He's never wanted a relationship before."

"But you want a relationship with him, right?" Nick clarifies, and I bury my face in my hands.

"Obviously," I say while my face remains hidden.

"Fuck, how would that even work?" he asks, voicing my fears. "It's not like you could leave Montana, and he sounds pretty established in Chicago from what you've told me with his job and family."

"I have no idea." I sigh, feeling absolutely defeated, and sit up to take a sip of my coffee. "It was incredible seeing him again, though. I got to meet his whole family and all of his friends at the hockey game we went to. Everyone welcomed me like they'd known me for years. They were all so kind—wanting to get to know me, saying they were so happy that Beck met me. I've never felt such a sense of family and belonging outside of joining Kyla," I admit.

Nick nods along like he knows what I'm talking about. "That sounds really cool, Cody. I hope you guys can work something out, and you can see them again."

"Thanks. Hey, after meeting his family, I was thinking that you've never really talked about yours. Do you get to see them much?" I ask, shocked that I don't know more about my best friend.

His shoulders sag and he gives me a small smile before shrugging. "You know how it goes. We were never that close, and they didn't like how much money the Kyla stuff costs. They couldn't understand the investment," he explains. "They were really against me moving here, said that I was throwing away my degree, coming to work for the company that 'I was giving all of my money to'. I haven't talked to them much since coming here." He sounds sad talking about them, and I'm even more surprised that it hasn't come up before. "But if they can't support what makes me happy, then why should I even want to talk to them?" He adds that last part sounding determined, like it's what he wants to believe, even if he is still bummed about it.

"I'm sorry, Nick, you don't deserve that."

"It is what it is. I've heard a lot of similar situations around here," he says casually, but I had no idea. "It sucks that some people can't understand what makes their kids happy if it doesn't align with what they had planned for them."

I'm so grateful that my parents have always supported me. I might have wished to be more present in their lives, but I know so many people have it a lot worse.

Nick shifts the conversation to something lighter, and I realize how common that is around here—people avoiding heavy topics like we're afraid to admit when we're unhappy. Kyla's programs emphasize finding happiness, but that doesn't mean we should ignore other emotions.

People have always commented on how positive I am and how happy I always seem. That's just who I am naturally, and I guess I assumed Kyla attracted more people like me who are naturally optimistic.

But if it took me almost thirty years and someone else pointing out to me that I'm attracted to men, what else have I missed?

That thought leaves me unsettled. Are people here genuinely

happy, or are they afraid to express when they're not? Is there an underlying pressure to always appear content? And does Viktor know about it?

I make a mental note to talk to him during our next one-on-one. For now, I try to focus on the fitness classes Nick is planning for the upcoming week instead of worrying about what else I might have missed.

CHAPTER NINETEEN

Beck

GOLDIE

ZERO MORE DAYS!

GOLDIE

Good morning!

GOLDIE

SO EXCITED!

SALEM

Good morning, can't wait to see you. About to board the plane now.

I tuck my phone away as I grab my carry-on bag to board this flight. It's the smallest commercial plane I've ever been on. My family might be able to afford private, but it seems like such a waste of resources if it isn't necessary.

And I kinda hate that my first thought when I saw this tiny plane was that I should have just taken the jet.

Might make me an entitled asshole, but I wish I had.

The flight lasts a little over three and a half hours, and I try to get ahead on some work, but the business class seats that were the best option for this tiny aircraft are just slightly bigger seats at the front. The person next to me is chewing loudly, and I'm too distracted thinking about seeing Cody to get anything done anyway.

It's been a really long, annoying, frustrating month since I last saw him. We've talked every day; constantly texting, talking on the phone, or video calling whenever we could. Cody and I have shared countless orgasms over video calls, and have even sent dirty pictures and videos, teasing the other person when they're busy, but talking over the phone could never compare to actually being with him in person. I want to fall asleep with him in my arms, not on a video call propped up on the pillow next to me.

The Werewolves had a great run, but we were eliminated in game six of the semifinals. I was devastated we made it so close to the Cup, and just like that, the season was over. The players were pissed, the fans were a mix of angry and heartbroken, and the office felt like a funeral.

Obviously, I was also very, very sad.

But there was a tiny part of me—maybe it's Cody's glass-half-full attitude rubbing off—that felt a flicker of relief. I could finally shift my focus to planning this trip.

Sure, I wasn't able to visit until after the draft, regardless of our loss, but there was still a ton of work I had to wrap up before I went on this trip. If we'd won, it would have significantly delayed my departure, not only with more games but with the press, parades, merch, and all the chaos that comes with winning.

I've decided next year is the year the Werewolves will take it all, and for now, I can focus on what the fuck to do about Cody.

Not that I've been able to think of anything yet. I've been

doing some research into Kyla, but other than their marketing campaigns for their programs and their required public tax filings and business statements, there isn't much about them online.

I even asked Jordan if he'd heard anything unofficial about them, and he said he vaguely remembered someone from Kyla giving a seminar at his company, but nothing beyond that.

I was hoping to find an easy solution, maybe a way that Cody could relocate to Chicago, but it isn't that simple. Their only offices are located in Montana, and I know how much Cody loves working for Kyla. I could never ask him to quit. *And what the fuck would I do in Montana?* Working for the Werewolves has been my dream for as long as I can remember. My friends are in Chicago, and my family. I can't imagine living anywhere else.

I've finally admitted to myself that I want a future with him. I know that I should have accepted it sooner, given how much I think about him and how amazing he makes me feel when we're talking or spending time together. Even just thinking about him makes me happy.

My relief at losing our shot at the cup this year made one thing very clear.

I love him.

I don't know why I kept trying to convince myself that it was just a fling that would fizzle out when we got bored with each other.

There's no moving on from Cody. He's it for me.

I want the wedding, the dogs, and the whole damn happily ever after—whatever he wants, I want it too. But I also want us to be happy. It might make me a selfish asshole that I'm not willing to pack up and join him in Montana permanently, but I want both of us to have fulfilling lives as individuals so we can make each other stronger by being together. I want to find a way for that future to exist, where one of us doesn't have to sacrifice everything to make the other happy. Even I know that can only lead to resentment and problems.

I can't settle for anything less than the kind of future Cody deserves. I'll do whatever it takes to make that happen, but leaving Chicago and everything I love there doesn't feel like the right decision.

Every morning since I finalized a date, I've woken up to a countdown text, followed by a "good morning" from Cody. Each message feels like it's piecing my bitter, untrusting heart back together. I know in my bones that Cody doesn't give a fuck about my family's money or influence and is excited to spend time with me *for me.*

I'm still not sure what makes me so special, but I'm trying to ignore those doubts and embrace how lucky I am to have met him. I never thought I could meet someone I'm able to trust so completely.

His boss, on the other hand, seems to really care about my family's name. Viktor's been sending me emails asking about what my specific interests are in Kyla, if anyone else in my family wants to join a program, and even if I'll pose for some pictures with him that he can use in their marketing. Despite that sounding like literal torture, I agreed because I don't want to disappoint Cody or create any issues with his boss when I'm hoping to spend more time with him in Linna.

Finally, we land and I've never been happier to deplane. I was surprised to find out there's a small international airport close to Linna with flights directly from Chicago and other major cities. Cody explained that it was one of the reasons Viktor chose Linna for their headquarters, which makes sense.

I rush to get my checked bag, which is already there because this place is so tiny, and when I pass the security checkpoint, my giant smile might rival Cody's. I spot him waiting for me with a pick-up sign that just has a poorly drawn cartoon cat on it in black marker, and I can't help but laugh.

The second he sees me, he drops the sign and breaks out into a full-blown sprint. I barely have time to drop my bags in anticipation before he launches himself at me.

He wraps his legs around my waist like he isn't a giant who probably has fifty-plus pounds on me. My lifting time in the gym has clearly paid off, though, because I'm able to catch and hold him as he squeezes me with his entire body.

He cradles my face in his hands and leans in for a surprisingly sweet kiss. I wasn't sure how he'd react to seeing me again, but this is way better than anything I'd pictured.

Clearly, Cody isn't worried about PDA. I wasn't sure how accepting Montana would be of same-sex relationships, but when we finally pull apart, and Cody hops down to take my hand with one of his and my bag with his other, the only looks I notice are smirks at our over-the-top display.

"Hi," he finally says, and I chuckle.

"That's the only way I want to be greeted from now on," I tease, and he blushes. I fucking love making him blush. I follow it up with a wink, watching his cheeks darken further.

"Sorry if that was a little obnoxious. I'm just so excited to see you," he explains, sounding shy.

I don't want him to ever feel like he needs to hold back around me. "Cody, I love how excited you get about things. There's never a need to apologize to me about something making you happy," I reassure him and lean in for a quick kiss on his cheek.

"Okay," he agrees with a huge grin.

"So, what's the plan for today?" I ask as we finally head outside.

"We'll stop by my house first to drop off your stuff, and then Viktor wants to show you around headquarters. We'll probably be there for most of the day." He sounds excited, so I attempt to squash down my disappointment that his answer wasn't *hang out at my house naked.* "Then we'll do dinner at the Old Mill," he continues. I'm assuming that's a restaurant, so I nod, giving him a smile. I like that he wants me to like his city as much as he does.

During the drive through town, he catches me up on his morning and points out different things about the area as we pass.

Linna is a small city of just over ten thousand people, nestled beneath a stunning mountain. Cody explains how the town was first established during the construction of the Northern Pacific Railroad in the 1800s. Over time, factories employed most of the locals, but as younger generations moved away and technology reduced the need for workers, the population began to dwindle. With the factories gone and the airport at risk of closing, the town was full of empty, abandoned homes.

"Viktor had a dream one night about building a state-of-the-art campus for the company headquarters beneath a beautiful mountain right next to an airport so that everyone had easy access," Cody says with a sense of wonder. "He wants everyone here to always have a reason to look up and remember to keep striving for their next peak."

Does Cody actually believe this guy had some divine vision? More likely, it was a strategic land grab—cheap property with convenient access. Viktor clearly has a flair for dramatics, and Cody is so trusting and positive that he probably buys into the whole story.

"When they started building the campus, it created a lot of local job opportunities for the people who were still in the area. Viktor offered them free Kyla programs so they'd know more about the company that was moving in. Most of them still participate in courses today."

Awesome, a whole city full of people drinking the Kool-Aid. I shake off that disturbing thought. I'm sure it's not like that.

Obviously, Cody is into it too, so they're not all bad. But the emails I've been exchanging with Viktor, combined with the weird vibes I got during the classes Cody didn't teach in Florida, have me wary of this place.

Cody being genuinely happy all of the time is adorable and refreshing, but a place where *everyone* is like that seems unrealistic.

As we drive, he points out the high school, grocery store, police department, post office, and fire station, naming all his friends who work there. It's like he knows everyone. Growing up in Chicago, I can't imagine knowing anyone everywhere I go, but I guess that's normal in small towns.

We pass a neighborhood of very cookie-cutter McMansions with a sign advertising available lots. I'm surprised to see so many new homes, honestly. I wonder how many people have moved here just for Kyla.

We drive through the quaint downtown that looks straight out of a made-for-TV movie. Old buildings with small stores and businesses line both sides of the main street, with people walking around enjoying the weather. Every single one waves as we pass, and Cody continues naming people and pointing out his favorite places.

Then we pull onto a side street not far from downtown, and it's full of older-looking homes. They're all well-maintained with a lot of character and charm. I'd definitely rather live in one of these than the new builds.

Cody pulls into the driveway of a beautiful white Victorian farmhouse with a wraparound porch, complete with a swing. It's the quintessential American dream home and fits him perfectly.

"I'm surprised you don't have a dog. This yard would be great for one," I say, looking around the spacious grass enclosed by a white picket fence.

"I'd love a dog," he says, a little sadly. "But I travel so much, it wouldn't be fair to them."

I want to tell him I'll get a dog for him. I'll let it live with me, and he can see it whenever we're together. I want to tell him I'll do anything not to hear that sadness in his voice again. But I know I'm getting ahead of myself.

"Hopefully, one day," I say instead, making him smile.

The inside of his home is beautiful. Hardwood floors stretch throughout the space, and everything looks like it's been recently updated with a brand new kitchen. It's so clean, it looks like a model home ready to be shown.

"Wow, Cody, are you always this clean, or are you trying to impress me?" I tease. I have people who clean for me, but if I had this giant house to myself, there's no way it would look like this.

He looks around, almost like he's taking in the space for the first time. "Oh, I guess it's always like this. I don't spend a lot of time here, and I have someone come in and clean it when I'm traveling," he says offhandedly as we head up the stairs.

"Have you lived here long?" There's a surprising lack of personal touches. I'd assume my happy guy would've filled his home with memories of his friends and family, but other than some Kyla awards, it really does look like a staged home.

"Yeah, I've been here since I moved to Linna five years ago. I'm so excited to have you at my house! I've been thinking about it nonstop," he admits a bit bashfully as he opens the door to what I'm assuming is his room.

I drop my bags and walk up to him, wrapping my hands around his waist. "Me too," I say, tilting my head up for a kiss. It's another sweet kiss, both of us enjoying the moment for what it is, knowing we don't have time for anything else.

All too soon, we pull away and share a small smile. I can't believe how lucky I am to have such a perfect man looking at me like this, like I'm everything he wants.

I want to deserve that look.

"Alright, if you need to change, I'll give you a minute. Then we can head into the office. Do you need to eat or anything?" he asks.

"No, I ate on the plane, thanks," I answer and pull out a suit. If Viktor's there, I'm sure I'll be photographed.

Can't wait.

CHAPTER TWENTY

Cody

Driving toward the Kyla campus, my leg is bouncing up and down with a mixture of nerves and excitement. Beck is finally here, and even though we talked every day, I've missed spending time with him even more than I realized.

I'm not totally sure why I'm so nervous, though. It's not about being with him in person—I couldn't stop myself from running into his arms when I saw him. Our physical connection is definitely just as hot as I remembered. I'm honestly regretting that we have so many plans for the day, but Viktor asked me to bring Beck in, and it sounded like a great idea at the time. Now, I wish we'd just stayed home.

Maybe I'm nervous he won't like Linna as much as I do or that he'll pick up on some of the less-than-ideal things that I've been starting to notice. Thinking about him coming to visit and how things might seem from an outside perspective has me noticing for the first time just how unique our community is. I'm worried that he won't want to stay for the entire month that we have planned. Or that he won't want to visit again.

"Here we are, my home away from home," I announce as we pull onto the campus.

Towering trees line both sides of the drive as we enter a giant roundabout. There's a large open green space in the center with paths and outdoor tables for people to spend time outside. On our right, we drive past the massive three-story fitness center. Then there's a strip mall with the coffee shop, a small grocery store, and some doctors' offices before we pass the emergency medical center.

Finally, we reach the main Kyla offices. It's the tallest building in Linna, made mostly of glass with huge windows that allow natural light to flood the entire space. Inside, it has offices, event spaces, a quick-service cafeteria, boardrooms, production studios for the Kyla videos—anything a company might need.

I point everything out to Beck, filling him in on details about some of my friends who work in the different spaces, just like I did on our drive this morning. "If we were to keep going, we'd be at the Old Mill, where we'll eat dinner. Then there's Village Bank and the childcare center. Viktor wanted to create a campus that rivals the big tech guys and other major companies who've revamped their headquarters to improve the work lives of the employees," I explain.

"Sounds like you'd never have to leave," Beck comments in a tone I can't read. He probably wasn't expecting this since I don't actually talk about the details of my job with him much.

We've spent so much of the last month getting to know each other more, and I've loved every moment. Even though we haven't officially labeled anything, I know that this is the best relationship I've ever been in.

I think he's finally over his concerns about me being so newly aware of my sexuality. The only reason I think we haven't had the relationship conversation is that neither of us can find a solution to the distance.

I'm not sure what Beck's thoughts are on the situation

because I'm too afraid to ask, but I know the long distance part has sucked. I also know that I'm not ready to give him up.

The more I've gotten to know Beck, the more sure I am that our connection goes far beyond physical attraction.

I love how unapologetically himself he is. On the surface, he might seem like a grumpy loner, but once you get to know him, you see the truth—he's an incredibly loving, fiercely loyal man who'd do anything for the people he cares about. I think he's just afraid of trusting the wrong people.

I love how funny he is. His dry sense of humor and sarcasm, always delivered with the most serious expression, has me doubled over in laughter almost daily.

I love how thoughtful he is, whether it's the little gestures when we're together or how he remembers the smallest details from our texts and calls. He always follows up on things I've mentioned or asks me to expand when he can tell I'm excited about something.

I realized it this morning—I love *him*.

I should have clued in sooner, but considering my track record for being oblivious, I think this was a pretty quick turn-around for me. When I saw him in the airport, something clicked. As I ran toward him, it hit me—I realized that my feelings for Beck are love.

I've never been in love before, but this has to be it. No one has ever made me this happy by just existing.

And yet, I have no idea what to do with that information. It feels ridiculous to tell him when I have no solutions for us.

A part of me hoped that maybe Beck would come to visit Linna and fall in love with it like I did all those years ago. But the more I've tried to picture Beck here, the less realistic that outcome seems.

I can't imagine Beck checking in every day with his fitness group chat or sending pictures of the meals he cooks like I do. And I know he wouldn't work for Kyla. He already has such a great job that makes him happy. There's no way anything in Linna would be a better fit for him.

I also don't think Viktor would appreciate his humor as much as I do. No matter how I spin it, I don't think his life would be better here than in Chicago.

And even though I've started to see the cracks in my life here, leaving Linna wouldn't be easy for me. I'm not even sure it's an option.

I push those thoughts aside and try to focus on the present as Beck and I pull into the underground parking garage below the tower.

We take the elevator to the lobby, where Viktor asked to meet to give us the tour. This whole situation is unprecedented, usually, you need to be personally invited by Viktor to visit Kyla headquarters. The last visitor I can remember was a European royal who'd participated in some of my California programs three years ago.

Luckily, Viktor's my friend and he respects my opinion, so asking to bring Beck here was possible.

Viktor likes to give the tours himself so visitors or new members of the community can hear his vision directly from the source. When we exit the elevator, he's standing near the mountain sculpture in the center of the large atrium, and he greets us with his warm smile.

"Beckett Caldwell, welcome to Kyla headquarters," Viktor says, pulling Beck in for a hug.

"Thanks," Beck mutters, looking uncomfortable with the embrace. Over Viktor's shoulder, he's giving me a wide-eyed *what is happening* expression that makes me silently chuckle.

"Well, we're all so pleased to have you staying with us," Viktor tells him.

"Yeah, I'm really excited to stay with Cody," Beck says, emphasizing my name for some reason.

"Before we begin the tour, I was hoping to get a few shots

here in front of our sculpture with the company name on it," Viktor gestures toward the mountain. Beck gives a slight nod before following in the direction of a photographer I hadn't noticed who'd been standing with Viktor.

They take a few photos: Beck and Viktor shaking hands, then a side hug, and another with Viktor's arm around Beck's shoulders, which looks a little awkward since Beck is taller than him. Finally, they do one with their hands in front of their chests in the mountain pose used in the Kyla programming. Viktor instructs Beck to straighten his fingers and interlock them to form a triangle—a symbolic "mountain," with the fingers above the triangle representing the potential peaks yet to be reached in life.

When they finish, Viktor thanks the photographer and asks him to follow our tour to take some candid shots. Beck looks less than thrilled about the idea, but doesn't say anything against it.

We spend the next hour or so exploring the tower, and then Viktor excuses us for a lunch meeting. He promises that he'll find us in about thirty minutes to continue the tour of the campus.

Beck and I head to the quick-service cafeteria on the top level with fantastic panoramic views of the city. I love that this view is a public space so everyone can enjoy it.

We make our way through the line, and both end up with grilled lemon chicken and asparagus—one of my favorite options here. After grabbing bottles of water, we head for a private table near a window facing the mountain in the distance.

"Are all of the options always so..." Beck trails off before finishing his question, "healthy?"

I laugh at the twisted expression he's aiming at his plate.

"Yeah, there's a huge emphasis on having a healthy mind and body here," I explain. "Everyone works with a dietitian to establish a personalized health plan and a personal trainer to maintain a fitness regimen."

He gives me a skeptical look before finally nodding. "I guess free health coaching is a cool perk of working here. I'm surprised everyone wants that, though. I can't imagine my employees' reactions if I got rid of the unhealthy options in our cafeteria." He snorts a laugh at the thought.

"Oh, it's not free," I clarify before digging in.

Beck gives me another quizzical expression. "So, it's optional, right?"

"Well, no. Everyone here is enrolled in the health and wellness program and assigned an accountability group," I explain. "But it's not just for employees. Everyone in Linna who participates in Kyla's programs is enrolled. The cost goes toward paying the nutritionists and the trainers and running the gym and stuff."

"Wait, your gym membership isn't free?" He sounds shocked now.

"No?" I answer like it's a question. "If it were, how would they afford to cover operating costs or pay the employees?"

"My company covers the cost of a gym membership of the employees' choice as a part of our benefits. They can even choose to put that money toward home gym equipment or streaming memberships that offer workouts," he says casually, like that's not the coolest thing ever.

"Wait, really? That's amazing."

"Yeah, it's better for health insurance purposes too," he adds.

"I don't mind paying for ours," I clarify. "I love the people I get to work with. You know Nick, he's my best friend here, but he's also my trainer. I know the cost ends up supporting him."

Beck gives me an indulgent smile and nods before he finally starts eating.

"So when do I get to meet Nick?"

"Tomorrow!" I blurt out a little too loudly. "He's leading a hike in the morning that I already signed us up for. I hope that was okay. I was just so excited about you meeting him that I didn't think to ask first." I give him a hopeful look, and he smiles, nodding.

"I'll do whatever you want, Goldie."

The nickname makes my cheeks heat as I smile, and I can't stop myself from rambling on about all the people I'm excited for him to meet and all the fun things he'll get to experience. The thirty minutes fly by, and we barely finish our meals in time with how much we're talking.

We meet Viktor back in the lobby, and he continues his tour of the campus, explaining the purpose of each building and how it supports the community.

Beck seems interested in everything and asks polite questions throughout the tour. Viktor and Beck speak in a lot of business terms that kind of go over my head, but I love that they're connecting. As the tour went on, Beck relaxed, asking me more casual questions and even making plans to visit some of the spaces again.

By the time we wrap up the tour, it's somehow already almost seven. "See you at dinner." I wave to Viktor before he heads back into his office. He waves, and I grab Beck's hand to lead him toward the Old Mill.

"Do we finally get to eat?" he asks hopefully.

I laugh before answering. "Yes, I promise I won't let you starve."

"I don't know. I think I'm pretty close to my hunger limit, I can't be held responsible for my actions if I get much hangrier," he warns solemnly.

"Well, we'd better hurry then," I say, walking faster as I grin at him.

I love having him here.

CHAPTER TWENTY-ONE

Beck

I'm so fucking hungry by the time we get to the restaurant.

Only when we arrive, it becomes abundantly clear that the "Old Mill" is not a cutesy name for a normal restaurant. Instead, it's a gigantic open-concept building that looks like it can fit at least a thousand people, all seated at long picnic-style tables beneath a large stage. Along one wall, there are windows into what must be the kitchen, with lines of people forming before each one, presumably to pick up food.

This is… not what I was expecting.

The building doesn't even look old. Despite the spinning mill wheel outside in the river, it's clearly as new as the rest of the campus. There's no way this was ever a functioning mill. *This is really weird.*

But, like I said, starving. So I shove the judgment down and follow Cody into one of the lines. As we wait, I try to keep my tone neutral while asking him about what the fuck this place is.

"So, this is unique?" I say, like it's a question.

"Yeah, isn't it cool?" Cody says, excited as ever. "Everyone eats here at least once a week, but because I'm in upper management, Viktor likes me to eat here more often," he says like it's a special perk. "He likes to encourage community bonding and allow opportunities for everyone to interact outside of work. He also likes it when management is here to show how we're just regular people, too. He thinks it helps us remain approachable.

"The stage is where Viktor, senior management, or people with positions in the community make announcements," he points out. "Viktor also likes to close out the night with a guided meditation, and throughout dinner, he makes his rounds around the room so that even people who don't work directly with him can still spend time with him."

"So, everyone is required to eat here?" I clarify, still trying to wrap my head around its logistics. *How can they possibly require that? What would happen if they didn't?*

"Yeah, just once a week unless Viktor asks you to come more. There's a schedule since not everyone can fit at the same time." He explains matter-of-factly.

I can't imagine enforcing anything like that at my company.

When we finally reach the front of the line, we're handed plates of chicken casserole packed with lots of veggies. The portion is way smaller than I'd like, but at this point I'll take whatever I can get.

We snag a spot next to each other near the stage, sitting shoulder-to-shoulder at one of the long tables.

"Viktor noted that in most societies today, people spend most of their time outside of work isolated. They go home and only interact with the people they live with. Or, if they go out, it's usually with the same people," he tells me.

He says it as if spending time with your family is a bad thing. I know Cody doesn't actually believe that because he's always asking about my family and telling me how amazing he thinks it is that we spend so much time together. *I think he's just repeating what Viktor told them.*

"These habits perpetuate feelings of isolation and depression. They prevent any sense of community and the support that comes with it," he goes on. "Then, the isolated people are more susceptible to harmful consumerism habits—shopping on their phone, only caring about social media views. Viktor says these behaviors prevent people from thinking for themselves and hold them back from reaching their full potential. So, his solution was the Old Mill to increase community interactions over dinner."

I make a noncommittal *hmm* sound in reaction, digging into my dinner, hoping that Cody can't tell how fucked up I think this all is by the look on my face.

He introduces me to everyone around us, adding, "I wish it were Nick's night to be here, but I'm glad we're doing the hike tomorrow." I do want to meet his best friend, so I nod in agreement.

The rest of the meal is full of polite small talk as I answer questions from everyone around us. I can't help but feel a little bummed when Cody introduces me as "his friend." We clearly need to have a conversation about labels sooner rather than later.

They don't all work for Kyla, the woman across from us is a police officer, and her husband works for the post office. One of the men owns a store in the downtown area, and says his family has been in Linna for generations.

Everyone seems so fucking happy, and not in the adorable way that Cody is where you believe he actually cares and is excited. With these people, it's like any answer I give is met with a "That's so amazing" response that sounds scripted and forced. I'm tempted to fuck with them and say something really awful, just to see how they'll spin it to find a positive way to respond, but I don't want Cody to be worried about whatever I'd come up with.

As pleasant as it all is, I can't help but feel a little cheated out of my time with Cody. I wish we were alone instead of surrounded by people. I try to focus on the fact that I'm staying with him and we'll have plenty of time together, but without a solution to our distance, our time feels so limited.

I can see Viktor walking around the space, being his usual overly touchy self. He does the weird mountain handhold thing with everyone he greets, kissing some of the people right on the mouth and standing way too close.

What's even weirder is how much everyone seems thrilled by his attention. I know that everyone around here is obsessed with the guy, but I still don't understand why.

I notice other people throughout the large space interacting in similar, overly familiar ways. At first, I'd have assumed they're couples since they're all touching so freely, but then I realized they act like that with everyone.

"What's with all the touching and kissing?" I murmur to Cody, keeping my voice low, hoping the people around us won't hear me. I lift my chin toward a group of people at the next table who are all kissing the person who just walked up like it's a completely normal thing to do.

"Oh, a lot of people here greet each other like that," he laughs. "It's all about reinforcing community bonds and the endorphins that come from casual physical touch."

"Random people won't come up and kiss me, will they?" I ask with obvious terror in my tone.

Cody laughs. "No, don't worry, no one should greet you like that if they don't know you. It's all very consensual. They all already know each other and have established that as a greeting they're comfortable with. If someone wanted to, they'd ask you first, and you can tell them that isn't something you're comfortable with. They won't be offended, it's never been something I've done. It's not like required or anything."

"Oh, thank god. You're the only person I want to kiss," I say, letting out a big exhale before laughing, and he flashes me a dazzling smile.

I finish my food too quickly. The size of the portion was way smaller than I'm used to. I really hope Cody has some snacks at his place, even if they're the healthy crap he likes.

It feels like an eternity waiting for everyone to finish their meals, though I suppose serving a thousand people takes a while. Then, Viktor gets up on the stage, and the room immediately falls into a hushed silence without him having to say anything.

To my absolute horror, he makes eye contact with me before speaking.

"Good evening, everyone. I hope that you've all had a successful day full of happiness. We have a very special guest staying with us here in Linna for a few weeks. I would like everyone to give a very warm welcome to Beckett Caldwell," he announces into a microphone, opening his arm out toward me, and people start to clap.

"Beckett is a member of the prestigious Caldwell family in Chicago. You may know them as the owners of the Chicago Werewolves ice hockey team, the Caldwell Hotel chain, or from one of their many other companies that are part of the Caldwell Corporation," he brags.

I hate when people lead with all of my family's info, like that's the only reason I have any value.

"Beckett began his Kyla journey a few months ago, and some of you might also recognize him from the retreat we had in Florida," he adds, and I see a few nods of recognition near the front of the room. "He'll be staying with Cody Richardson, so make sure that you embrace him as a new member of our village and help him to see how amazing our little city of Linna is!"

He finally finishes my introduction, and I'm very glad to have the attention off of me when he transitions to other community announcements.

I tune him out almost immediately. It's nearly 10 p.m., and I'm way more interested in how adorable Cody is. Here in his element, he's so excited about everything, and watching his reactions to Viktor is way more entertaining than anything Viktor could possibly be saying. I know that we need to have a serious conversation about the feelings I have for him. Ideally, before we take things further physically, but all day, I've had to stop my mind from picturing all the things I want to do with him while I'm here.

My cock probably has a zipper-shaped indent on it from being half-hard for so long.

Cody gives me a playful nudge with his elbow and nods toward the stage to focus my attention. Apparently, Viktor has moved on to the guided meditation portion of the evening. Not wanting to disappoint Cody, I mimic the others, clasping my hands together in the "mountain" prayer pose everyone else is already in.

Of course, my thoughts immediately drift back to Cody. We've had a lot of fun during our naked video calls and in the dirty texting conversations when one of us couldn't call over the last month. Cody has remained vocal about wanting to bottom for me, and whenever I tell him to play with his rim, he finishes quickly. I don't think he's actually lasted long enough to explore his prostate, and I'm very eager to introduce him.

The sound of shuffling fills the room, pulling me out of my thoughts. I open my eyes to see Cody standing, smiling down at me.

"Really into that meditation?" he teases, raising a brow.

"You know me, very dedicated," I agree with a serious expression that makes him laugh.

"Let's go home," he says, pulling me up.

I know he means his house, but the idea of our home being the same place makes me smile.

CHAPTER TWENTY-TWO

Cody

Tonight is the night. I *need* Beck to fuck me.

I feel like he's been edging me all day with his heated glances and casual touches. It's super awkward to be hard at work, especially in front of your boss, and I've been struggling all day.

Having him here and seeing him in my favorite places has only made everything better. But if I don't get to see Beck naked soon, I think I might cry.

The short drive back to my place feels like it lasts forever. I ignore a few speed limits, and the second I throw the car into park, I'm out the door, practically sprinting to unlock the house.

I can hear Beck laughing as he climbs the steps up to the porch behind me, and a whine slips out of my mouth when he wraps a hand around my throat from behind. He pulls me down slightly, pressing his hard body against my back as he brings his mouth to my ear.

"What's the rush, baby?" he whispers, and it feels like all of my blood rushes south. I'm already panting, and I subconsciously grind back into him while I finally get the key in the right spot to open the door.

Words are tough right now, so I spin to face Beck and pull him inside by his shirt, kicking the door shut behind him.

"We seem to have a habit of barely making it inside before one of us pounces on the other," he says in a flirty tone before I use my hold on him to push him back into the door, devouring his mouth with my own. I kiss him desperately with all of the longing and desire I haven't been able to properly channel since I last saw him in person.

My hands roam over the muscles of his broad chest before I slide them under his shirt to trace his abs. He shrugs off his jacket, and I race to unbutton his shirt as he works on mine, neither of us breaking the kiss.

When our shirts hit the floor, I run my hands over the muscles of his arms and back, wanting to know every inch of him. My lips move to kiss up his jaw, behind his ear, and down his neck, committing his taste to my memory.

"I can't wait to fuck you, baby," he murmurs with a deep, commanding tone. I love when he gets bossy. That tone of his voice alone would make me hard, and his confirmation that *tonight is finally the night* has me harder than ever.

"Please do," I manage to get out between kisses.

He grinds his bulge against mine, and I moan.

"Are you going to be a good boy for me?" he teases in that same tone. "Beg to have my cock inside of your tight, virgin hole?"

He grabs my ass with both hands, squeezing and grinding me against him again. I nod desperately. *I've wanted him inside me for so long.*

"Have you used any toys or anything here?" he asks, dipping his hand beneath my pants and underwear before sliding his fingers closer to my hole.

"No, only my finger and never very deep. I wanted it to be

you the first time," I admit, feeling my cheeks heat. He cups my face with the hand that isn't down my pants and runs his thumb over the blush, staring at it.

"You're the most beautiful thing I've ever seen," he whispers reverently.

The change in his tone throws me for a moment, and I almost miss what he said. My cheeks grow even hotter at his compliment, and I don't know how to react, so I move my lips back to his, sucking his bottom lip between my own before licking into his mouth.

He pulls back slightly and cups my face in his hands as he looks into my eyes, his gaze filled with emotion.

"There's a lot that I need to say to you about how much I like you. How I wish we could spend every day together. Where I want our relationship to go," he says, making my breath hitch. My chest feels like it could explode with how happy his admission makes me.

He looks almost desperate as he continues, "I don't think I can hold back much longer, and I want your first time to be perfect, so can we promise to talk after sex and move this into your shower so that I can enjoy you properly?"

"Okay," is all I manage to get out. My heart is racing as he grabs my hand to lead me up to my bathroom.

He turns the water on, quickly stripping us out of the rest of our clothes before leading me under the warm spray.

"Can I wash you?" he asks, and I nod. I swear my brain has stopped working properly since he admitted that he wants to spend every day with me and said we're in a relationship. I've wanted to hear that word from him for so long, but my rock-hard cock is too focused on his callused hands rubbing soap all over my body for me to properly form words right now.

Orgasm first, relationship talk later.

Once all the soap has been rinsed from our bodies, Beck quickly towels off before grabbing another to help me.

"Sit on the edge of the bed," he directs, and I immediately comply. He grabs some lube from my nightstand and a pillow, coming to stand between my legs.

"Are we still okay to not use condoms?" Beck checks, and I nod.

He kisses me deeply, tackling me back onto the bed. When he pulls back, he props the pillow under my lower back so I can angle my hips, holding my bent legs up. The position leaves me feeling very exposed, but I relax when Beck rubs his hands up my thighs, looking at my ass like it's the greatest thing he's ever seen.

"Can I taste you?" he whispers like he's afraid I'll say no.

"Yes, please," I exhale, my body trembling in anticipation.

I've been slightly obsessed with rimming porn during my month away from Beck, and I feel like I've been fantasizing about this moment for forever.

Finally, Beck places his hands on the globes of my ass, leans in, and licks a strip right over my rim. My dick twitches, leaking as I let out a deep moan. I feel like a million nerve endings in my body light up at once, and I never want him to stop.

"Please, do that again," I pant out, and he flashes a huge smile at me before repeating the motion.

Only this time, he stays there, eating me out like he's a starving man, and I'm his favorite meal. He spears his tongue inside of me, and I swear I could come from that feeling alone.

Just as I'm about to lose control, Beck pulls back. I whimper at the loss of sensation as he leans over me, holding two fingers toward my mouth.

"Suck," he growls, his voice sending a jolt of heat through me.

I do, licking and sucking his fingers like I want to do with his cock. When he's satisfied they must be wet enough, he kneels back down and resumes feasting before pushing a finger in with his tongue past the tight ring of muscle.

It doesn't hurt, and I love the new sensation of the added pressure.

I realize I'm rocking my hips back onto his finger, and it must be all the way in. Beck pulls back enough to repeat the process with a second finger, and it burns slightly as my body stretches, but it still feels good. After I'm able to relax again, he starts to fuck the digits into me, still using his tongue to drive me wild as he carefully stretches his fingers apart, preparing me even more.

Then he curls his fingers, and I cry out, pleasure jolting throughout my entire body at whatever he just did. My cock jumps, and I almost come, my hand flying to squeeze my base, trying to prevent the release.

"That's your prostate," Beck teases with a smug smile.

"Whatever it is, you need to not do that again unless you want me to finish before you're even inside of me," I warn, sounding completely out of breath.

Beck chuckles to himself as he continues to move his fingers in and out of me with maddeningly shallow thrusts. Then he pulls out and adds lube onto three fingers before slowly and gently pushing all three in.

The new sensation feels… strange. It's not painful exactly, he's being so slow, but the pressure is kind of overwhelming. My cock starts to calm down slightly before Beck distracts me by swallowing it down his throat.

I'm completely overwhelmed by the dual sensations and am quickly back to being hard as a rock. He teases me, licking and kissing my dick without taking me fully into his mouth again, no doubt trying to manage my pleasure without pushing me over the edge. He continues to stretch me with his three fingers, and after a little while, the sensation in my ass is no longer unpleasant. I fucking love it.

"More, Beck, please, I need you," I whine, rocking back onto his hand. "Please fuck me."

He immediately abandons my cock, pulling his fingers out and leaving me feeling empty as my muscles clench around nothing.

"Bear down," he soothes as he uses his hand to grip the base of his erection. He guides the swollen head to my slick, prepped hole and his lubed-up cock pushes against the tight ring of muscles. I try to relax as he pushes in.

"Look at you, baby," he says, his tone full of awe. "You look so fucking hot. All needy and whining, begging for my big cock to fill you up. Fuck, that's so good," he continues as he slowly thrusts into me. "You're so good for me. This is the best hole I've ever had, so fucking tight and warm. You were made to be filled up by me," he's rambling now, and I'm obsessed with the effect this is having on him, how blissed out and desperate he looks.

His praise relaxes me further, and eventually his hips meet mine, so I think he's all the way in. He doesn't move, allowing me to adjust to the new sensation. Beck leans down to kiss me, and I get lost in his intoxicating taste. When he gives a slow experimental thrust, a deep moan escapes from my throat. Each glide of his cock inside of me lights me up in a way I've never experienced.

The pleasure is truly indescribable as he keeps up his slow pace, angling his hips until each thrust brushes against my prostate. This is spectacular, I always want to have Beck inside of me.

"Fuck, don't stop," I beg, finally remembering how to speak. I can't seem to prevent the thoughts from leaving my mouth as I try to match his motion. "This is amazing. Why haven't we done this before?"

He picks up the pace, and I can feel my release building. I'm so close, and nothing is even touching my aching cock.

"I've wanted nothing more than to fuck you, to be the only man who's ever been inside of you," he says. "To fill your perfect ass with my cum and mark you as mine forever."

His words make everything even more intense. "Fuck, I'm gonna—"

"Come for me, baby," he practically growls, before biting down on my collarbone.

Pleasure explodes from the base of my spine, spreading throughout my entire body. My vision goes dark as the most intense orgasm I've ever had wrecks me—without anything even touching my cock.

He lets out a deep moan and I can feel the warmth and added lubrication of his cum as he finishes inside of me. I love knowing his release is still there when he finally pulls out of me.

"Good boy," he murmurs, and my spent cock twitches at his praise.

He stares at my ass for a moment before collecting the cum that's leaking out of me on two fingers and shoving them back inside my hole. My cock twitches again.

"Apparently, I have a breeding kink," he murmurs, and I laugh.

"I think I do, too."

"I've never had sex without a condom before. I had no idea how hot it would be." He smiles up at me, and it feels like my heart is going to burst.

"Me neither."

"Wait here." He places a soft kiss on my lips before getting out of bed and heading into the bathroom. He returns a moment later with a warm washcloth to carefully clean me up. When he's done, he tosses it into the hamper and helps me get into a more comfortable spot on the bed, crawling in with me so that we're both lying on our sides facing each other.

"That was even better than I'd hoped it would be," I admit.

"I meant what I said," he replies with a huge smile. "Best sex I've ever had."

"So why didn't we do that sooner?" I hesitantly ask, afraid of his answer. It's been bothering me since my last visit when we'd talked about not needing condoms but he hadn't even tried to fuck me.

He gives me an apologetic look, taking a moment to think about his answer. Then he takes a deep breath.

"Because I'm an idiot," he begins. "Cody, I don't know how to say this. I never have before, so I'm probably going to completely mess up the delivery." He's rambling, and now I'm worried.

But then he says the words that I didn't dare to dream I'd be hearing from him anytime soon.

"Cody, I love you. I'm *in* love with you. And I think I have been for a long time," he admits, looking shy but determined. "I've never met anyone I've wanted to spend all of my time with —until you. You make everything better with your positive attitude and your dazzling smile. I'd sell my soul to make you laugh."

He grabs my hand, holding it between us as he goes on. "But I want to be there all the time, not *just* when you're happy. I want to be there for you to lean on when you need it. I want to be your boyfriend and your partner, and one day, if you'd want it, I want to be your husband. I want to give you the close family you've always dreamed of. I want you to be at my grandparents' house for family dinners. I want you to be friends with my brothers, Adrian and Jordan. I want to give you dogs to chase around the yard. Or if you want kids, we can have as many as you'd like so they never feel alone like you did growing up."

His face blurs as tears fill my eyes. I never thought someone would care enough to truly see me like this, let alone offer me a future and a family I've longed for.

"I love how much you care about everyone and want to help make them all happier. How you remember little details about people that you haven't seen in years. Anyone lucky enough to talk to you is better off for it. *I* am so much better off having met you, and I can't believe that, for some reason, you want to be with me too. Or, at least, I hope you do," he trails off, and I nod desperately as he continues with a relieved laugh.

"The reason I was so afraid to fuck you in Chicago is because I want to be able to give you the perfect future you deserve. A future where neither of us has to sacrifice everything to be with the other. And it's been driving me insane that I can't find a solution to make it work."

His eyes flicker with emotion as he continues. "I knew that after we were together like this, I wouldn't be able to stop myself from blurting all of this out, but I couldn't wait any longer, and fuck, now you're crying!"

His tone sounds slightly panicked, but I can't stop the tears from flowing.

"I tell you I love you, and now you're crying, but you're also smiling, and I'm so fucking confused," he whispers, squeezing my hand.

I burst out laughing, sitting up to lean against my headboard as I attempt to wipe away my tears. Beck sits up too, both of us still angled in toward the other so our eyes meet when I finally say, "Beck, I love you too."

His entire expression relaxes into one of pure joy before he leans in for a slow, sweet kiss. We take our time before finally pulling apart, and he wraps me in his arms with my head resting on his chest, listening to the steady beating of his heart.

"I was drawn to you from the beginning," I admit. "Looking back, even before I realized how attracted I was to you, I knew I was way more excited to go to dinner with you than I'd been with anyone else I met through the courses or while traveling."

Beck runs his fingers through my long hair as I speak, and I love how calming the sensation is, how connected I feel to him.

"I love your sense of humor. How you can always make me laugh," I continue. "I love how different we are, how we seem to complement each other so perfectly with our different strengths. I love how smart you are and how hard you work, even though you don't need the money. I love that you're unapologetically you. Not some trust fund kid rebelling against his family or attempting to fit into their perfect mold." I trace the tattoos on his arms and chest as I speak, wanting to memorize every detail of his perfect body, to know the story behind each one.

"I love how fiercely you love the people you trust, how you treat your friends just like you do your family. I love how you make me feel seen, like I'm allowed to be myself at all times, even in moments when I'm not happy. And I love that you can work to make me smile again in a way that doesn't make me feel bad or guilty for being sad," I trail off, realizing just how untrue that is about almost everyone else in my life.

"I want it," I whisper. "That future you talked about, I want it all."

"Then I'll make it happen," he promises, kissing the top of my head.

And as much as I want to believe him, we both know it isn't that simple.

CHAPTER TWENTY-THREE

Beck

That stupid fucking alarm tone goes off well before the sun rises, and I cannot fathom why in the world anyone would *choose* to wake up this early. We can still work out and be healthy after the sun rises. I'd seriously much rather still be awake at four a.m. than be starting my day at this hour for fucks sake.

The things I'm willing to do for love.

I already knew I loved him. But hearing Cody say the words back to me last night, and finally getting to be inside him, was incredible.

I've never been happier.

It only cements how much I want to share a bed with him every night and how fiercely I want to keep my promise to him. Hopefully, that will involve some actual sleep, though. Or at least missing out on sleep for more fun reasons than a fucking sunrise hike.

Despite the very minimal rest I know he got, Cody is staring at me with a giant smile on his face when I finally crack one of my eyes open.

"Good morning, I love waking up with you in my bed," he says with a happy sigh.

"I'd love it more if it wasn't four a.m.," I grumble, making him laugh.

He leans in and kisses me on the tip of my nose before rolling out of bed. "Come on, sleepyhead, let's get you some coffee."

I finally open both eyes at the promise of caffeine, practically falling out of bed because my body refuses to cooperate at this ungodly hour. I brush my teeth, then put on all the hiking shit I got specifically for this trip. I'm a fit guy, but there aren't any mountains in Chicago—my home gym works just fine and doesn't require me to wake up this fucking early. I head to Cody's kitchen, following the scent of coffee as I walk down the stairs with my eyes still only half open.

"Here you go, boyfriend," Cody says in a tone so chipper it would annoy me on anyone but him.

I do like the upgraded title, though.

I attempt a smile, though it's more likely just me baring my teeth as I take the coffee and plop onto a chair at his breakfast bar. I close my eyes, focusing solely on consuming enough caffeine to become a functioning human.

"I'm glad to meet Nick," I grumble after chugging most of the cup. "But I don't think I can do another four a.m. wake-up call."

"You probably don't have to since you're not assigned to an accountability group or anything, but I'll have to get up this early almost every day so I don't get fined," Cody says with a laugh.

"Why would you get fined?"

"It's part of the wellness program I was telling you about." He adds powders and vegetables into a blender, making what I assume will be a very healthy smoothie.

"So, you have to pay if you miss a workout? Who are you paying?"

"It gets added to your gym membership fees. It's a great motivator," Cody explains casually as he blends up his health concoction, as if the whole system isn't completely absurd.

"And what about the accountability group? Who are they?"

"It's a group of about fifty people, and we all follow each other on this fitness tracker app. You can see who's completed their workouts and stuff." *That part doesn't sound too bad.* "We also help each other stick to our meal plans. If we eat anything outside of a Kyla-provided meal, we have to send a picture to the group chat," he says as he takes a photo of his smoothie with all of the ingredients artfully placed next to it on the counter. I've obviously noticed him taking pictures of his food before, but I thought he was just one of those people who posted it to a social media account I don't follow.

He shows me his phone where he sent the photo to a group chat, and the *likes* are already pouring in. *I guess everyone has to be up this early.* "Will they all be on the hike?" I ask.

"Nah, only some of them will be. There are a lot of different class options to choose from. That's why we have the fitness app —it lets everyone pick the class they enjoy most, but we're still connected."

I nod like I understand, but the whole thing still feels controlling. Especially if everyone is required to participate or they get fined.

The fines sound insane, but I'd be willing to pay Cody's fees if it meant we got to stay in bed together until after the sun came up.

"How are you feeling this morning?" I change the topic, hoping Cody won't be in pain for this hike.

"A little sore, but it doesn't hurt," he answers. "I like the reminder of our night, if I'm being totally honest." His smirk is adorable, and his admission makes my chest feel full.

We both finish off our coffee, and I reluctantly drink the

smoothie Cody made for me. It wasn't as gross as I expected, but I wouldn't order it at a restaurant.

I'm still hungry even after the smoothie. I seriously need to get some real snacks.

WE MEET the hiking group in a parking lot at the base of the closest mountain. Apparently, there's a lake about two miles up, and the plan is to hike there and back this morning. Cody said about twenty people were expected to do the hike, and judging by the crowd, we're one of the last to arrive.

It's my fault entirely because moving quickly at this hour is impossible.

We approach the group gathering at the trail entrance. People are putting on sunscreen and tying up their hiking boots, and I see a man as tall as Cody looking right at us with a smile just as big as Cody's lighting up his face. He's got stylish dark hair and pretty eyes, and he obviously works out a ton.

He's definitely hot, but he's got nothing on Cody.

"Nick!" Cody yells, even though he's clearly already spotted us. "Come meet my boyfriend!"

He doesn't bother lowering his volume at all, and I love that Cody's so excited to claim our label so publicly. I feel a little guilty that we didn't have that conversation sooner, but I'm glad we've gotten to this point.

"It's official now, huh?" Nick teases, raising an eyebrow as he pulls Cody in for a quick hug. It's a normal, friendly greeting— nothing like the overly familiar ones I witnessed at dinner yesterday.

"Yup, we decided last night," Cody says proudly, and I reach out to grab his hand, giving it a squeeze.

"Sorry, it took so long," I murmur, and he squeezes my hand back with a big smile.

"Worth the wait."

"I'm the best friend, Nick," he says, holding out his hand in greeting, and I shake it, appreciating that he didn't assume I'm a hugger.

"The boyfriend, Beck," I introduce myself proudly.

"I've heard a *lot* about you over the last few months."

"Hopefully good things?" I question with a teasing tone.

"Mostly about how you're so hot and funny and perfect that you made him realize he's bi," Nick responds with a laugh.

"For the record, I don't usually go after straight-identifying men," I clarify. "I thought he was flirting with me."

That makes Nick laugh even harder. "He probably was. When he came out to me, all excited about his newfound sexual identity, I had to tell him I thought he was already bi and out—because he unintentionally flirts with literally everyone all the time."

Cody groans, already laughing, and Nick adds with a wink, "He was shocked. If I were into guys, I would've gone after him years ago."

I can't help but laugh, too, because that sounds exactly like Cody and his adorable, oblivious kindness.

"Well, I'm very glad for the confusion," I add, and Nick smiles fondly at me.

"Me too, Cody has seemed... brighter since the two of you met. Don't get me wrong, he's always been super happy, but it's like he's more present now. I hope you guys can keep finding ways to spend time together," he says earnestly, and I decide Nick is probably my favorite person we've talked to since my arrival. It's clear that he cares about Cody as an actual friend and not just as someone important to Kyla.

I'm glad Cody has him, even if he is making us wake up so fucking early.

The hike itself is fairly easy, with a slight incline. It takes us about an hour to reach the lake, and when we do, the view is gorgeous. I can understand the appeal as we watch the sunrise over the water.

But what really steals my attention is Cody. Watching my sunshine man light up at the spectacular view makes every yawn I'll have today worth it.

Nick and I get along really well. He played hockey growing up all the way through college, so the three of us talk about the play-offs that just wrapped up and how I'm determined to make next year the year the Werewolves finally go all the way.

Because I *obviously* have that kind of power.

By the time we're back in the parking lot, it's almost eight a.m., and we say goodbye to Nick after he and I exchange numbers.

Cody and I head back for a quick shower, where I get to wash him—a task I absolutely love—and then we're on our way to the headquarters again.

Viktor mentioned wanting to show me more in the studio today, so I assume we'll be reviewing the marketing materials they've likely already put together from yesterday's photos. But the moment we step inside the studio, my stomach drops.

There's a full-blown production stage with employees running around to prepare for filming. A set's been prepared to record an interview in front of cameras, and Viktor is sitting in the slightly larger armchair on the right, where someone is applying powder to his face.

I really need to start paying more attention to this guy.

I'm almost certain Viktor never mentioned filming videos or interviews. When we talked about taking my picture and there being some cameras around, I thought he meant candid shots of me and Cody.

Clearly I was underestimating Viktor, and that needs to end.

As soon as we're spotted on the set, another makeup artist

appears seemingly out of nowhere to add makeup to my face as well. I'm covered in powder, and a stray hair is plucked from above my left eyebrow. *Seriously? Was an errant hair going to fuck up the video?*

Once my appearance is deemed appropriate for whatever's happening here, I'm led over to the seat opposite Viktor.

The chair is comfortable, but I'm on edge as I look around. I don't understand why Kyla even needs this large of a studio. All of the videos I've been shown in the classes must have been filmed here, but they only featured the speaker. This place has room for an audience and has multiple stages, so they must film more than the program videos I've seen.

I have no idea what to say or do, so I look to Viktor, hoping he'll clue me in on what's happening. He gives me a small smile and nods in greeting before waiting for a camera operator to raise a hand, signaling that they're recording.

"Today, I have a very special member of Kyla with me," Viktor starts, looking into the camera.

My thoughts snag on the word "member."

I'm not a member. Am I?

I guess that I have taken multiple day-long courses and spent a lot of money in the process. Plus, I did go to the retreat in Florida, and now I'm here for an extended amount of time...

Shit, I guess I probably am a member. That realization really snuck up on me, and I don't know how I feel about it.

Meanwhile, Viktor is going on about who I am and my family, just like he did last night. I'm trying to keep the panic off of my face since I've been told I'm not great at keeping my thoughts and emotions out of my expressions, and the last thing I want is to offend Cody if I look upset by Viktor's statement.

I also don't want to piss this guy off.

I'm starting to really question Viktor's motives and teachings, and I don't want him to suspect I'm anything less than an enthusiastic participant in whatever the hell is happening in this town until I can figure out what's really going on here. Cody mentioned getting Viktor's approval for me to be here, and I don't want to find out what happens if I lose it.

"So, Beckett, I would love to hear a little more from you about your Kyla journey and how your life has improved since joining the Kyla family," Viktor prompts me, and I note that the leading way he phrases it makes it clear he's only expecting a glowing, positive response.

I don't think I have any choice but to fake a smile and bullshit my way through this so that Viktor doesn't try to make me leave Linna and Cody.

I force the same practiced smile I use during media events for Werewolves' business, and attempt to sound genuine.

"Well, I was first introduced to the company when Cody hosted a seminar for my family's company." I figure the more truth I use, the less likely Viktor is to question my answers. "I was intrigued," I continue—by Cody, but I leave that part out. "So I signed up for the individual program that weekend, attended the Kyla retreat in Florida the next month, and now I'm spending the summer here in Linna."

I glance over at Cody and see him smiling at me encouragingly.

"I've found my family here," I say, holding his gaze. "A renewed sense of purpose. I'd say that my life has improved dramatically in that time."

"That's great to hear," Viktor says, returning my attention to him. "And certainly a common story among those who participate in Kyla's self-improvement programs," he adds sagely.

He asks me a few more leading questions about how great everything here is and how much I love Kyla. I manage to bullshit my way through it with short answers, mostly just echoing his phrasing. Despite my best efforts, my comments start to sound more sarcastic as we go on, and Viktor must decide he has enough footage, because he interrupts my commentary on how everyone is so healthy here and quickly wraps up the interview.

After a short goodbye to Viktor, Cody and I are able to escape to his office on the second-highest floor. Unfortunately, we both have actual work to do, so I set up my laptop on a table in his office. The rest of the work-day flies by, interrupted only by another disappointingly small and overly healthy lunch.

We have dinner again at the Old Mill, and just like the night before, a lot of the people are overly familiar with each other. There are also a lot of pregnant women in the crowd, and I think back to last night, realizing that there were quite a few then too.

When I ask Cody about it and question if birth control isn't a thing here, he just laughs and says there are a lot of people here in their childbearing years, and that Kyla has such great maternity leave and childcare options that more women here feel like they're supported in having children.

By the time we eat, socialize, wait for the announcements, and close with meditation, it's almost eleven p.m. when we return to Cody's, and I'm exhausted. Cody is able to keep me awake with the promise of mutual blow jobs, but the moment my head hits the pillow after that, I'm asleep.

THE REST of the week flies by in a similar routine. Cody convinces me to join him for some sort of group fitness session before the ass crack of dawn, usually led by Nick, then we spend the day at his office.

We avoid any more one-on-one interaction with Viktor—I don't know if we're really that lucky or if he's avoiding me. *No complaints from me.*

It turns out that Cody eats at the Old Mill *every* night when he's in town because he travels so much. So, we spend our evenings there, Cody socializing and me avoiding talking to anyone but him and Nick. In my opinion, we're not eating enough food. I think I've already lost weight being here, and I don't feel like that's necessarily a good thing. Combined with the lack of sleep, I can only deal with so much bullshit conversation, so I'm glad Cody finds my short, sarcastic responses amusing.

We can't even fill up at home. Cody only has healthy, fresh options at his place, and we haven't had any time to grocery shop for me to get actual snacks. I've always been a healthy eater, but I need something fried and covered in salt every once in a while.

When we get home at night, we fall into bed, exchange orgasms, and pass out. Cody hasn't expressed any interest in topping yet, but I think that's only because he's been enjoying bottoming so much—I've been following his lead.

It's Friday night now, and apparently, we finally get to sleep in tomorrow. Our spin class isn't until eight a.m. and I don't think I've ever been this excited to wake up at seven.

Cody and I are curled up naked in his bed after he just rode me for the first time. I was far too exhausted to attempt anything else. When I suggested it, Cody eagerly helped me undress, practically pushed me onto the bed, and climbed right on top of me —it was amazing. Sex with him always is, and his enthusiasm when it comes to having me inside of him is hot as fuck. I don't know how he has so much energy, he's been getting just as little sleep and food as I have, but he still managed to ride my cock like he had all of the energy in the world.

His head is resting on my chest now as I run my fingers through his gorgeous hair. I accidentally snag his necklace and realize I've never asked him about it. Now that I think about it, I don't think I've ever seen him without it.

"So, is this a Kyla thing?" I ask, pulling at the silver chain to see the three mountain peaks dangling from it.

"Oh, yeah, I'm so used to it by now I forget it's there most of the time. Everyone in Linna gets one as a part of the welcome ceremony that Viktor throws when you move here," he states.

"You start with a bronze one with only a triangle on it, and as you spend more time here, achieve different things, advance in the company, stuff like that, then you can earn more peaks and different metals," he explains. "I have the highest-ranking one because of my title, but I think they all look cool. Everyone gets excited when they get to exchange theirs for a new one."

"Do you ever take it off?"

"Oh, I can't," Cody says casually. "It has a special locking mechanism so it doesn't fall off and can't get lost."

My stomach twists. He says it like that's totally normal, *but he's wearing a fucking collar put on by his fucking boss.* It's a short chain that's snug against his neck, so there's no way it would fit over his head.

"So only Viktor can put them on or take them off?" I clarify. I'm really trying to keep my tone even so that Cody doesn't catch on to my growing rage, but I'm not sure how successful I am.

"Yeah, I guess so," he answers. "I never really gave it much thought since I tend to lose jewelry. I just thought it was cool that I wouldn't have to worry about that."

I keep playing with Cody's hair, trying not to alarm him, even as the horrible sinking feeling in my gut spreads throughout my entire body. The hairs on my arms stand up, and I think I might be sick.

This isn't normal.

I've always had my reservations about the company he works for. I've ignored a ton of red flags because my focus has always been on Cody—trying to spend more time with him and getting to know him.

I brushed off the Kyla stuff as unimportant baggage, something I just had to tolerate to be with him.

But now, the pieces start to come together.

I think more about the classes, how expensive they are, and

the strange content. I think about Linna and the forced happy people here and the weird, overly familiar touching. Then there are the mandated diets and exercise, fines, and internal policing. Fuck, even the actual police in Linna participate in the Kyla courses and eat in the Old Mill. I've met some of them.

Then there are the necklaces. *The collars.*

And Viktor.

And then, something clicks. Hard.

I know Cody has joked about being oblivious, but apparently, I must be too.

Kyla isn't just some weird self-help company.

Kyla is a fucking cult.

I joined a fucking cult and didn't even realize it because I was so focused on the hot guy I wanted to hook up with.

We need to get out of here. Like right now. Tonight, before Viktor catches on that I know.

But fuck! How the hell am I supposed to convince Cody to leave with me? He loves this place—the town, his job, the people.

For a split second, a dark thought creeps in—*does he know?* Cody's on their management team. Could he be a part of it? Complicit even?

But as soon as that pops into my head, I know it's impossible. There's no way that this kind, sweet, genuinely good man that I love with everything that I am could possibly be involved in a scheme to manipulate people out of their money—and god only knows what else Viktor is doing to these people.

Clearly, he's controlling their food and exercise, even their sleep, to an extent, keeping everyone at dinner so late and making them wake up to work out so early. If he has everyone in town in these programs—the local government, the police and fire departments, the medical professionals—his control of this city could be absolute.

We seriously need to get the fuck out of here.

"Cody, we should go somewhere for the weekend," I blurt out, and I can't quite manage to keep the desperation out of my tone.

He laughs, sitting up to look at me. "What? Why?" he's giving me a concerned look, and I'm obviously doing a terrible job keeping my cool right now.

"Well," I begin, trying to think of an excuse that will get him to leave without completely shattering the way he views his entire life.

"I miss my family," I say quickly. "I was thinking we could call my brothers in the morning, maybe see if they want to meet us halfway. We could drive somewhere to show them how beautiful it is," I ramble. I know I'm not really making sense, but I worry that Viktor would somehow know if we tried to take a plane, and driving seems smarter. Using my family seemed like a good excuse in at the time, but even I know it sounds suspicious.

"Why wouldn't they just fly here?" Cody questions because obviously, they could.

"It would be fun," I insist. "I can call them now. I'm sure they're still awake."

I go to reach for my phone, but Cody grabs my arm to stop me. "Beck, you're freaking me out." He sounds so concerned, and I hate that I'm the one who's going to have to tell him. "What's wrong?" he pushes, and I know I have to stop stalling and just say it.

"Cody, I need to tell you something. Well, a lot of things, actually," I start, wanting to warn him. "And you're probably going to be really upset about it, but I need you to understand how much I love you and that, no matter what, I'm here for you. We have each other now, so we can get through anything, okay?" I'm gripping both of his hands in mine, holding his gaze so that he can see the sincerity in my eyes.

He nods. "Beck, whatever it is, just tell me. You're really scaring me."

"Cody, it isn't normal for your boss to lock a necklace onto you. That's called a collar, and it's a symbol of ownership," I say gently. His expression shifts from concerned to confused.

"It doesn't seem healthy to limit what you're eating so drastically, especially with all of the exercise you do. And the sleep you're getting, Cody, it's barely enough to function. I've had a lot of concerns about this place, and about Viktor, but I kept dismissing them because it seemed like your job and the company made you so happy," I admit. "I'm sorry that I kept my concerns to myself until now. I didn't realize I could be hurting you by ignoring how harmful all of this could be."

I take a shaky breath. *How am I supposed to tell Cody that everything he knows and loves is a lie? That a person he clearly admires and respects has been manipulating him to hurt people?*

My throat tightens as I finally whisper, "Baby, I think Kyla is a cult."

His confused expression only seems to deepen. I have no idea how he's going to react, so I go on, trying to get out as much as I can in case he tries to shut me down. "I'm worried Viktor is a cult leader and that he's built the company to scam people out of their money, claiming all of this 'wisdom' about self-improvement and success, while taking more and more money from them. I think that he selects people to be promoted to work here in Linna based on their commitment to his ideas and values. That he's manipulating everyone here to see how much power and control he can take from them."

I sound like the crazy one now, but I'm desperate for him to believe me.

"That stuff that you told me about everyone casually touching him and the 'enlightened relationships,'" I keep talking, waiting for him to say something. "Do you think he's sleeping with them too?" I voice the thought as I have it, but it feels sickeningly true as I say it.

Cody's brows are furrowed together tightly, and his eyes squint as they bounce around the room, not focusing on anything. He doesn't look at me, and I can't tell what he's thinking.

I have this overwhelming feeling that this could be the most crucial moment of my life, that whatever happens now could change everything.

"Cody, we need to leave before he realizes we're onto him." I'm begging now, I don't think I've ever been more desperate for anything in my life. What he says next could determine my entire future, if I'm ever able to be happy again.

He still won't meet my gaze as he finally murmurs, "I can't leave."

My whole body freezes in response to his refusal. The pain in my chest is unlike anything I've ever felt as my heart completely shatters. The pieces pierce through my lungs, making it impossible to breathe.

This is it then. It doesn't matter that we love each other. Love isn't enough. Just like that, it's over.

I'd really started to believe we would make it, to hope.

I never wanted a happily ever after with someone until I met Cody. But now, knowing what it's like to be *his*, I'm ruined. There will never be anyone else.

What the fuck am I supposed to do?

CHAPTER TWENTY-FOUR

Cody

"I can't leave," I admit, afraid to look at Beck and see the disappointment no doubt written all over his face.

"Cody…" he chokes out on a sob, and when I finally look up, the heartbreak on his face guts me.

"Wait," I rush to explain because he doesn't understand, he can't when he doesn't know everything. I grip his hands back tightly, afraid that he'll let go, and force myself to hold his gaze. "Beck, I don't mean that I don't want to go or that I don't believe you," I clarify. "I mean that I literally cannot leave."

"What do you mean?" he pleads, obviously desperate for me to explain. There's hope shining in his eyes now, despite the confused expression that's replaced his previous anguish.

"I think you're right," I admit. As much as I really, really don't want to believe him, I'd be lying if I said his claims don't seem true.

I don't want to believe that Viktor, someone I thought was my friend, has been manipulating and abusing my trust this entire time.

But... is he really my friend? Are any of the people here?

They don't treat me like Beck's friends treat him, or hell, even how Beck's friends treat me. Nick is the only person here who ever really seemed to care about *me* and not my position in the company.

Viktor has never asked me why I wanted Beck here. He doesn't care that I love him. It's always been about how Beck could help the company.

I've been noticing more and more things around here that have felt *off* since meeting Beck a few months ago. And now, when he spells out the reality of everything—I can't deny his accusation. He doesn't even know the full extent.

It took me nearly thirty years to realize I'm attracted to men. I guess it makes sense that it's taken me almost ten to realize I've been in a cult.

"But Beck, I can't just leave. There's a lot you don't know," I explain. "When we move here, as a part of 'proving our commitment and dedication to Kyla',"—I say with air quotes—"we have to give Viktor proof of that dedication."

"What kind of proof?"

"A notarized secret. Something so personal that we'd never want it to be public knowledge. It had to be submitted to him so that if we ever betray the company, it'll be released," I say. Hearing it now, I feel so stupid for going along with it.

"Viktor downplayed its importance," I continue. "He explained that everyone does it, and it's never been needed. He said that he's the only one with the information, so it's safe." I feel even more idiotic as I go on. "I was fresh out of college when I started with the company. I had no reason to think that I'd ever betray it, and they made Linna sound so amazing. I was so excited to move here," I add.

"Hey," Beck interrupts, cupping my face. "Don't do that. Don't beat yourself up over any of this," he says with such conviction that, despite myself, I do feel a bit better. "Cody, there are over ten thousand people in this city being manipulated by this man, clearly, he's good at what he's doing. None of this is your fault."

I give a small nod. He's right, of course. Feeling bad or guilty about this isn't going to fix anything right now.

"He also has access to all of my bank accounts and credit cards," I confess. "I can't go anywhere without him knowing. I can't even withdraw large sums of money without Viktor's pre-approval with the bank," I explain. "So, I literally can't leave. If it were as simple as choosing Kyla or you, it wouldn't be a decision. I've already chosen you, Beck. I just don't know *how* to leave. I'd have no money, and he'd release my secret. I don't know if I'm ready to deal with the fallout of that," I admit weakly.

"Cody, you wouldn't need money. You could come live with me," Beck answers softly. "I've loved us sharing your house this week, but if you're not ready to officially live with me, then we can get you an apartment or something," he adds when he sees the hesitation still in my expression.

"Beck, I'd love to live with you," I chuckle. "But how can I let you pay for everything like that? We've only been officially dating for a week."

"This might make me sound like an asshole, but money doesn't mean anything to me—I have more than I'll ever need," Beck says with a shrug. "I'd love to pay for anything you want for the rest of our lives. I meant what I said when I told you I want a future together. You don't have to give Viktor that kind of control over you anymore. Please, Cody, let me help."

I take a deep breath, needing a moment to think about his offer.

It would be so easy to let him do it, to let Beck try to fix everything. *But easy doesn't always mean right.*

"Beck, I love you too." I cup his face with my hand, holding his desperate gaze. "I do want that future with you," I reassure him. "But, I still want to be my own person. I just found out that Viktor, a man I've respected and considered a friend for years, is abusing the power I gave him in my life. I know you'd never do that, but I can't give *anyone* that kind of control over me again." I sound as defeated as I feel, but I know I need to explain everything.

Beck nods, thankfully not looking hurt by what I've said. "I get it, Cody. I want us to be individuals who make each other stronger. I wouldn't want to rely on anyone that much either," he says, making me fall in love with him all over again.

I lean in for a soft, slow kiss. Beck's lips on mine immediately calm my racing heart. I might not know what happens next, but if we're together, I know I'll be okay.

Eventually, he pulls back, still looking concerned. "So you agree with me though, you're not freaking out?" he asks.

"No more than when I first realized I wanted to kiss you in Florida," I say with a shrug.

"You're amazing." He laughs, leaning in for another short kiss. When he pulls back, there's a determined look on his face. "We'll find a way to get you out of here," he says with a nod. "We'll keep acting like we don't realize how awful Viktor is, maybe come up with an excuse to transfer out some of your money that he wouldn't question, and we'll figure out how to get back whatever secret you gave him as collateral."

He makes it sound so feasible that I don't hesitate to agree. "Okay, let's beat him at his own game." I let out a breath of relief, happy to have the beginning of a plan, but the calm feeling is short-lived, replaced by more anxiety as another thought hits me. "What about everyone else? He's manipulating thousands of people, we can't just run away and let him continue to hurt people," I point out, and Beck smiles fondly at my concern.

"I love how much you care," he replies, then lets out a big sigh. "You're right. I've only really thought about how to get *you* away from Viktor, but we should probably try to gather some proof of what he's doing, try to expose him somehow."

"I should be able to get proof. I have access to a lot of stuff with my position, and I've never given Viktor a reason not to trust me," I say with more excitement.

"I'll call Jordan. Maybe see if he can do some research while we're still here and figure out what kind of evidence we'd need. He's always wanted to do more investigative pieces. Maybe he could even write an article for his company," Beck says, sounding hopeful.

Then his expression falls, becoming serious again. "You don't have to tell me anything you don't want to, but how bad will it be if the secret does come out?" he asks with concern. "Even if we do get the document back, Viktor could still tell people."

"Oh, I don't care if *you* know," I say honestly. "I've just never told anyone before. I guess I didn't know how to bring it up—thinking about it always bums me out because I have really mixed feelings about the whole thing," I explain before launching into the story.

"In college, one of my frat brothers did one of those ancestry DNA kits, and I thought it sounded fun. My grandparents had all passed by then, and I didn't know much about where either side of my family was from. So, I got the kit, spit in the tube, and sent it away. I'd honestly forgotten about it by the time I got the results email a few weeks later," I say, pausing to take a deep breath before I get to the difficult part.

"I wasn't expecting much, especially not in the relatives section. Both of my parents are only children, so I figured it'd be blank. That's why I was shocked to see a result claiming that I had a relative—a probable half-sibling," I say, stopping to gauge his reaction.

Beck's face lights up. "That's great, Cody! You've always wanted siblings!" he responds, sounding so happy for me. *I love how excited he is over something that he thinks will make me happy.*

"Well, the app allows you to create a public profile if you'd like, and you can choose to let family members see it. So, I went to their profile and found out that we're the same age." I watch his expression fall as he realizes what that would mean.

"So, your dad cheated on your mom while they were still together?" he clarifies, and I nod.

"He must have. The guy had his full name and picture on the app, so it was pretty easy to find his social media. He also grew up in California, and there were some posts about his mom, and how amazing she was for raising him on her own. I have no idea if my dad knows or not, and even though they split up a few years later, my mom's never said anything about him cheating." I take another deep breath, trying to collect my thoughts so that I can explain everything properly. I know a secret about my dad cheating almost thirty years ago might not seem like that big of a deal to some people, but I hate the idea of hurting my mom, even if it isn't actually my fault.

"My mom is already really hard on herself," I say. "My entire life, she's constantly made comments that she isn't pretty enough, young enough, interesting enough. I think the rejections over the years in Hollywood and comparing herself to the women she was auditioning against took its toll on her self-esteem. Even though they didn't stay together, I know their marriage was important to her. It's always been a point of pride for her that my dad, a successful, popular man in the industry, chose to marry her, to have a family with her, and that he never remarried anyone else. It made her feel special in a way that nothing else really has. I didn't want to hurt her if she didn't know he cheated," I explain, and Beck guides me to lie down with him.

I rest my head on his chest, letting the steady beating of his heart calm me as he runs his hands through my hair. It feels amazing when he plays with the long strands, and I focus on how connected I feel to him, on how lucky I am to have Beck here lending me support as I continue. "If the other woman never told my dad, I'm sure she had her own reasons not to. I didn't think it was my place to bring it up. And then there's my dad. He's always been known as one of the good guys in Hollywood. He doesn't have the predatory reputation that so many men in his industry do, and he's helped so many people get housing with his charity. If news of a cheating scandal, especially one that resulted in a secret child, got out, the media would run wild with it. You know how things get twisted to fit whatever narrative will sell the most copies or earn more clicks. He isn't a bad person, but his secret could ruin everything that he's worked so hard for."

Beck is quiet, probably waiting to see if I'm done. As much as I want to be, I force myself to admit the real reason I don't want Viktor to share the secret with anyone. "I hate the idea of it being my fault that any of them are hurt. I'd never want to hurt the other woman or her son. And, I love my parents, but they already make so little time for me. What if they blamed me for the fallout? I don't want to lose either of them."

"I'm so sorry you had to deal with that on your own, especially when you've always wanted more family. And I know you'd never intentionally hurt anyone, baby," he says quietly, placing a kiss on the top of my head as he continues to stroke my hair. "Did you ever reach out to your brother?" he asks after a few moments of silence.

"No, I was too afraid to," I admit. "He's never reached out to me either. What if he hates me because I grew up with our dad?" I whisper.

"Or what if he's always wanted a brother too, and ends up being really cool?" Beck counters.

I give a noncommittal hum as I think about that possibility. "Let's deal with the Kyla stuff first and then if the secret isn't forced out, I can think more about my options," I suggest, and Beck kisses me on the top of my head before agreeing.

"We should try to get some sleep," he murmurs, sounding halfway there already.

"Okay. Goodnight, babe," I whisper, knowing he's right.

We have a lot to talk about and plan, but it can wait until tomorrow. Beck kisses my head again. "Night, baby."

218

"Okay. Goodnight, babe," I whisper, knowing he's right.

We have a lot to talk about and plan, but it can wait until tomorrow. Beck kisses my head again. "Night, baby."

CHAPTER TWENTY-FIVE

Beck

I'm still really fucking pissed about this entire situation, but I'm trying to channel all of my energy into fixing it so that I don't jump the gun and storm into Viktor's office to confront him.

I don't see that going well, and we need proof if we're going to stop him from continuing to hurt people.

Cody and I both agree that keeping up with our routine is going to be the most important thing. If Cody suddenly stopped showing up to his fitness classes or skipped dinners at the Old Mill, it would draw attention to him, and that's the last thing we want when he's going to be gathering potentially damning information on Viktor and Kyla.

We still make our way to the fitness center for Nick's eight a.m. spin class and decide to wait until we're back at Cody's to kick off our plan. Waiting gives us plenty of time to explain things to Jordan and my brothers before we need to be at dinner tonight.

"I wish I could tell Nick what we suspect," Cody says when we get into his car after the class.

"I know," I sigh sympathetically. "But I think the fewer people we involve in this, the better. We don't know what Viktor's capable of, and we don't want word getting back to him somehow."

"I just hope it doesn't take us too long. The faster we can expose him and stop him from manipulating everyone, the better," Cody says, sounding determined.

When we're back at Cody's house, we set up my laptop at his kitchen table and call Jordan.

"Hey, man, how's Montana? We miss you in Chicago." His deep voice calms me as he greets us on the video call. I didn't realize how much I miss him.

"Not great, actually," I answer honestly. "Cody and I need to talk to you about some weird things happening here to see if you might be able to do some digging into it from the outside to find out more."

"Shit man, what's going on? You know I'll help however I can," he answers, looking worried.

I knew he'd want to help, not just because of his career, but because my friends are amazing, and I know they'd do anything for me. Still, actually hearing his offer eases some of my stress.

We launch into the whole story, starting with all the red flags I ignored while I was too focused on Cody. I tell Jordan about the outrageous cost of the classes, and the way they practically worship Viktor and praise the city. I describe the overly familiar touches I first noticed at the Florida retreat, and how eager Viktor has been to have me join because of my family's name and potential influence.

Cody cuts in, adding details I hadn't known. "As a coach, they push the idea of cutting out 'toxic' friends and family," he says, using air quotes. "But ever since I visited you guys in Chicago and saw firsthand how amazing Beck's family is, I've realized how few people here talk about their relatives.

"I started asking around. It seems like I have one of the best relationships with my family of any of the people here. My parents never cared enough to ask for details about Kyla or how much money I was spending on it. They were just happy I seemed so happy and had a job," he explains. "But I've found out most people in Linna have stopped talking to their loved ones who 'don't support their success.'" He uses air quotes again on that last part, and it's strange to see how he's already distancing himself from the teachings that have been his life for years.

I love how confident he is in himself. Just like he was able to quickly embrace his attraction to a man, it seems he's already accepted Viktor's teachings as manipulation and is making a conscious effort to separate himself from it. I hope that he knows how much I admire him, how fucking strong he is. I squeeze his thigh under the table next to me, and try to focus on what he's saying.

"When I asked Viktor about it, he brushed off the topic and told me that those people are lucky to have found the Kyla family to replace their unsupportive ones," Cody says.

"That's horrible," Jordan responds, and I nod, a bit shocked. I can't imagine not talking to my family. I know that mine is better than most, but from what Cody's describing, it's obvious that Viktor encourages them to cut out anyone who questions Kyla. That means people have probably stopped talking to their loved ones simply because they were worried about them. *We seriously need to stop this asshole.*

I take a few deep breaths to center myself before describing the things I've noticed since coming here—the strict diets and exercise programs enforced with fines, the loyalty to Viktor to report other members who don't follow the rules. The communal dinners and long work hours. How everything is packaged in this pretty facade; Linna as a utopian city, with Kyla being the epitome of a perfect place to work.

Cody's cheeks turn pink, and he sounds embarrassed when he explains the necklaces and collateral, but Jordan, being the amazing friend that he is, responds with support.

"Cody, I hope you know none of this is your fault. It sounds like this Viktor guy is a master at gaslighting everyone into thinking his ways are normal," he says fiercely, like he really wants Cody to believe him.

"Thanks," Cody murmurs, sitting up a little straighter. "It's been difficult to accept that everything I thought I knew is basically a lie. But, like I said, I already had doubts about what was happening here since meeting Beck. I bet I'm not the only one. But they build up Linna as this amazing place where everyone is always happy, and even being here, it does come across that way. Now I'm wondering if people are just afraid to break that mold. I was starting to think there was something wrong with me for noticing these things when everyone else didn't seem bothered by it," he admits.

I squeeze his thigh again, wanting him to know I'm here, that he isn't alone in any of this. He places his hand on mine, aiming a small smile my way before turning back to Jordan on the screen.

"It definitely sounds like a herd mentality situation," Jordan agrees. "I absolutely want to help. I'll start to do some research on Viktor and Kyla and maybe see if I can find anyone who's left the company. Cody, can you think of anyone who's moved away from Linna?"

He thinks about it before answering. "Yeah, it's very uncommon for people to leave here permanently, so I remember their names. It's usually sudden, though. Viktor always has a story, like a family member died and they needed to help take care of things, or that they got a dream job opportunity they've always wanted and had to leave quickly, stuff like that. He always made it seem like a positive thing that they had to leave, never that they didn't want to be here anymore," he explains.

Cody texts the list of names to Jordan from my phone instead of his own. We're afraid to use his devices just in case Viktor somehow has access to them. We're pretty sure his house is safe, Viktor's never doubted Cody's loyalty, and there's no security system he could have access to.

"I'll start digging right away," Jordan promises. "If it's alright with you both, I'd like to see if I can get my boss's approval to investigate the story officially so I can use the company resources too," he adds, and we both give him our consent.

"Just don't publish anything while we're still here," I clarify. "We want to get as much dirt as we can while we're on the inside before we leave."

"Got it. Send me anything you can find, and I'll do the same," Jordan agrees before we all say our goodbyes.

Next, we call my brother, Oakley. He and I are close, so I want to tell him anyway, but we're also hoping for some advice from his best friend, Parker. Parker's in finance, and we're wondering if he might have advice for what Cody can use as an excuse with Viktor to transfer out as much money as possible into a new bank account so he'll have it when we get back to Chicago.

I'd support Cody financially, even if things didn't work out between us in the long run. But I respect his wishes to remain independent, and if he needs his own money to feel free, then I'll do whatever it takes to make it happen.

"Hey, man! How's Cody?" Oakley says after answering on the third ring. It looks like he's walking through his apartment and isn't actually in the camera's view yet.

"I've been better," Cody replies with a small laugh before saying hello as Oak finally props his phone up so that he's on the screen sitting at his kitchen table.

"We have some stuff to tell you, and we were hoping Parker might be around to get his opinion on it too," I add.

"He's around, but I don't want to bother him," Oakley says. It's weird enough that they're not already in the same room. *Are they fighting or something?*

"Come on, man, this is serious. Can you just get him?" I complain.

"Shit, okay, sorry. One second." I can hear him call out for Parker. After a minute, he's on the screen.

"Hey guys, what's up?"

Once again, we dive into the whole story, telling them everything we told Jordan, going into more detail about the financial situation and seeing if he has any advice on how Cody can get his money out of Viktor's control.

He has some ideas, and after agreeing to rope Adrian into our plan, we promise to nail down the details and update them later. Then, they spend some time updating us on their girlfriends and chatting. They seem like nice women, but the whole dynamic of their double dates seems a little off. I'm not about to say anything when my own life is such a mess right now, though. It's nice to have a few minutes that feel normal after how crazy the last twenty-four hours have been. Eventually, we say our goodbyes, and I stand up to wrap my arms tightly around Cody, where he's still sitting in his chair.

"I'm glad we have a plan," I admit, kissing the top of his head.

"Me too," he agrees. Then he tilts his head back to kiss me, and I get lost in his taste, content in feeling like we have a shot at a real future together for maybe the first time.

CHAPTER TWENTY-SIX

Cody

Pretending that everything is normal for the past few days has been harder than I expected.

I'm mentally questioning everyone that I talk to—*do they know? Are they a victim, or are they helping him? Am I hurting them by not somehow stopping him sooner?* I've tried to stop that line of thinking because I can't change the past, and I do think that almost everyone here is a victim to some extent.

As much as I hate to admit it, I'm sure there are probably people within the upper management team who are actively helping Viktor blackmail people or squeeze more money out of them. But then there's also me, and I had no idea. I don't know what he's told people to justify his actions, and until I have more information, it isn't my place to pass judgment.

"Here's another external hard drive that's been uploaded," Beck says as he hands it to me to put away and find another.

Beck and I have been attempting to download any and all information that I have access to as a member of upper management into a cloud that he and Jordan can both access from anywhere. Viktor's distrust of cloud technology means nearly everything is stored on external hard drives, which works in our favor.

Beck has been pretending to work in my office, just like when we first arrived, but now his only task is uploading as many files as he possibly can. Adrian's been a lifesaver, covering for Beck's actual work back in Chicago, allowing him to focus on our plan here. Meanwhile, I've been uploading my entire email history to the cloud.

We both agree we want to be in Linna for the least amount of time possible. The goal is to take as much information as quickly as we can and then sort through it when we're safely in Chicago.

I'm not sure when that will be, but we've packed go-bags in case we need to literally run. We each have one in the trunk of my car and another at my house. I have no idea what Viktor is capable of—whether we're in physical danger or if we're being dramatic—but I'd prefer not to find out.

The hardest part has probably been my guilt over not telling Nick. I'm certain he's just as much a victim as I am, and keeping him in the dark feels wrong. Beck actually suggested that I tell him because he can see how much it's been bothering me to keep him out of the loop, but ultimately, I agree that it's safer for now if we don't.

"It's almost time for my meeting with Viktor. I should head down there," I say, handing Beck the next hard drive.

"Are you sure you don't want me to come with you in case he starts asking questions?" Beck asks me for the hundredth time.

"I'm sure. I think it'll seem less suspicious if I'm alone, and if I can't answer a question, he'll assume it's because I'm not great with money. He already knows that about me," I explain.

"Fiiine, I'm sure you'll do great, I just hate you being alone with that asshole," Beck mutters, and I lean in for a quick kiss before leaving my office and heading down the long hall toward Viktor's door.

I knock three times, just how he prefers, two short knocks followed by a long third, then wait for him to say I can enter. It's such a small, strange demand and one of the countless ways he asserts control over everyone. Things like this seemed harmless before, but now they feel ridiculous. I hear the short click of the door unlocking, something I know he can control from his desk, and I step inside.

"Come on in, Cody. I'm so glad that you suggested this meeting today," Viktor says, sounding so genuine. *I'm sure that's how he's conned so many people.* "You wanted to talk about a business opportunity?" he asks, motioning for me to sit in the chair opposite his desk.

It's smaller than his. Everything about this place, the size of the giant office, the mini bar on one wall, the full conference table set up, and a sitting area with plush couches, supports the image of how important he is.

"Yeah, Beck mentioned it to me," I reply, trying to sound casual and like my usual cheery self without overdoing it. "He has so much money that other people handle it for him, but I'd told him about the money I have from my parents and that it's just been sitting in my account, not doing anything," I say, starting the speech I rehearsed with Beck. "I've been thinking I'd like to use it to help people somehow."

"That's a great idea, Cody," Viktor nods, squinting his eyes a little as he meets my gaze like he's really concentrating on what I'm saying. "And it couldn't have come at a better time, I've been thinking about ways to help even more people learn about Kyla's programming. I know there are so many people out there who could improve their lives with our courses, but they don't know about them yet. That money can be used to spread our knowledge, can help so many people," he says, as though we've already agreed to use *my* money this way.

"Really?" I ask, perking up, trying to make it seem like we're on the same page.

"Of course, I've had so many great marketing ideas that we've had to postpone due to limited funds," he explains.

"Well, when I mentioned it to Beck, he suggested that I invest it first so that I can have even more to help people with," I add hesitantly, like I'm waiting to hear Viktor's opinion.

"Investments can take a long time to see results," he warns.

"That's what I thought, too," I enthusiastically agree. "But, he told me about this business he'd planned to invest in and said that I could do it instead if I wanted to use the money for good," I continue with our script.

"There's this small business that went viral on social media," I explain as I pull out my phone to the fake webpage Adrian made for us. Beck and I told him everything, and he immediately offered to create an online presence for the company we'd made up for this scheme.

"Apparently, they've designed an at-home frozen yogurt machine that sells out every time they post about it, but it's just two guys making them, and they don't have the money to buy the supplies to make more than a few machines at a time."

I show him some pictures of "the guys" and "the product" as I talk. In reality, it's actually just pictures of Adrian and Parker posing as the business owners on the fake social media page Adrian set up for Froyo-yo-yo.

The website and social media page have a lot of aesthetically pleasing frozen yogurt photos that I'm sure they purchased at a shop and then transferred into pretty bowls to place in front of the countertop machine. The machine he actually bought from a frozen yogurt place near his house after paying them three times what it was worth, then covered in the fake company's logo.

He did a great job of making it look like a home appliance instead of one you'd see in a store. I'm kind of convinced that Adrian can do anything at this point.

"Beck had already reached out to them to find out if they'd be interested in an investor to split the profits with if he paid for the supplies they needed to create more. They said that making them is super easy, and there's a large profit margin; they just don't have the money to buy enough supplies to meet demand. They've agreed to split the profits evenly if someone funds them," I say, hoping to convince Viktor to sign off on the "investment" so that I'll have his approval to transfer a bunch of money out of my bank account into a new one he can't access.

"So you want to give these random guys on the internet a bunch of money and hope they'll use it to make more of their product, sell it, and actually pay you back?" he asks skeptically.

We'd anticipated Viktor questioning the idea, so I stick to the plan. "Beck was going to do a trial run with a smaller amount, and then if it worked out, invest more heavily. His lawyers had already vetted them and drawn up a contract, so he'll do it if I don't." We'd talked about using an excuse to need a much larger amount of money and only doing one transfer, then running. But, we ultimately determined that this plan would allow us the best chance of him agreeing, while also giving us time to gather intel.

I'm worried my practiced responses sound too eager, so I try to tone it down a bit as I remind him about the potential for more money. "Beck just saw how excited I was about the idea of helping people, so he wanted me to be able to do as much as possible," I say with a shrug.

At the mention of me reinvesting the profits—profits Viktor no doubt assumes will go to Kyla—he perks back up. "I think that the smaller initial investment sounds like a solid plan," he agrees, and a huge weight lifts from my shoulders. *He agreed! I won't need to rely on Beck's money.* I literally pinch myself under the table where he can't see, hoping the sting will distract me enough to keep a smile off of my face. "How much were you hoping to initially invest?" he asks.

"Fifteen thousand." I found out that the bank allows transfers of up to ten thousand dollars before alerting Viktor. We want it to need his authorization so that we can test the process, but not be so large that it would seem unrealistic to quickly spend.

Viktor nods, "I'll be sure to approve the transfer when the bank calls. Is that all then?" he asks, turning back to his computer in a dismissal.

"That's it," I answer with a big smile. "Thanks, Viktor. See you at dinner."

I wait until I'm all the way back in my own office before breathing a sigh of relief. We checked pretty thoroughly, and the only security camera in my office is pointed at the door from behind my desk. Viktor could potentially see what I'm working on, but he'll just see me with my emails open. The desk that Beck has been working at is perpendicular to mine, so what he's doing isn't visible. I know none of the security cameras have audio because Viktor has complained about it to me before, so we're free to talk in here.

"He bought it," I say as I shut my door behind me.

Beck perks up. "Really?"

"Yeah, he was too excited about potentially having more of my money to ask any tough questions," I explain with a laugh.

I head straight to my computer and log in to Village Bank's website. I enter the details to transfer the funds into the new online account we set up on Beck's laptop, and as I hit "confirm," a sense of relief washes over me, leaving me feeling lighter than I have in days.

"I STILL CAN'T BELIEVE that the grocery stores don't have any actual food," Beck complains as we get ready for bed.

"There's plenty of food," I say with a laugh as I start to undress, but his side-eyed glare makes it obvious he disagrees.

"Fine. There isn't any *good* food," he amends. "I'm a healthy guy, I watch what I eat. But zero processed snack options? Not even a diet soda? If we hadn't realized this place was a fucking cult already, one trip to that store would have clued me in," he huffs.

I can't hide my grin in response to his temper tantrum. "We won't be here much longer," I remind him.

"Thank fuck for that. I'm exhausted. If you want to have sex tonight you either need to ride me or fuck me, because I don't think I have the energy to do more than just lay there," Beck says as he strips off his clothes.

"Wait, seriously?" I'm frozen in place where I stand naked at the foot of the bed as I process what he just said.

"Um, yeah? I have no idea how you have so much energy with how fucking busy we are and how little food we get," Beck groans collapsing onto the bed.

"Not that! You'd let me fuck you right now?" I ask, practically bouncing onto the bed next to him. My tone is definitely not hiding how shocked and excited I feel at his suggestion. Obviously, I've fantasized about topping him, but I haven't gotten around to actually asking if he'd want me to. I've always been so eager to have him inside of me when we make it past using our hands and mouths, that I've never remembered to bring up topping him in the moment.

I don't know why, but I assumed it would be a bigger deal, an exception on a special occasion if he was even interested at all. Not a random night because he was tired.

Not that I'm complaining. At all. I'm very much on board with this suggestion. Bottoming with Beck is the best thing ever, but I'm also eager to have this new experience with him too. I want everything with Beck and the thought of being inside of him has my already eager cock twitching.

"Did you think I wouldn't bottom if you wanted me to?" Beck asks, sounding alarmed as he sits up to look at me. "I'm sorry if I gave you that impression. I thought you were just enjoying bottoming too much to want to change anything."

"Don't worry, I've definitely been enjoying it. That was a very accurate assessment," I agree, nodding my head. Hopefully, from the giant smile on my face, he believes me. "I guess I didn't think that you *wouldn't,* I just wasn't expecting it right now." I lean in to kiss him, intending for something soft, but I'm quickly consumed by his taste and end up tackling him back onto the bed in my enthusiasm.

Our rock-hard erections line up as I cover his body with mine, managing to maintain the kiss. The feel of our cocks rubbing together is amazing and I grind my hips down into his to create even more friction. Our mouths devour each other, and I know that Beck joked about not being an active participant tonight, but he's fighting me for control of the kiss. *I love it.*

"How do you want to do this?" I force myself to ask before I can get swept up in this position, his hands are now roaming my sides and when he squeezes my ass I almost ask to start with him inside of me, but I'm way too excited to risk finishing before I get the chance to be inside of him.

"Do you want me like this?" he asks, moving his mouth to my neck to leave a sloppy kiss before continuing. "Or, would you rather me get on my hands and knees, so that you can watch your cock filling me up for the first time?" he offers in that deep tone that he only uses during sex.

I let out a groan as that image fills my mind and I try to focus on what he asked me, pretty sure there was a question in there. "As much as I want to keep kissing you, now that you've put that picture in my head, I think I need to see the real thing." My voice sounds whiny and desperate, which might be embarrassing if I didn't know how much Beck loves it.

He chuckles before repositioning himself on his hands and

knees on the bed while I grab the lube from my nightstand. I get on my knees behind him, sitting back on my feet to stop and really enjoy the view for a moment.

"Babe, I hope you know how hot your ass is," I say as I squeeze the perfect round cheeks in my hands. It's not the first time I've admired his bubble butt, but it is the first time I've looked at it knowing I was about to be inside of him, and I seriously need to hurry up with how much my dick is already leaking just thinking about it.

"It'll be even hotter with your cock splitting me open," he taunts and a whimper escapes from my throat.

"Okay, I'm going to start with a finger," I warn, adding some lube and slowly rubbing it into his rim. He relaxes his head down onto his forearms, and this position has definitely gone straight to my head. Having Beck, a man who is so strong and confident, so commanding, on his knees, waiting for me to fuck him, is seriously blowing my mind.

I know that Beck loves me, and that he sees me as an equal partner in our relationship. I'm so grateful for that. But honestly, I usually like him taking control. Sure, neither of us holds back, and we'll fight for dominance when we're kissing or teasing each other. But, when it comes to who is fucking who, I've been more than happy to welcome Beck inside of me.

So I was definitely not expecting to have this dramatic of a reaction to swapping our positions. I'm not about to declare myself a top and give up bottoming or anything, but the control this position implies is super hot.

I add pressure to my finger as he relaxes and I work it in until he's shifting his hips back to meet my hand. The feeling of his tight warm body squeezing around me, even when it's just a finger, has my cock weeping.

I repeat the process with two fingers and then three, spreading them around and using plenty of lube to get him relaxed and ready for me. As eager as I might be to swap out my hand for the real deal, I don't want to rush things and end up hurting him. Beck always makes sure bottoming is so good for me, I want him to enjoy the experience too.

My fingers brush over a soft spot that must be his prostate, and Beck lets out a soft moan as he moves his hips back to meet my hand more forcefully. It's so hot seeing him like this, I'm so lucky to be able to share this with him.

"Baby, I need you to be a good boy and fuck me already," he commands. I love that even on his knees, with his ass in the air ready to be fucked, Beck is still so in control.

I withdraw my hand, adding more lube before gripping the base of my swollen cock to guide the tip to his entrance. Slowly, I push my way in past the tight ring of muscle and I have to stop myself from slamming home as his ass seems eager to swallow my dick. "Fuck Babe, you're so tight and warm, it feels absolutely incredible. There's no way I'll be able to last long like this," I warn him.

Still, I force myself to take my time, slowly pushing in deeper, allowing him time to adjust to my cock inside of him. Then he shifts his hips back, forcing me the rest of the way in, and another whine escapes from my lips. I don't move, afraid I really will finish too soon.

"Baby, I promise that I'm fine. But I won't be if you don't move and actually fuck me in the next two seconds."

I laugh as I pull out a little before working my way back in, repeating the motion and picking up my pace, trusting that Beck won't let me hurt him as I give into my pleasure. I grab his hips to pull him back into me, meeting the movement of my thrusts, all caution completely gone and forgotten. The bed is rocking, knocking into the wall with each motion, but I can barely hear it over the moans and gasps coming from the two of us.

"Fuck. Yes. Baby, just like that. Harder. Such a good boy. Faster. So good. I'm so close," Beck praises between gasps as I fuck him harder than I thought I was capable of. One of his arms has shifted so that he can stroke his leaking cock as I continue to thrust into him. As much as I want to be the one working his dick, I don't think I'm capable of slowing down right now to reposition myself. His tight, warm hole feels incredible squeezing my cock—*I can't believe I've lasted this long*— I try to make sure my angle is working his prostate, noting his sounds of pleasure when I get it right, and eventually I feel Beck's muscles tense. He lets out a strangled moan and his ass clenches around me, the intense pressure around my dick sending me right over the edge with him. My cock jerks and I fill him with my release as I continue to fuck him through our orgasms, trying to draw it out as the pleasure that had been building in my spine consumes my entire body.

We both collapse forward, completely wrung out. I hate that I can't remain inside of him for hours, for the rest of the night. I roll off of him, but watch where my cum is slowly leaking out of his hole. I scoop it up and copy what Beck loves to do to me, gathering my release and pushing two fingers back inside of him, remaining there in a comfortable silence as I rest my head on his perfect ass like it's my pillow.

Eventually, Beck breaks the silence. "That really was so hot, baby." He's mumbling, like he's already half asleep. "You did such a great job fucking me, filling my hole with your cum, and marking me as yours from the inside out."

I feel like I could float away with how light his sleepy praise makes me feel. I push myself up, crawling to place a kiss on the back of his neck before finally standing, intending to get wipes to clean him up. Beck grabs my wrist as I turn, stopping me from leaving, and pulls me back to him. His eyes are closed, but his lips are pursed, and I laugh before bending down for a soft kiss.

I still can't believe that just happened. He lets me go, his hand falling away slowly like maybe he's already asleep. I get us both cleaned up before snuggling in, bringing the blanket over us both. I'm way too hyped after that to sleep, still I force myself to try. Beck wasn't kidding about how little rest we get around here.

I'm so glad that even in the midst of so much negativity and all of the problems we've been uncovering about Kyla, Beck and I have still been able to find these moments together.

I'm so in love with him and I'm so grateful that I get to call him mine.

CHAPTER TWENTY-SEVEN

Beckett

*I*t's been almost three weeks of pretending like I'm super invested in this stupid company and this fake ass city with its annoying people.

Cody keeps reminding me we're all victims and to focus my hatred on Viktor, not the members, but it's hard not to let my frustration bleed into some of the people around him.

At least the fake frozen yogurt machine worked. Two weeks after Cody sent the initial transfer to his new account, I sent another ten grand for him to transfer back into the Village Bank.

Cody was concerned that transferring money like this might get us in trouble somehow, but technically, all he's doing is transferring his own money between accounts he owns. And I'm just his supportive boyfriend. It isn't illegal for me to send him money, I didn't even send enough to be taxed. I think my sweet man just doesn't like having to lie about everything.

I was more worried that Viktor would rightfully question how many people want to make their own frozen yogurt, but all he seemed to care about were the profits. He even suggested Cody make a more significant investment next time. By now, Cody has successfully moved $300,000 out of his Village Bank account. He said he has a lot more money in there, but that would be plenty for him to fall back on if needed.

We've been able to upload a ton of stuff to the shared cloud, and Jordan even found a few ex-Linna residents and other people who have left Kyla. At first, they were very hesitant to talk to him, but after I offered to pay them a lot of money for their exclusive interviews, a few of them agreed to share their experiences if they could remain anonymous.

So far, they've had really sad stories similar to what Cody and I suspected. They've described how their lives fell apart after losing everything to the classes, isolating themselves from friends and family, and feeling trapped by the very community that promised to save them.

The most shocking claim came from a woman who left Linna last year. She claimed Viktor is obsessed with passing on his "superior DNA" and that he grooms women into sleeping with him and carrying his children. She estimated that a large percentage of the children in Linna could be biologically his.

She even quoted Viktor's teachings to husbands of these women in "enlightened relationships". Saying that, "Children are our community's future, and it takes a village for any one individual to succeed. So, it shouldn't matter who the biological father of a child is because you are actively choosing to shape the future and better your community with every moment you spend with any child."

She also said that Viktor requires all women to track their cycles in the fitness app they all use, and he specifically requests that his "chosen ones" support his so-called enlightenment during their most fertile days. *What a load of manipulative, predatory bullshit.*

I'm so fucking over spending time with this creep, and I know my friendly act is starting to slip. Viktor requested a meeting with just me this afternoon, and I have a feeling this could be my last day here.

"Good luck, babe. You'll be great," Cody says as I give him a quick kiss on the top of his head before leaving for Viktor's office.

I knock on the door when I get there, noticing an intense keypad that is certainly not on Cody's. I hear the lock click as it opens, and he calls for me to enter.

"Hello, Beckett. Come in and have a seat." Viktor sounds friendly enough, so maybe this won't be a complete shit show. I sit down in one of the chairs across from him at his desk and wait for him to continue.

"Beckett, having you here has been a unique situation for our company," he starts, folding his hands on his desk in his signature mountain pose as he holds eye contact. "We've had visitors here at our headquarters, of course, but most of them stay a few days and then are on their way. So to have you here for such an extended amount of time has been a... delicate situation," he says carefully, his tone still conversational, but each word is measured. "Obviously, you've shown interest in our company, what we stand for and believe in," he continues, and I try hard not to have any sort of negative facial response to that bullshit statement.

"It's nothing personal, but I worry about having *anyone* be so privy to our interworkings for such an extended time without any assurances that they won't take that information and try to use it against us somehow. Perhaps sell it to competitors, or use it for themselves in some other way," he explains apologetically. "Beckett, it's time for you to either prove your loyalty as a member of Kyla or leave Linna."

Looks like it's my turn to provide collateral.

I've been expecting this, so I've had some time to decide how I want to play it. At first, I thought I could just feed him a bullshit secret and keep playing nice, but the longer I've been here, the more my focus has been shifting to getting back Cody's collateral. I want us to be able to leave without making him feel like he's hurting his family if Viktor uses it against him.

"Oh, I think I know what you're talking about," I agree confidently, working to make myself appear at ease. "Like with Cody's brother," I add casually. "You want me to tell you a secret to prove that you can trust me, that I won't hurt the company, right?"

"You know about his brother?" Viktor questions, looking genuinely surprised. "I was under the impression that I was the only person he'd ever disclosed that information to."

Viktor doesn't look happy that I know, so I push it further. "Oh yeah," I say offhandedly, leaning back in my chair, stretching an arm over the back and spreading my legs like I'm super relaxed. "After he met my brothers in Chicago, it got him thinking about his own. We were actually just talking about him reaching out to his brother this weekend," I throw in.

Viktor looks kind of pissed about it, but then takes a deep breath and forces a more relaxed expression like he's trying to remind himself to stay focused. "Well, that's good," he finally responds. "I guess you already understand the process, then. Have you decided what information you'll be sharing with me to prove your loyalty?" he asks expectantly, with an edge of excitement.

I decide to toy with him a bit, I feel like it's now or never, and I want to get him flustered. "Well, I do have some pretty sensitive information that could really damage my family," I say kind of dramatically, without going too over the top. "But before I share anything, I need to know it's safe," I explain seriously. "What do you do with this information once you have it?"

"Oh, you don't have to worry about that," he reassures me. "I'm the only one who has access to it. Everything's locked up here in my office, and you've seen all of the security measures required to get in here. I'm the only one with the key," he explains, waving his hand toward the filing cabinets that line the room.

I take a moment to pretend to consider. "Prove it to me," I challenge. "How do I know what's in those cabinets? I already told you I know Cody's secret—show me his. Prove to me that it's still here."

Viktor looks annoyed as he reluctantly stands and heads to a filing cabinet with an R on it. Eventually, he locates Cody's file. It's a secure manila envelope, and he slides it across the desk to me.

"See? Safe and sound, right where it's been since he came here," Viktor says, sounding smug, like he's got me right where he wants me. *Jokes on you, asshole.*

I open the envelope and quickly scan the document. It's a notarized letter, addressed to Viktor, explaining his family's secret and expressing Cody's trust in Viktor to help him navigate the situation.

"Well, this won't be worth much when he tells his whole fami-ly," I point out casually. "He's planning on telling his parents soon and finally finding out if they know." *That's complete bullshit, but Viktor doesn't need to know.*

He looks even more pissed as he tries once again to earn my cooperation.

"Would you like me to get a notary up here so you can tell me whatever your secret is?" Viktor pushes.

"I'm not telling you shit," I say in a cheery tone, and his look of confusion makes me seriously happy. "Look at how easily you just handed over Cody's secret," I point out, holding it up for emphasis.

His expression hardens. "So, you're leaving? What's your plan? You're just going to break up with Cody that easily? Go back home? I guess you don't care about him like I thought you did," he taunts.

"We don't need to break up," I assure him.

"Well, if you're not prepared to prove your loyalty, then I think your stay here in Linna has surpassed your welcome. It's time for you to go," Viktor says with authority.

"Well, maybe he'll come with me," I argue to gauge his reaction.

Viktor's smirk turns into a full-blown laugh. "Cody would never leave because of *you*," he scoffs. "Cody is one of my most valuable assets on the Kyla team. He's brought thousands of people to our seminars. He loves this place more than anyone. Cody *is* this company. There's no way he'd choose you over me," he says confidently, and I know I need to act fast.

"If Cody's information is worthless now anyway, with him telling his whole family soon, why don't you just give it to me? I'll take it when I leave," I challenge.

"I'm not just going to hand it over to you when he hasn't even told his family yet," he sneers.

I shrug, feigning indifference. "He was planning on doing it this weekend, so if you want to hold onto it, that's fine. But I have more money than I know what to do with, so I'd pay you for it."

Viktor perks up at that. "How much are we talking?" he prods, trying to sound nonchalant but intrigued.

"I don't know. How much are you thinking?" I ask.

"A million dollars."

I can't believe the fucking guts of this asshole to ask me for that much money.

But Cody is worth so much more than that, so I don't hesitate.

"Fine," I say, pulling out my phone. "Give me your info, and I'll call my banker right now." He hesitantly tells me, and I make a short call. I don't spend crazy amounts of money like this often, but my family is well connected, and I know who to call.

"You didn't actually arrange to send me a million dollars, that could have been anyone," he scoffs when I hang up. He sits back at his computer to no doubt confirm the information, and when he sees the scheduled pending transfer, he looks genuinely shocked.

"Fine," he huffs, with a tone of annoyance, even though I just gave him a million fucking dollars. "Take it with you. It won't do me any good anyway," he says confidently. "I've never really needed leverage on Cody. There's no way he'd ever leave me. He's one of my most loyal members. He loves Linna. He loves me. Cody's not going anywhere," Viktor rants.

After securing his letter and the envelope, I slip my phone out. Viktor's too busy hitting a button on his desk to call security and asking them to escort me out to notice when I hit the screen to call Cody, quickly placing it on speaker and then lowering the volume so we can't hear him, but he can hopefully hear us.

With my phone screen against the envelope in one hand, I raise both hands in surrender. "Maybe you know Cody better than I do," I say loudly. "But I've got his collateral, and I don't want to hang out in this creepy city anymore. So, I guess I'll leave, and we'll see if he follows me."

Security quickly arrives and escorts me out of the building into one of their cars. For a minute, I fear I've underestimated Viktor, and that I'm about to be driven to the top of a mountain to be murdered, but then we pull up to Cody's house. They proceed to follow me inside to get my bag, looking a little confused when they see it's already packed.

"I knew my time was up," I explain with a shrug, and they don't say anything.

From there, they drive me straight to the airport and escort me inside to the ticket desk, where they watch me buy a ticket to Chicago on a flight that leaves in a few hours. It feels archaic to buy a plane ticket in person, but I don't complain.

Once I'm through the small security line, I watch them finally turn to leave, and I immediately pull out my phone to purchase Cody a ticket for my flight as well.

I really fucking hope that he heard my call. It had ended by the time we were in the car, but I'm praying to anything that will listen that he heard enough to know what's happening and that he can get here in time for the flight.

I'm definitely not leaving without him.

CHAPTER TWENTY-EIGHT

Cody

As soon as I heard Beck say he had my collateral and was leaving, I hung up the call, erased the call history, and ran to plug my phone into the charging station that sits on a side table far enough away from my desk that I can't reach it. I sit back down just as I hear the knock on my door.

"Come in," I answer, and I'm pleasantly surprised by how normal my voice sounds. "Oh, hey, Viktor. I was expecting Beck after your meeting."

Viktor comes in and sits down across from me. I see his gaze catch on my phone so far away from me, and he sits up straighter in his seat. "Cody, I'm so sorry to have to be the one to tell you this, but Beckett is gone." He manages to sound remorseful. *I hate how fucking manipulative he is.*

"During our meeting, he threatened me. He said he was going to take everything he's learned about Kyla during his stay, use the information in his own company, and try to shut us down unless I agreed to sell to him. When I refused, he started yelling and became aggressive. I'm so sorry, Cody," he continues. "I know you really liked him, but I had to have him escorted out, and I've got the security guys following him back to your house to make sure he doesn't steal anything. Then, they'll take him straight to the airport."

I nod along, trying to look sad and confused, as I think about when I can sneak away to the airport myself.

"Wow," I mutter, trying not to look excited that we can finally leave.

"I know this must be shocking for you. I can show you the footage from outside of my office if you'd like," he offers.

I don't want to draw this out any longer than necessary, so I try to think of how he'd want me to respond. "You don't need to go through the trouble," I say softly. "I mean, I obviously trust you, Viktor, so I'm not questioning you. I'm just so surprised he'd have these ulterior motives," I explain.

Viktor straightens in his chair again, looking a bit smug. "It's my fault. I never should've allowed someone like that to be around you for so long," he tells me. "Cody, you're so important to me, and I'm so lucky to have you here. I should have protected you more, I apologize," he says, and I nod along, hoping he'll leave.

After a moment without him moving I decide to keep talking. "So, you said he'll be gone when I get home?" I question.

"Yes, I promise you won't have to see him again," he says. "He should be on the way to the airport any minute."

"Alright, thank you so much, Viktor," I say, then decide to push my luck. "Do you think I could maybe skip the Old Mill tonight? I'm kind of embarrassed about how easily I was manipulated," I say, attempting to sound reluctant, like I'm admitting a hard truth. "I think I need some time to figure out where I went wrong."

"Of course, Cody. I'll tell them you weren't feeling well after work if anyone asks," he promises.

After work, because, obviously, I'll stay to keep working. *What an asshole.*

"Thank you, Viktor. Will you be at tomorrow morning's quarterly recruitment report?" I ask. Trying to keep the conversation casual.

"Yes, I can't wait to hear how well your team has been doing," he replies, and I smile at him.

"See you then, Viktor."

"See you then," he echoes, standing and finally leaving my office.

I wait a few more agonizingly long minutes, just in case he's watching the cameras, and finally try to make it look like I'm casually retrieving my phone. I open it up, and I've never been happier to see a text.

SALEM

Let's get the fuck out of here!

Attached is a screenshot confirming a plane ticket in my name for a flight to Chicago leaving at eight p.m.

I sit at my desk for another hour, uploading as many final things as I possibly can to the shared cloud. When it's finally almost seven—around when I'd usually head to the Old Mill—I go down to my car, waving goodnight to the security guards as I pass.

I don't bother to go to my house, I don't need anything there.

Everything I could ever hope for is waiting for me at the airport, ready to take me home.

EPILOGUE

A FEW MONTHS LATER

Beck

*J*ordan's article came out about a month ago. It was a huge career break for him, the story blew up, and his company has him running non-stop with follow-ups and interviews as more people come forward.

The story got enough attention that Viktor and some of the other top executives were arrested on racketeering charges, and there are talks of more charges being added as the investigation continues.

Cody was questioned because of his role in the company, but we'd already turned over all of the information we gathered and explained our role in getting Jordan involved, so his interrogation was pretty short, and Cody was quickly cleared of any charges.

My family started a nonprofit in Linna. We're really concerned about everyone who's still there, and we've hired a few therapists, and even someone who specializes in helping victims of cults with deconditioning the learned cult behaviors and ways of thinking.

We've set up a fund for the victims to help pay their bills and cover the cost of living now that the company has been shut down and so many people are out of work. My family started with a fifty million dollar donation, and we've set up ways for people who've seen the news stories to donate to the victims, but it's not a long-term solution. Some people left, attempting to rekindle the severed relationships with their families or seek new job opportunities, but the majority of ex-Kyla members are still in Linna.

The government has seized all of Kyla's former assets as a part of the investigation, but I've already expressed interest in purchasing the properties after they've concluded. I'd like to eventually use the campus to help rebuild the town and turn it into something more positive, find a way to give all of those people employment again.

I know that Cody misses Montana and would love to go back to help, but for now, we're helping from Chicago and staying near our support system.

We've been back for a few months now. The Werewolves preseason has started, and I'm excited about our chances this year—although yesterday, I found out our captain was served divorce papers in the locker room in front of reporters. I'm not looking forward to the media shitstorm that will cause.

Apparently, he was completely blindsided, and his wife kicked him out, changed the locks, and everything. He was afraid of the media at hotels, and to my complete surprise, is now staying with Adrian at his condo. Roy said something about wanting to be away from the team while he felt like his life was imploding, and Mr. Fix-it, Adrian, is now his new roommate.

It's giving Roy's agent and the team's PR team a second to figure out a plan for him, though, so it works for me.

Cody had reached out to Nick before we were even on the plane to give him a very quick explanation about our sudden departure and to apologize for leaving so abruptly. After we were settled here, Cody and Nick talked extensively. Nick was a little apprehensive at first, but after a few days of thinking over everything that Cody had told him, he booked his own flight to Chicago and showed up on our doorstep unannounced.

Jordan, Adrian, some of my brothers, and Parker had been over for dinner when he arrived. Jordan was talking with us about his plans for the next phase of the article when Nick walked in, and I swear, I thought I'd have to scrape Jordan's jaw off the floor. He couldn't stop staring.

Having Nick here has been great for Cody. It gives him a tie to this "old life" without all the bad parts. I also think it's good for him to have someone he didn't meet through me.

Even though Cody loves my family and friends, and is absolutely one of us now, I know he still worries about giving someone else too much influence over him again. He was so relieved when we were able to cut the necklace off—I never want him to feel trapped like that again.

He's also gotten pretty close with Adrian and Parker after they helped him with his finances, but Oakley and Parker have been acting weird around each other lately, making it hard to hang out with them. Oakley came over the other day *without Parker* for the first time that I can ever remember, and he asked Cody a ton of questions about his experience realizing he was bi after assuming he was straight his whole life. *He wouldn't explain why he was so curious, though.*

There's definitely something going on with them that they aren't telling me, but as far as I know, they're both still dating the girls from their building, and with everything that's been going on with my own life, I haven't pushed it. They'll talk to me when they're ready.

Cody ended up reaching out to his half-brother, Jameson, who was completely surprised. Apparently, he hadn't checked the app after getting his own results, so he'd never known about Cody. He was thrilled, though— they've been texting and calling every day since, and he seems like a great guy. He's still out in California but is planning to visit soon. They still haven't confronted their parents about it yet. Cody's hoping to do that after he actually meets him to make sure they're on the same page about how to approach it.

Cody also isn't sure what he wants to do for work yet, but the therapist that he's been working with recommended he volunteer at a shelter for victims of abuse that she's involved with, and he's been loving it. I know that we both still have healing to do after our time in Linna, but I'm so happy we ended up where we are, together.

Cody moved in with me as soon as we got back to Chicago. Spending a month together in Linna proved we fit well in the same place, but having him here, in my home, is so much better than I could have ever fantasized about.

Some of my family members were concerned that it was too soon for us to be living together, but after everything that we've been through, it felt right for both of us. Every night that he's in my bed feels like a gift, and every morning, waking up with him in my arms *after* the sunrise is perfect.

Cody says he likes my condo just fine, but I have a surprise for him on the way to dinner at my grandparents' house today.

"This isn't the street we normally take," Cody notes after I pull into their neighborhood and turn away from their house.

"Very astute observation," I tease.

"So, where are we going?" he laughs, but I just smile and keep my eyes on the road.

A few moments later, we pull into the drive of a beautiful white Victorian farmhouse that's been completely restored. The details on the architecture are painted yellow, and when I first saw the pictures, it made me think of my sunshine man. The wraparound porch reminds me of his house in Montana, and the huge fenced-in yard would be perfect for a dog.

I offered to go with him to adopt one shortly after we came

back, but said he couldn't picture a dog in my fancy condo. I started looking at real estate listings for houses that night.

"What is this?" Cody asks, sounding happily confused as he smiles up at the home.

"Ours. If you want it," I answer, and his head whips around to look at me.

"You bought me a house?"

"Technically, I put in an offer on a house. I didn't want to take the decision away from you," I explain, making him smile.

"Thank you for not making a major life decision without me." He chuckles and throws the car door open, running up the porch steps, unable to hold still as he waits for me to get there with the code that lets us inside.

"This place is amazing," he says, the wonder evident in his tone, as he bounces from room to room. The inside has been completely modernized, and it looks even nicer in person.

"There are six bedrooms, and an office down here," I tell him. "So plenty of room to grow."

"It's perfect," he announces as he comes to meet me in the center of the kitchen.

"Do you really like it?" I ask. "We can look at others, too. I just saw this listing and it reminded me of your home in Montana—and I didn't want someone else to grab it before we could..." I realize I'm rambling now, but I can't seem to stop.

Cody cups my face with his big hands, pulling my lips to his. I forget where we are for a moment, deepening the kiss, moving my hands to his ass to pull him in closer to me before he playfully shoves me away.

"We'll have plenty of time to fuck all over this house," he says with a laugh. "But I really want to see it all first."

"Whatever you want, Goldie," I promise as I follow him up the grand staircase.

And I hope he knows I mean it—*whatever he wants for the rest of our lives.*

I was so afraid I'd lose my chance at a future with this perfect man. Now that we're here together, in the same place, with no end date in sight, I'm never letting him go again.

THE END.

AFTERWORD

If you'd like to read a bonus epilogue where Cody finally gets his dog, (and some much better jewelry) sign up for my newsletter at https://dl.bookfunnel.com/dj8noarb39

For Jordan's article and a few more details on Viktor/Kyla check out the free tier on my Patreon at https://patreon.com/LexiAmber?utm_medium=unknown&utm_source=join_link&utm_campaign=creatorshare_creator&utm_content=copyLink There will also be lots of fun extras there as well so let me know what you'd like the different tiers to look like!

Join my reader's groups on Discord at https://discord.gg/esrCnR4Srf or Facebook at https://www.facebook.com/share/g/162srUeNMd/?mibextid=wwXIfr to stay up to date on my latest release information and for other fun updates!

Thank you so much for reading my debut! As an indie author I really appreciate every single person who took a chance on a new name and I still can't believe people have read a book that I wrote!

If you have the time I'd love for you to rate and review wherever possible to help other people find Cody and Beck!

I'm sorry if you were hoping for more info on what happens

to Linna/the former cult members, but their story isn't finished. The Chicago Awakenings series will feature interconnected standalones, and book three (Adrian and Hudson) will include more detailed updates on what happens next in Montana and will hopefully be out later this year!

Oakley and Parker are next, keep an eye out for Accidentally Falling For My Best Friend, a best friends-to-lovers MM romance releasing this summer!

Check out my store at lexiamber.com for Werewolves merch, signed paperbacks, character art, stickers, and other Lexi Amber exclusives.

<u>**Also by Lexi Amber**</u>

Chicago Awakenings

Accidentally Joining His Cult

Accidentally Falling For My Best Friend, Expected August 2025

<u>**Co-authored with Bec Benson**</u>

Love Without Labels

The Reality of Wanting Him, Expected July 2025

A reality dating show MM romance, **KEEP READING FOR BLURB REVEAL**

THE REALITY OF WANTING HIM
BLURB

Blake

When my parents threatened to cut me off if I wasn't married by the time I turned thirty, I thought finding a wife would be easy. But apparently, I'm not very good at dating, and almost two years later, I'm still very single.

My birthday is coming up fast, and unless I want to give up the comfortable lifestyle I'm used to, I need to find someone willing to settle down fast. I'm desperate and out of ideas, until my best friend suggests I apply for a new reality dating show.

Now I'm a contestant on the first season of *Love Without Labels*, a completely blind reality dating show where we talk to each other through distorted voice technology and texts. No photos, ages, genders, or even names will be revealed until we decide to move in together.

I knew all of this when I signed up, and even though I'm straight, I assumed it would be easy to tell if I was talking to a woman.

Apparently, I was wrong.

Liam

It's my final season working for the family farm before I take over for my dad. I'm ready to find someone to build a real future with, but I know they aren't in my small hometown.

Love Without Labels feels like the perfect chance to find my person. I've never cared much about labels anyway. All I want is someone who's loyal, honest, and I can share my dreams with.

As we narrow down our matches, there's only one person I can imagine a future with. Someone who listens, makes me laugh, and feel wanted in a way I haven't in a long time.

But while I've kept my mind open about who I'm falling for, apparently, he's been convinced I was a woman this entire time.

Will he still want to continue building on the connection we have now that he knows the truth? Or was this relationship doomed before it could really even begin?

ABOUT THE AUTHOR

Lexi is an American author who is obsessed with queer happily ever afters. Most of her time is spent with her two kids, but if they're asleep then she is either reading, writing, or watching hockey.

Professionally trained as a nurse, Lexi decided to start writing when she became a stay at home mom and the characters in her head haven't stopped talking since.

Lexi also loves Diet Coke, traveling, and Halloween. Her house is probably obnoxiously decorated for whatever holiday is next because she thinks that little things that make people smile are important.

You can find her attempting to stay up to date with all of the social media below, as well as the MM wire and discord

ACKNOWLEDGMENTS

Thank you so much to everyone who helped make this book possible!

Both covers were created by the super talented Rebecca at Story Styling Cover Designs and the amazing cover image was done by Michelle Lancaster. Spectacular copy edits were done by Becca at Remain Unedited, sensitivity feedback by Lindsey Middlemiss, and proofreading was done by Brittany at Campfire Edits who was a complete lifesaver—I seriously can not thank you enough for dropping everything to step in at the last minute. Everyone was so fabulous to work with and were so so helpful in bringing this debut to life.

The biggest shout out and thank you to my beta readers! Kelsey H, Elizabeth N, Bryoni H, Jennifer R, Lauren W, Anna R, Christina S, Crystal K, Zephyr W, Cath V, Alyssa G, and Ronan M, I seriously don't know what I did to deserve such a fabulous group of people to first read this story, but I am so thankful that each and every one of you helped make it better. From the actual story feedback, to answering my messages at all hours, you are all rockstars! I am so glad this book brought us together and am forever grateful that I get to call so many of you my friends.

Ronan Marlow, I need to give you an extra special thank you because you went so above and beyond beta reading you were basically acting as my PA. Thank you for being such an amazing friend, I can't wait to attempt to return the favor with your debut and to come visit you so we can meet in person.

Lys, thank you for being such an awesome hype-girl and for always making me laugh when I'm stressed. Your encouragement has meant the world to me and I am so grateful to have you in my corner. You didn't say anything weird or awkward and I promise we're still friends.

Bec! Words can not describe how grateful I am to have you as my friend and to have had all of your help on this book! Not only your feedback in the actual making of, but also all of the emotional support and encouragement you've given me throughout this entire process! I am so glad that you were the first to meet Beck and Cody, and that we're now writing even more fun oblivious men together! I'm so excited to see where this crazy author journey takes us.

I'd also like to thank my very supportive husband who believed in this dream before I did, and who's encouraged me every step of the way. I definitely couldn't have done any of this without you.

Thanks to my parents who've been very supportive, even if I hope they never actually read this book.

And to my kids, thanks for napping, going to bed on time, and letting mommy work, even after I quit my nursing job to stay home with you guys. I'll love you forever and always no matter what.